I0687495

CHRISTIAN

A Mitchell-Healy Series

Jennifer Foor

Copyright © 2014 Jennifer Foor
All Rights Reserved
Cover Art: Wicked Cool Designs
Edited By: Pamela Snyder
Cover Photo : Toski Covey

Check out the other books by Jennifer Foor
(Contemporary Romance)
A Mitchell Family Series
Letting Go -Folding Hearts - Raging Love -Risking Fate
Wrapping Up - Wanting More - Saving Us - Blinding Trust
Losing Him - Loving Her
A Mitchell Healy Series
Noah
Isabella
Love's Suicide
The Kin Series
Repair Me - Replace Me - Restore Me
Remember Me – Reject Me – Redeem Me
Hustle Me (A Bank Shot Romance)
Hustle Him (A Bank Shot Romance)
Diary of a Male Maid
Twinsequences
Lustly
A Hope and a Chance

Beta Readers
Kayla Kennedy, Emma Clifton, Kristy Davidson,
Catherine Roberts, Lara Petterson ,
Jennifer Harried, Kasey Craig, Jamie Grant, Julie
Barley, Amanda Mooney, Toski Covey

Web Design and Marketing by: Inkslinger PR

Acknowledgements:
This book is for all of the women and men out there who have been a victim of sexual assault. There's help out there, and you're not alone.
Thanks to Inkslinger, and my publicist Danielle. I heart you!!

Thanks to Toski Covey for the cover shoot, and Nicole Thomas for posing.
Thanks to my kick-ass street team, Foor Players.
FOORWHORES – my super secret society
Thanks to all of my new friends on my FB, Twitter and Goodreads. Thank you for spreading the word and all of the support you give.Thanks to all of my other Independent Author Friends. (you know who you are) Thank you to all the book bloggers out there spreading the word for me and others who write.
Bloggers: I wouldn't be anywhere without you.
Thank you so much!

the Mitchell Family Series Reference Guide

Please use this guide to follow along with the characters from the original Mitchell Family Series

Each character is listed with a detailed background from the whole 10 book series

Notable Characters and Villains have also been listed as well as a list of Parents and Children

Main Characters

Colt Mitchell – The oldest Mitchell cousin who lives in Kentucky, and is the only son to the eldest of the original Mitchell Brothers. His father owned and operated the largest cattle ranching facility in the state. Introduced in book one when he came to North Carolina to help his uncle (father's brother) run his farm while his cousin Tyler was in a coma, after a near fatal car crash.

He fell in love with his cousin's long-term girlfriend and that became the whole plot of the first book. He battled with right and wrong, finally giving into temptation and straining his relationship with his cousin, Tyler.

Colt and Savanna were eventually married in book three. After Savanna miscarried their first child, Colt discovered he had a son (Noah). They had two daughters after that (Christian and Addison). Colt is an old-fashioned and serious man, who thrives on his love for family and religion to get him through any part of life's journey.

Even in the latter books he struggled with jealousy over his wife's friendship with Tyler. The two friends never crossed any lines, but Colt still worried. It wasn't until book seven where Colt finally understood that Savanna and Ty's love for one another was part of their bond from being first childhood friends and then cousins by marriage, instead of something else.

Colt tells the story in books One, three, four and a half, and seven.

Letting Go
Raging Love
Wrapping Up
Blinding Trust

Relationship to characters

Miranda & Conner Healy are his cousins. (Their mothers are sisters.)

Tyler Mitchell – cousin (Their fathers are brothers.)

Savanna (Van) Mitchell – Introduced in book one as the love interest to both Tyler and Colt, Savanna struggles with right and wrong and which man she's destined to love. After falling head over heels for her boyfriend's cousin in book one, she leaves North Carolina behind to start a future with Colt.

In the second book her friendship with her ex is tested, especially when he falls for someone close to her.

She's kidnapped by Colt's cousin Miranda's lunatic ex-boyfriend in book three and held for ransom-tied up in a basement. At the time she's pregnant and during an escape attempt she miscarries and kills her capturer, who happens to be her niece's (Isabella) biological father (Tucker Chase).

In Book eight she discovers that she has breast cancer, while struggling with the relationship with her step-son Noah.

Throughout every book Savanna grows as a strong woman. She's a major key to the family and the bond that they all share together. Not only does she continue to be close to her ex Tyler, but she's also a best friend to his wife, Miranda and even her sister-in-law Amy.

Savanna tells the story in books One, Three, Four and a half, and Seven.

Letting Go
Raging Love
Wrapping Up
Blinding Trust

Savanna has no blood relation to any of the original characters. She is the wife of Colt Mitchell.

Tyler Mitchell – As a main character in book one, Tyler Mitchell was known as the cheating boyfriend that everyone loved to hate. His family owns and operates a farm in North Carolina. After waking from his coma, he was left without a girlfriend, job or future. It wasn't until book two where he found love, starting with the birth of a young child (Isabella), and later turning into a relationship with Miranda Healy. Miranda, who is Colt's cousin on his mother's side, was no relation to Ty. It still didn't keep their family from forbidding them to be together. When Miranda's ex threatened her and the baby, she goes to stay with Ty to be safe. Their love was undeniable and to stay together they eloped. By the end of book two the family accepts them. New and old friendships are rekindled and the family feels complete in every aspect. This character tells the story in books two, four, four and a half, and nine.

Folding Hearts
Risking Fate
Wrapping Up
Loving Her

Relationship to characters
Colt Mitchell – Cousin (fathers are brothers)

He is not related to his wife, Miranda by blood. They only share a similar cousin, Colt, by both being related to him on different sides of his family. Growing up he and his wife considered each other cousins because the Healy's lived on the ranch with Colt. This was also a huge reason for their relationship being forbidden.

Miranda Healy (Mitchell) – This character is introduced at the very end of book one. Along side of Tyler, she tells the story in book two. It starts out explaining her failing relationship with her then boyfriend Tucker Chase. He's a criminal that wants nothing to do with her or their child. After threats are made, she flees, falling right into the arms of her new best friend, Ty. By book four the couple is happy. Tucker Chase has died and they thought that their fears have ended. She's found the perfect man that not only loves her, but also adores her daughter as if she were his own flesh and blood. After giving her his name they vow to take the secret to the grave. New threats come into play and to protect their child, they do something unthinkable. Miranda thinks that Ty has cheated on her and she leaves town, very pregnant. An accident on the road sends her into labor and she almost dies, along with her unborn twin boys. By book eight the couple has gotten away from the drama and trust issues. Instead it's their daughter that has all of the problems. It starts out with her being sick and then finally the discovery of Ty not being her biological father. At the end of the day it's the family that helps make everything right with the world. Miranda tells the story in books two, four, four and a half, and nine.
> **Folding Hearts**
> **Risking Fate**
> **Wrapping Up**
> **Loving Her**
> **Relationship to characters**

Colt Mitchell – Cousin (Mothers sisters)
Conner Healy - Brother

Conner Healy – The brother of Miranda and first cousin to Colt, this character was once secondary, only being mentioned in book one at the end of the book. He's a bigger character in the beginning of book two when he interferes with his sister's (Miranda) love life.

He's mentioned in book three because he works alongside of Colt on the ranch.

After being a huge part of book four and four and a half, where he risks his own happiness for his family, Conner gets the next two books, five and six. It follows the story of a drug abusing cowboy with no structure in his life, as he recovers and finds love with a married woman. Conner would do just about anything for his family, but even more for Amy. It takes them a while to admit it, but when they finally do there's no denying it. They end up having four children together, three girls and one boy.

Conner tells the story for books five and six.
Wanting More
Saving Us

Relationship to characters
Miranda (Healy) Mitchell – Sister
Colt Mitchell – Cousin (Mothers side)

Amy Healy– While introduced in the second book as Miranda's boss at the hair salon, she's later a main character playing the role of Miranda's best friend. Amy has lots of secrets, including a husband who drinks too much and takes out his anger on her body. Amy's story begins in the background of the other books, but is front and center in the fifth and sixth edition. Her struggles to get away from her husband (Rick) and finally be with Conner cause them to have two full books back to back. In their second edition Amy is pregnant and the family will do anything in their power to keep her safe, including sending them to Kentucky to stay. It didn't stop her ex from hunting her down and holding her at gunpoint. He meets his demise on the Mitchell ranch when Heather (his mistress and Ty's ex) shoots him to save Amy.

Amy is best friends with Savanna and Miranda.

When the series ends she and Conner are married with four children, Cassie, Cammie, Callie, and Joshua.

She tells the story in two books.
Wanting More
Saving Us
Relationship to characters
None

Villains in the series

Heather – Was introduced in the first book as one of the college girls that Ty was sleeping around with. In book two she's still attempting to win the affections of a newly single Tyler. Obviously he goes on to wed Miranda and they try to forget all about her. She runs into Ty a while after that in book four. He's married and in awe of his wife and adopted daughter. To protect them from Isabella's biological father's family they turn to Heather's brother for a forged paternity test. Heather forces Ty's hand, and she uses extreme measures to break them up, causing Miranda to leave town, distraught and nine months pregnant with his twins. She gets into an accident and not only almost dies herself, but also the twins.

This character continues to cause problems for the Mitchell Family throughout the series, until she is punished and taught a lesson by Conner Healy, Miranda Mitchell's brother, in book six. She ends up becoming the hero in that book when she saves Amy's life by shooting and killing Rick. In book seven she runs into Savanna and through a common medical diagnosis they share a heartfelt moment.

After that Heather gets her own book (Eight) and readers finally find out why she did all of those terrible things to torture the family. In her book we learn that while she was trying to change her life around she fell in love with Rick's (Amy's Ex) son, Jesse. Together they had a son named Jacob. In book eight they finally stop fighting about the past and move forward with a future together, as a family. Heather gets her own book to tell her side of the story.

Losing Him

Tucker Chase – This guy was Miranda's boyfriend in book 2. He was a thug, who didn't ever want to be a father to Miranda's baby (Isabella). It was a good thing that Ty stepped in and became the father that she deserved. In book three Savanna is kidnapped and held for ransom. She loses her baby in a struggle and ends up killing Tucker while trying to get free.

Tucker's mother- This woman shows her face in book three and four, after losing her son in the kidnapping episode with Savanna. She's sets out to gain visitation of her granddaughter, causing Miranda and Ty to go to extreme measures to keep their daughter, including forging a paternity test and almost getting a divorce.

Rick – Was once married to Amy. His verbal and physical abuse was derived from his addiction to alcohol. We later learned that his past secrets included murder and betrayal. Rick dies in book six of the series, after holding Amy and Heather at gunpoint. He is survived by two children, one being Heather's love interest Jesse.

Zeke – The brother of Noah's (Colt's oldest son) biological mother, Krista, is a rock star that comes back to town to get to know his nephew. He's always known that Savanna was his step-mother, but this book destroys his love for the only woman who has raised him. While struggling with breast cancer, Savanna is faced with the fear of losing Noah. We later find out that Zeke only wanted to use Noah for publicity and never cared about the kid at all. Once his secret was exposed, he left town and Noah never tried to contact him again.

Notable Characters

Lucy - This character is known as the housekeeper at the Ranch mansion, and best friend of Colt's mother. She is featured in almost all of the books at least once.

Karen – Miranda and Conner's mother, a widow who eventually marries the sheriff, John. Known as mom-mom to her grandchildren.

John – The town sheriff in Kentucky, who marries Karen. Known as Pop-pop John to the grandkids.

Krista – Noah's biological mother

Jesse - Rick's estranged son. The two characters are never in contact with each other. Jesse never even knew Rick was around.

Shelby – Rick's daughter.

Brina – The once best friend of Savanna in the earlier books. She dated Conner for a time when he moved into North Carolina, but enabled his addiction.

Toby – Heather's brother who falsified the paternity test for Ty and Miranda. He went to jail later on for similar charges.

Savanna's parents. – Known as Mr. and Mrs. Tate or mom-mom and pop-pop to the three children.

Colt's mother – Grandma to the three children.

Ty's parents – Mimi and Poppy to their three children. His dad is referred to as Uncle Mitch.

Harvey – The ranch hand at the North Carolina Mitchell Farm and Ranch. He was once mentioned to have a connection to Lucy.

Parents/Children

COLT AND SAVANNA (Mitchell)

1. Noah (Savanna is his step-mother)
2. Christian
3. Addison

TYLER AND MIRANDA (Mitchell)

1. Isabella, (Izzy or Bella or Bells) Tyler is listed as her birth father on certificate, but he is really her step-father
2. Jacob (Jake)
3. Jaxson (Jax)

CONNER AND AMY (Healy)

1. Cassie
2. Callie
3. Cammie
4. Joshua

The kids are all related to each other as first cousins.

Chapter 1
Christian

Sometimes I wonder if I was switched at birth with some other green-eyed baby. How could it be possible that I'd spent my entire life cast out from all of my other cousins? Surely there had to be some common ground that united us, besides our obvious blood connection. At the end of the day, or should I say family gatherings, I was left in the corner, while everyone else enjoyed being together.

I suppose the adults enjoyed my company, when they weren't talking about things I didn't care to hear. There was even a time when my brother liked having me around, up until he got engaged to a famous singer. Nowadays it's just me and the big world of college.

Choosing to live closer to campus was an easy decision. After having the dorm experience for the first two years of school, it was time for a change. Besides, I was getting sick of living vicariously through my mischievous younger sister's antics, so going home was out of the question. Between her hookups, and the constant trouble she found herself in, my parents were always cleaning up her messes, and making sure she was being punished for her mistakes. In some ways I was jealous of Addison. My sister could walk into a room full of strangers and somehow be friends with everyone in little time.

I was the opposite.

Always the quiet type, I spent most of my childhood behind a book, or shadowing my mother. As I got older nothing changed, except for my appearance. I remember going through an awkward stage, where only my family, including my brother Noah told me I was pretty. Maybe that's why I'm so self-conscious. When I look in the mirror I've never seen anyone beautiful staring back at me. Even though I resemble my gorgeous mother, with golden brown locks of wavy hair, and share my father's green eyes, I see myself as plain, and somewhat nerdy.

Perhaps it's derived from never being sure of myself, or having cousins that picked on me every chance they got. At the end of the day I was Christian Mitchell, oldest daughter of Colt and Savanna, second in line to the family ranch, and the least good looking of my two siblings.

I'd like to say that all of the above explanations led me in a good direction in finding myself. It would have been the educated decision they'd expect me to make. For lack of better terms

I'd reached a breaking point in life. It wasn't just about my looks, or my inability to communicate rationally with someone of the opposite sex. Surely I had a couple lasting friendships. I'd dated, even when my brother would threaten to chase them down our dirt road with a hunting rifle to keep them away.

Despite Noah's efforts, there was a special guy in my life that I hung out with all the time. We'd been best friends for years. He was the person I'd turned to when I wanted a night of release. We were human, each of us needing a physical connection every once in a while. It still didn't get me what I needed though.

My problems were about self-discovery, and it was time I finally found who the person was that I wanted to be.

I've heard college is the best years of a person's life. Perhaps that's true for most young adults. I'd seen my peers change in my first two years of attending the University of Kentucky. Like my father, I'd gotten a full ride, finding it easy to maintain a high grade point average with little effort. Socially I lacked confidence, which in turn caused me to be an outcast, just like in earlier years.

When I'd decided to live near the college my dad was leery about allowing me to live alone. It was then that we sought out housing looking for roommates. As nervous as I was to be around three female strangers, I knew it was impertinent that I forge forward with my anticipated need for change. It didn't take a rocket scientist to figure out early on that I had nothing in common with any of the girls. Not only was I the newbie, but they clearly had a long-standing bond with one another. Since I was used to being cast aside, I spent my first week organizing my new room, and staying out of everyone's way. It would've been fine with me if we passed in the halls with a friendly gesture and went about our days as if I was just a friendly acquaintance.

Unfortunately, they didn't share those feelings.

Becca seemed to be the leader of my three new roommates. There were all transplants to Kentucky, coming from all different states. Often they mentioned my strong drawl, though I never noticed it.

Becca was always in control of planning. It was she who came into my room, plopping down on my bed before forcing a conversation on me. I found it uncomfortable, as if she was invading my personal space, but longed for a connection with someone other than my own mother.

I wasn't so much impressed with Becca as I was with the way she was able to act so bubbly all the time. People seemed drawn to her, which in turn made her highly likeable. Her long hair had both brown and blonde in it, and it hung down half of her back. The way she dressed left little to the imagination. I'd overheard her talking about being a cheerleader, which completely fit the stereotype I'd provided in my head. Still, we weren't in high school anymore. I had to get over what clicks were like back then, and understand that people change. Just because she was well-liked didn't make her someone I had to hate. It was more like jealousy of wanting her life, her friends, and of course her confidence.

"So, us girls are going out tonight, and we want you to come with us." She threw up her hands before I could decline, or give her some convoluted reason why it would be a bad idea for me to tag along. "We aren't taking no for an answer Christian. Unless you plan on joining a convent, you're coming out with us."

"If you insist." I shrugged, still unsure of how I felt about it. The girls that I lived with liked to party I'd heard some of their crazy stories. I don't think that I looked down on them for being so open-minded, it was more like I was jealous that they were so easily social.

"We do. Now, do something with your hair, put on some makeup, and change out of those clothes. If you need to borrow something of mine, you know where my closet is. In fact," she put her finger up to her lips as she looked over my body. "I've got this red dress that would look hot as shit on you." She left the room, quickly returning with what I would call a long shirt. It was see-through red fabric, low cut, and very stretchy.

"Becca, I don't know about this. I've never worn somethin' so tight before, and clearly I don't have a body suit for underneath."

"Girl, you've got a rocking body. It's time you flaunted it. Besides where we're goin' you'll fit right in." She seemed sure, while I remained a skeptic. If this got me to meet new people, I was at least willing to give it a try. It couldn't hurt to come out of my shell for a couple of hours, and they were nice to invite me.

An hour later I sat in front of a vanity mirror staring back at a person I barely recognized. Becca had been nice enough to come in and do my makeup. I felt like she was making me look like a floozy, albeit the final result was something overwhelming. I'd never felt like I was beautiful, even though people had always complimented me. The reflection I was seeing was gorgeous. My hair, flowing with long curls, fell down over the middle of my back. My eyelashes were lengthened, and the dark shadow on the lids caused my green eyes to look so pronounced.

Becca stood back with her arms folded across her chest. "So, you're totally smokin'. I'd do you. With that body and your southern drawl, girl you'll be the talk of the night."

I rolled my eyes, paying little attention to her forward announcement. While I leaped to my feet, spinning around checking out my ass in the mirror, I felt sexy. It was something I'd never been comfortable with. "Impressive."

"Maybe after tonight you'll realize that hidin' behind those books ain't how college life is supposed to be. You need to experience things, Chris. God gave you that rockin' body. It's time you showed it off. I know I'd kill for your tits."

I looked down at my cleavage, noticing how the bra underneath shown through. "I'm ready when you are." She couldn't understand what it was like to never feel like you could fit in. I wanted to be liked, but changing myself to do it didn't seem like it was real. At any rate, I wanted to try.

Right before we went out my best friend, Ethan called to check on me. My stomach still got butterflies at the mere thought of him. It was probably juvenile to feel so excited about someone I'd known forever.

"Hi."

"What are you doin' tonight?"

I kept checking out my ass in the mirror as I spoke. "I'm going out with my roommates actually."

"Wow. Seriously? I thought you didn't like them."

I smirked, knowing he couldn't see. "I never said that. It was more like they didn't care for me."

"That's their loss. Listen, if you have a bad time you can call me. I'll pick you up and keep my questions to a minimum."

"Yeah right. I can already tell you're bustin' to hear about it."

He was quiet for a second. "Chris," he always called me that. "I wanted to talk to you about somethin' tonight, but I guess it can wait. Call me tomorrow, okay?"

"Okay, I will." As much as I'd become curious as to what he'd want to discuss, I was eager to have this night out, so that I could discover all that I'd been missing out on.

When we piled into Becca's compact car, I sat with my hands clasped together in the backseat thinking about Ethan. We'd been friends since middle school, and I guess I'd always had a crush on him. Like me, he'd been focused on school and not wanted a relationship to be damaging to his education, no matter how close we became.

Since we hung out so often we were comfortable being alone together. One night, years ago, we were alone in his living room watching a movie after quizzing each other for a final exam. His father had started a fire before heading upstairs, and the crackling set a romantic ambience. I think secretly his parents were always trying to get us to hook up, because they liked my family.

Our first kiss came after a long discussion about staying focused. We sat there side by side agreeing that being in a relationship would cause unwanted stress and break our strict study guidelines. Neither of us talked about having feelings for each other, and honestly, at the time, I hadn't given it much thought, although I know now that I was swooning hard. It was that night, in that very setting where we decided to satisfy our desires together. We made a pact to share all of our firsts. It was a pact that we'd kept since that night. If there was something new to discover we'd do it together.

The awkward kiss that started it all lead to something so much deeper for me. I'd had boyfriends, but never experienced something real. That intense feeling caught me off guard, and as our practicing progressed, I longed for more from him.

We slept together for the first time that following month, and had been sexually active with one another for a couple of years. I'd fallen hopelessly in love with him. We hadn't only lost our virginity with each other because we had feelings; it was also because we trusted each other. Somehow that trust became more for me.

Ethan must have noticed and gotten freaked out. He said he could only love me as his best friend. As much as the friendship meant to me I accepted it. Slowly he started pulling away, and ended up becoming interested in one of our friends. It took me two months to be able to be near him again, and when we were together I couldn't stop the longing to be closer to him.

After graduation we were still sleeping together often, and spending huge amounts of time either with each other or on the phone. He knew everything about me, and I him. I guess that's why it was so difficult to hide my feelings.

College had helped.

While we attended the same university, our schedules kept a good distance between us. Though still study partners, and the closest of friends, we didn't have much time to hook up, causing me to feel unwanted whenever were alone.

Lately he'd been calling more. It was odd to me how for so long I wanted his attention, and now when I was ready to open up and explore whatever else was out there, he was showing back up.

I looked down at my messages on my cell phone, seeing that besides Ethan, only my family ever called me. This night had to go well, because I was determined to break out of this shell and become something more than a boring nerd.

Chapter 2
Christian

A prude.

That's what I'd been for twenty years of my life.

The lights had been dimmed as we entered into the Lazy Horse Club. The tantric music played, creating an ambience as we located seats. Right away I knew where they'd brought me, and it was an immediate anxiousness when my eyes sought out the person on the stage.

A blonde female, probably my age, swayed her body, while her hands gradually played with the tiny straps on either side of her hips. I wanted to turn away, feeling ashamed for staring. This wasn't a place I ever thought I'd be.

While relaxing enough to find a chair, I sat with my back to the stage. My mind went to my mother, and what she'd say if she ever found out I was in this type of establishment. Surely my new roommates had been here before, because I watched two of them, Becca and Mandi, waving to the girl on stage. They whistled, causing my curiosity to make me turn to see what could be so interesting.

She was now topless, squatting down with her back up against a pole. Her arms were lifted above her head, her breasts at full attention.

To say that I was uneasy would have been an understatement. I couldn't fathom how I was intrigued, but yet as my eyes focused in on the confidence she held, a part of me felt jealous.

I'd always believed that women who dance for money had problems; like daddy issues, or even just for money. I felt like they were desperate and it was some last resort. This woman on the stage seemed happy, almost like she carried herself as if she was a queen. As her song ended, she hopped off the platform and headed in our direction. I turned my chair back around, trying to make it less obvious that I'd been in awe.

When she sat down beside me I almost wanted to cry, in fear that she would address the way I'd been watching her. Instead, she pretended that I wasn't even present. "So, what'd you think of the new song?"

Becca reached over the table and took the stripper's hands. "It was great. I noticed how many tips you got. The men loved it."

I tightened my lips and sat silently listening to the next song begin to play as a new girl was introduced to the crowd. Shell, my third roommate turned her attention to me. "Sorry, Chris, this is Amber. Her dance name is Charisma. She used to live in your room, before she started making the big bucks. Now she's got a studio apartment all to herself."

Since money was never an issue with my family, I was just learning how someone could struggle as an adult. I tried not to talk about my family much, so that people wouldn't want to be my friend for the wrong reasons. I'd been raised that money didn't make a person, but knew enough to see how people could be taken advantage of if they had it. In all honesty, it wasn't my money. It wasn't like I was helping out around the ranch in anyway. My parents wanted my focus to be on school.

Amber looked me up and down, taking in the dress that fit so snug against my curves. "It's nice to meet you, Chris. Is this your first time in a strip club? You seem uncomfortable."

I shrugged. "It's that obvious?"

She reached over and put her hand over mine, smiling fully as she spoke. "Don't worry. I felt the same way my first time. Trust me, coming from my religious family, I never would have stepped foot into one of these places if it weren't for Becca. One night out turned into a new life for me. Now I'm able to afford school and live lavishly without having to bust my ass every second of the day. Here these will help." She slid over two shots.

I looked down at them, contemplating if I wanted to drink or not. After watching her doing her own, I succumbed to the pressure.

They burned like my throat was on fire, and I puckered up my face to handle the extreme discomfort. "I suppose the hours would be better," I finally replied.

"Honey," she started. "I work three days out of the week, for four hours at a time, and still bring home a grand easy. I've even started doing private parties. I get three hundred bucks for an hour and a half. Usually I end up splitting it with whoever I take, even if they don't dance with me. It's peace of mind knowing I'm not alone with strangers, ya know?"

I nodded, still in shock with being in a strip club and sitting next to a topless girl. It was difficult, even for a straight person, to not have your eyes radiate to naked skin, especially when it was right in my face. "I get it. It's not something I could ever do, but it's great that you can spend more time on school. So, if you don't mind me askin', what's your major?"

She smiled. "Psychology."

I was impressed again that she was seeking such a difficult occupation. It took a certain kind of dedication to focus on the medical field. This girl wasn't a bimbo. She clearly knew what she wanted, and also how to make it happen.

While my roommates were having a good time, I was mesmerized that this lifestyle was nothing I'd imaged it to be. It was so intriguing, and I found myself wondering what each dancer's story was.

Before I could ask Amber more, she smirked and waved as a gentleman motioned for her to join him. She stood up and leaned forward. "I'll be back in a few minutes. This guy tips out the ass, and I don't want to keep him waiting."

For the next several hours, and drinks later, the four of us sat there watching the girls dancing around the stage. With each act, I could sense that same confidence with the performers. Maybe I picked up on it because it was something I lacked. Perhaps I was in amazement to be experiencing this type of lifestyle. No matter how I tried to spin that this wasn't something I'd ever be interested in being around, I was drawn with curiosity. Not to mention that as I sat there watching someone of the same sex dancing around, I became very aware of how turned on it was making me. When Amber came back to our table she was pulling five dollar bills out of her G-string. "It's a good night, ladies."

A group of guys at a table next to us started cat-calling. We all turned to see that they were asking us to join them. Of course, all of the girls except for me thought it was a fun idea. I felt someone tugging on my arm, and noticed that Amber was pulling me along. "You remind me so much of myself. Is your name Christina?"

"No, it's Christian."

She giggled as we sat down at the new table. "You're shitting me."

I shook my head, finding humor in her shock. "No, I'm not."

"Wow. Let me guess, catholic school girl. Your parents are still happily married, and they never miss a Sunday in church?"

"Are you psychic?"

She grimaced before continuing. "No. I like to think that I'm a good judge of character. Believe it or not you're lucky. Not many kids live with both parents nowadays. It's part of the reason why I want to be a psychologist. I feel like if people tried a little harder then marriage wouldn't be such a failure."

"Are you from a broken family?" I wondered if my question was too personal after I'd asked.

"Actually I'm not. I'm the middle child to a doctor, and a teacher. My dad's a surgeon, and my mother works with special needs kids. They've never needed to work on their marriage, because neither is around each other enough to fight."

"I'm sorry." I felt bad for her.

"Don't be. We spend holidays together, and vacation during the summer."

I needed to change the subject, but the guys we were now with wouldn't stop addressing us, so I let them do it for me.

We both turned to see what they wanted. Immediately I caught eyes with one in particular. His brown hair was disheveled on the top of his head, while white teeth brightened his smile. "My name's Seth."

"Christian."

"Is that your dancer name?" I was flustered that he'd ask that, assuming I was a stripper.

"No! This is my first time at a place like this."

His eyes traveled from my chest down to my legs. I crossed them when his glaring made me uncomfortable. "You would kill on the stage."

It was a good thing that the room was dark, because I didn't want this guy to see how much I was blushing. I narrowed in on his hand, tracing the condensation on his bottle of beer. There was something about the way he caressed it that made me think about how he touched a woman. Perhaps I was horny, or maybe this kind of place brought a sexual arousal out in people. Whatever the case, I began licking my lips before I could respond. "You think so?"

He leaned in close to me, so that the other people at the table couldn't hear us. "I know when I'm in my bed tonight I'm not going to be picturing the women that work here."

Our eyes met as I took in his compliment, wondering if he was actually hitting on me. "Do you go to school here?"

He sipped his beer. "We have two classes together. Since you sit in the front, I knew you wouldn't notice."

During class I remained focused. I'd always sat in the front of the room, and been the first person to participate. Clearly everything else in the room was unimportant.

"Sorry. I'm very studious." A barmaid delivered a round of shots to our table. As one was slid in front of me I waited for the cue and downed the liquor. It burned going down, but seemed much easier than the first couple. I was feeling relaxed as Seth replied.

"If that's the case then what are you studying right now?"

"What...nothin'! I came here with friends," I said defensively.

"Right. First timer." He looked over at topless Amber. Right away I felt a wave of unexpected jealously. Her perky breasts were exposed and she downed a shot with several guys at the table.

"What about you?" I interrupted. "Do you come here a lot?"

Slowly he directed his eyes to me. "It depends." I watched the rim of his beer bottle surrounded by his lips. His Adam's apple bobbled as he swallowed. This place was like a natural aphrodisiac. I'd never felt so drawn to a man before. As naked women danced on the stage in front of us, all I could think about was what it would feel like to kiss this guy.

"Occasionally." He put his arm around me as he talked. "Take a night like this. I didn't really feel like going out, but a friend of mine shot me a text that said the ladies tonight were the best he'd seen. It peaked my interest."

"The dancers are very pretty," I added.

He smiled and drug his index finger over my bottom lip. "Yeah, I don't think he was talking about the dancers."

I pulled away quickly, getting a sense of presumption out of his comment. "That's flattering."

He flipped me a grin, turned his attention to the stage, and then back to me. "Would you feel better if we got out of here?"

Stumbling for an answer, I was saved by one of my roommates. "How about we all get out of here? Y'all can come back to our place if you want to party. We've got plenty of booze." Becca seemed excited, and I got the feeling that she knew the guys pretty well.

"Yeah, and I could come by once I get off. I'd love to see what Chris did to my old room." She winked at me before climbing up out of her seat and walking away.

I fidgeted with my clutch purse, trying to avoid making eye contact with Seth. He was sexy, sure of himself, and clearly out to get my attention. Just because I was dressed like a slut didn't mean I was one. He obviously had the wrong impression if he thought I was ready to take him back to my room and get freaky, or did he?

As we all climbed back in Becca's car I started wondering what would have been so bad about hooking up with a hot guy. We were both adults. It wasn't like it was against the law. If I wanted to be treated like a normal person I had to step out of my shell. Even though I knew sex was never an answer, there was a possibility that I'd become so worked up that I may not be able to decline.

Chapter 3
Christian

With a car full of guys pulling up behind us we didn't have much time to prepare the house for visitors. Although we kept it pretty clean, my room had clothes all over the floor, including underwear. I rushed inside and began shoving my bras and panties into a pile. When I heard someone laughing I turned to see Seth leaning against the doorframe. "You don't need to straighten up on my account. I'm not here to admire your furniture."

I noticed how he was looking at me as I sat down on my mattress. "What are you here to admire?" It was a rhetorical question.

He crossed his arms and chuckled to himself. "I think we both know the answer to that."

Looking at my nightstand, I noticed that it was still early. Laughter could be heard from the living room, and a part of me knew that we should go join everyone else. After only three shots I was feeling adventurous. It was unlike me to drink at all, combine that with my low weight and I knew I was already buzzed.

I crossed my legs, noticing immediately where his eyes lingered. "So you think that since we shared a moment I'm going to put out?"

He still didn't move from my doorframe. I suppose someone else could have been listening, not that I cared. I wasn't close enough to any of them to give a damn.

"I don't think anything." Slowly he walked into the room and closed the door behind him. At first I assumed he'd make his way over to my bed, but instead stood in the same place. "Invite me over there with you."

"No!" He was crazy if he thought I was going to ask. When I didn't respond right away he located a chair under my computer desk and walked over to it. After turning it around to face in my direction he sat down and placed his palms on his knees.

"Is this better?"

"Actually, it was probably a mistake for you to assume that any spot in my room would be a good one." I let my words sink in for a moment. He needed to know I wasn't easy, even though every single time I looked his way I thought about what it'd be like to date someone like him. "I'm not going to sleep with you, Seth."

He seemed disappointed, but for only a short time. "I get it. You don't know me. Nice girls like you don't usually put out. That's a good thing, even if guys like me don't like it."

"I'm impressed that you have both looks and brains."

His chuckle let me know that he took it as a compliment. "Since you have me pegged, and you certainly have every right to, tell me something about you."

I looked down at what I was wearing, suddenly realizing how uncomfortable I felt. I motioned to the garment. "For starters, this isn't what I'm about. Becca let me borrow it for tonight. I know you're probably thinkin' that I look cute, but I feel ridiculous. "

"For what it's worth, you look hot. I think we've already covered that though." I was getting this vibe from him that he wasn't like other guys. He kept paying me compliments like he was determined to win my trust. Seth was sitting far enough away to assure that I wouldn't feel uncomfortable. "If you want to go change I can wait right here for you to get back," He raised his brow and paused. "Or you could show me what you learned at the club tonight."

I laughed at his comment, until realizing he was being serious. "That's not happening!"

"Well that's a shame because I've got a feeling you'd give those girls a run for their money." His half-smile made me feel like he was being cocky. Did he expect me to dance around my room?

"How about I just take off my clothes and spread out on my bed for you to join me?" I waited to see his reaction.

Sure enough, his face filled with excitement. In a way I was flattered that the idea was appealing to him. "Seriously?"

"No. I'm not serious. We may be adults, but I've got no intentions of flaunting my naked skin to you tonight."

He stood up and walked toward the door. "It's obvious you don't want me in here. It's a shame, because I'd rather hang out in this room with you than be out there with those drunks. Maybe in time we'll become friends. Until then, it was great talking to you tonight, Chris."

Chapter 4
Christian

As he exited the room I stood there staring at the door. Had he really just walked away without an argument? I'd never known a guy to give up so easily. After sulking for maybe losing an opportunity with a perfectly decent guy, I decided to get changed and join my roommates. They'd taken me out and been so nice. I couldn't just hide out in my room all night.

It took only a few minutes to throw on a baggy t-shirt and a pair of shorts. I then followed the laughter into the large kitchen where I found everyone conversing. Since I'd assumed that I had chased Seth away, I was surprised to find him standing there amongst the group of people. Our eyes met and I couldn't help but smile.

My attention was grabbed when Becca pulled me up to the counter and slid a glass of some liquor concoction my way. "Come on, Chris. We're playin' a drinkin' game."

Even though I didn't feel like participating, I knew it was imperative to make a good impression if I wanted to find friends.

Two hours later I couldn't feel my face. Everything that was said was somehow hilarious, and my shyness had suddenly ceased to exist. It was also very obvious that Seth was still interested in me. As the game progressed he'd ended up sliding in closer to where I sat. Most of the people had exited the room once it was over, leaving only a few standing around. Seth brought his lips up to my ear. I closed my eyes, feeling turned on that he was so near. "Let's go back to your room."

I mumbled my words, speaking softly with intentions that nobody else could hear. Unfortunately, in my drunken state I wasn't as quiet as I thought. "Definitely."

At some point Amber had showed up. Thankfully she was clothed, because I liked talking to her, but felt uncomfortable when we'd met. Throwing herself in between Seth and me, she got up close to my face. "Is this guy giving you trouble?" Even in my condition I could tell she was drunk.

"No. He's fine." I looked to Seth as I answered. He was mid sip on his drink and pulled away with a smile on his closed lips.

She placed her palm on his chest. "We go way back, Seth and I. Don't let him fool you. He's a smooth talker."

I giggled. "I didn't think otherwise."

"Just so you know I have firsthand experience with this guy. He likes to be in control."

While laughing at her comment, Seth rushed forward, gently grabbing my arm and leading me out of the kitchen. "Don't listen to Amber. How about we go somewhere quiet?"

He may have felt embarrassed, but I appreciated her honesty. If I were sober it may have bothered me that he'd been with my new stripper friend. Apparently I was too emaciated to consider what I was actually doing.

By the time we'd made it into the confines of my room, we were already lip-locked. Seth had his hands on my ass as I pressed him against the door to close it. Mid-kiss I backed away, noticing his intent-filled eyes watching me. He licked his wet lips and stepped forward toward me as I continued moving backwards. "We're back to the same place," I noted.

"Are we still strangers?" He gained inches on me, finding my waist before my butt reached the bed. "I can still leave if that's what you want?"

I could feel his breath on my face, as well as the lingering smell of the whiskey he'd been drinking all night. This was it. I could tell him to leave like the old Christian would have done, or I could take a leap of faith and let my new found freedom guide the way to happiness.

It was no secret that I was attracted to this guy, and with the amount of alcohol we'd both consumed it would be easy to let go. The truth was I wanted this to happen. There was some necessary desperation to feel accepted by not only this guy that I barely knew, but the people in the next room.

I needed to fit in, and if I could do that and receive some much needed satisfaction I was up for the challenge.

It was time for the new me to shine. "I'm not going to ask you to leave, Seth." Our eyes met, and I could see the excitement shining across his face. "In fact, I'm thinking that I'd like you to stay."

Our lips connected, lightly brushing together. I could taste the liquor on his tongue as it coursed over mine. His gruff whiskers tickled my face while our kissing intensified. Large hands cupped my ass, lifting me onto my soft mattress. I pulled away to back up so that he had room to join me. I didn't have to ask. Seth leaned forward bringing one knee up before the other. I could feel his weight on the bed as our mouths connected again. Immediately he brought one hand up and cupped my breast. My normal instinct would have been to push him away, but I refused to be that person. I couldn't be that innocent little girl that my parents expected me to always be. Independence was something I strived for; something I needed to find on my own.

That same hand pushed the fabric of my shirt up to reveal my naked abdomen. The cool air in the room was apparent, even though parts of my body were numb. His warm touch sent chills all through me. As one hand traveled up and underneath my underwire, I lifted my knee to feel his eagerness, becoming turned on more. He took my hand and guided it over his groin. "Is that what you want to feel, baby?"

Him calling me that sent me into a frenzy. Ethan and I had experimented with many things, and he liked to call me babe on occasion. Somehow it always made me feel like I was his, in a teenage-girl kind of way. Even though this was just casual sex, it felt different for me, which in turn was quite exciting. I wasted no time reaching my hand down his pants and feeling the smooth skin of his erection. Despite it being squished in between fabric I could tell his girth was impressive. My kisses became more aggressive when he began grinding himself into me. "You want it now, don't you?"

I closed my eyes to try and rationalize with myself on the answer. The right thing to do was kick him out and forget all about it happening, but I didn't want to be a good girl. I wanted to feel like Amber did when she got up on that stage. I wanted to be in control for the first time in my life, instead of the girl that hid behind the books.

I shoved Seth off of me and stood on the mattress. He leaned up on his elbows as I began swaying to music that didn't even exist. There was no real rhythm involved. I was far too drunk to attempt to be graceful. Through the madness I grabbed the edge of my t-shirt and slowly lifted it over my head. My midriff beckoned to be touched, so I looked down as my fingers trailed the skin beneath my navel. Seth licked his lips as he observed the show catered for his amusement. He didn't scrutinize as I wriggled out of my pants, letting them drop to my ankles. "Is this what you wanted to see tonight?" I asked as I flipped around shaking my ass while playing with the elastic on my thong.

His warm hands grasped my calves and started rubbing the skin on my legs. Thankful that I'd shaved, I removed my bra and tossed it across the room. When I finally turned around to face Seth I was completely naked, covering my breasts with my own palms. "Show me," he said as he stared at my chest. I froze in place, knowing that only a small thong kept me from being without clothes in front of this man that I'd just met. My fingers inched away from my nipples, revealing the brown circles in the center of each breast. "I want to taste you."

He may as well have put his mouth up to my pussy already, because that's how hot I got when I heard him saying it. I dropped to my knees, allowing him to remove my panties himself. In no time at all he'd pulled me on top of his face, immediately going to work with his tongue. I threw my head back and let the tantalizing sensations devour every part of me. His skilled tongue flicked over my clit, causing me to shiver and cry out words that made no sense at all. The harder he did it, the more difficult it was for me to hold still. I was convulsing over his face, and he seemed to be getting off on it.

When Seth knew he'd taken me to new heights, he pushed me to the side. There was no need for him to ask me to participate. I was already longing to touch him and discover what else he could do to my body. The comfort of the alcohol was allowing me to feel relaxed; to not worry about what he might be thinking, or if I was bad at something. All I wanted was to keep going, even if that was hard to admit to myself.

After unzipping his pants, and pulling out his thick cock, I took him into my hand. His fingers played in my messed up hair as I jerked him off. His girth made me wonder about oral sex, and if my lips could even fit around it. The good thing was that I wasn't about to find out. That was something I'd never done before. Using my saliva as a lubricant, I let my palm give him pleasure, while moving at a steady pace. Being that he was pretty drunk, I knew I was safe from having him ejaculate all over the place. I was being careless, but I couldn't stop.

Seth pulled my hair, forcing me to back up. "I need to stop before I do something I'll regret. I'll be right back."

Honestly, from the moment he walked out of the bedroom, I felt like it was over. Maybe he'd lost interest in me and this was his excuse. Perhaps I was just bad at making out, or the way I'd handled him going down on me. I know it seemed irrational, but nothing else made sense.

After locating my sheets, I pulled them up to my chin and looked at the ceiling wondering how I'd always ended up in the same situation. A single tear dropped from my eyes, and I began to sniffle.

Then my door opened.

Seth came walking back inside, locking the door behind him. He reached into his pocket and pulled out a condom, holding it up as if it were a prize. "Sorry it took so long. It was in the bottom of the glove compartment." He noticed the way the covers were pulled up. "Did you change your mind?"

Using my feet, I kicked them down. "No, that's not it."

Desperate for the connection, I patted the mattress beside me. Seth headed in my direction, dropping his pants before joining me under the covers. His kisses weren't aggressive, but subtle and kind. He took his time caressing my skin, savoring the moment as if we had all of the time in the world.

Even though I could still taste the liquor on his tongue, I cared less about it. It was very apparent that he being responsible had given me an extra bout of confidence. I felt like he was a good guy, and maybe, just possibly he'd want to see me again after this was all over. Seth could be my way in with improving my social life.

This one-night-stand had serious potential.

Being with a stranger, even if we'd talked for several hours before, had me worried. I'd never done this, albeit that casual sex was something that happened quite frequently with people my age. Maybe if I hadn't been raised by my church-going, ten-commandment, abiding parents I'd have different morals. There again, my sister didn't seem to have my struggles with fitting in and breaking rules, nor did my older brother Noah. Their free spirits made me envious, which was yet another reason why I was allowing this encounter to take place.

As our kissing intensified, Seth's hands explored my body. He'd already spent enough time between my legs that I felt more comfortable being naked in bed with him. I ran my fingers down his back as he sat up to apply protection. The crackle of the wrapper was another reminder of what was about to happen. When he turned to face me our eyes met. I wouldn't call it a cosmic connection, but I absolutely knew we were both on the same page. My buzz had eased the nerves leaving me ready and willing.

Seth started out on top of me, entering me with ease. I was already so wet between my legs that we didn't need any more foreplay. My muscles were contracting in all of the right places each time he coursed in and out of me. He leaned forward to kiss me several times, and I found it reassuring to know that he cared enough to make sure that I didn't think he was selfish.

When we went to flip positions he slid back inside of me, but stopped to stare at my face. "You're so beautiful."

I looked away as the heat rushed to my cheeks. "Thank you."

"I'm serious. You're gorgeous. I knew when I saw you in class that I wanted to see you naked." He laughed and brushed a strand of hair away from my face.

"That's a drunk statement."

"No," he argued. "It's not. I noticed you the first day of the semester. You wore this red shirt that said something across the chest. You had shorts with rips on the thighs and I couldn't help but notice the skin it revealed. I wanted you to notice me, but you were too busy reading your syllabus to even notice me standing next to you."

I felt flattered, and a bit saddened. Perhaps we could have been friends before having to meet officially in a strip club. "Sorry. School is important to me. I guess you could call me a nerd."

"Na. I'll stick with beautiful." He leaned forward and kissed my lips slowly, seeming like he was savoring them. "Now, where were we?"

As goose bumps covered the outside of my skin, new sensations filled my insides. His strides became faster as he pumped inside of me. Seth reached between us, rubbing hard against my clit. My own body began to twitch and shake as uncontrolled bouts of pleasure overwhelmed me. I knew he was enjoying seeing me lose control, because the next thing I knew he was holding me still and clenching up his face. When he finally relaxed he rolled us over to be lying side by side. "You okay?" He asked.

I shrugged. "I've never had a one-night stand before. Honestly, I don't know how I feel about it."

Seth rolled over on his back and looked up at the ceiling fan as he spoke. "I feel so good right now." The bed was moving a bit, and I understood it was because he was removing the condom. I grabbed a napkin off of my nightstand that I'd been using for a coaster and handed it to him. After confiscating the used rubber, he turned to face me.

Even with feeling uneasy over my actions, I managed to smile.

"You know, it's not a one-night-stand if it happens again."

"Are you asking me to sleep with you tomorrow?" It was a simple question.

"That depends on your answer," he teased.

"I'll probably say yes," I taunted back.

Shortly after that we both passed out. I didn't know about Seth, but I for one couldn't hold my liquor very well. After the buzz wore off I was left exhausted. Falling asleep was easy, so much so that I didn't even care that a stranger was asleep in bed with me, locked in my room.

My parents would have been so disappointed in me, but somehow I couldn't stop smiling. All of the years they'd spent educating me on how to be the proper kind of lady had just gone to shit. It didn't matter to me, because this was my chance to reinvent myself, and I was damn sure going to do it.

Chapter 5
Christian

The early morning light illuminated the room even though I had the blinds closed. The reminder of what had happened last night was a muscular forearm draped over my chest. Considering that I was about to pee myself, I knew I had to free his limb without waking him.

As slow as I could move I slid off the bed, almost tumbling to the hardwood floor. I crept out of the bedroom before I noticed any movement. Once inside the confines of the bathroom, I stared in the mirror at the person I wasn't sure I knew anymore.

It was true that I'd known exactly what I was doing with Seth. Even though I wanted it to happen, a part of me hated that I'd allowed myself to change in an effort to fit in. My red eyes were probably from the amount of alcohol I'd consumed, but I saw them as regret; a reminder of the lengths I was willing to go to seek acceptance. After brushing my teeth, and cleaning up a bit, I marched into my room prepared to face whatever came my way. I just didn't expect it to be empty.

Seth was gone, and even though I was clothed, I felt naked.

The utter humiliation of knowing I'd slept with someone that didn't even have the decency to say goodbye was devastating. I'd stooped to a whole new low, and been left to suffer the consequences. Just as my butt made contact with the mattress my bedroom door flew open. Becca rushed in, placing her hands on her hips even before she came to a halt in front of me. "What's Seth Radcliff doing coming out of your room at the crack of dawn?"

I shrugged and looked over at my furrowed sheets. Dismay was written all over my face. "Do I have to spell it out?" I said in an undertone.

"Did you sleep with him?"

Was she really that naive? "What do you think?" I may have been quiet, but I wasn't blind. He was sexy, kissed with passion, and made me weak in the knees. From the moment we first touched I knew that I secretly wanted him.

"Girl, don't be surprised if you get a visit from Mila."

"Who's that?"

"His girlfriend, well, on again off again. They break up all of the time. As soon as Seth hooks up with someone new they have a huge blowout and then make up for a couple of weeks. When she finds out he slept with you she's going to shit her drawers. There's no way she can compete."

It was another nice compliment she'd paid me. I appreciated how it wasn't about me looking like someone else to fit in. She was saying I was beautiful, and it meant so much to me that I forgot about the seriousness of the conversation for a few short moments.

"I didn't know he had a girlfriend."

"He doesn't, technically. It's so complicated. I should have mentioned it last night, but you were the last person I saw hooking up with a guy you just met. Clearly I have a lot to learn about you," she teased.

"I'm an open book, I can assure you. Last night was a mistake. I drank a lot, and so did Seth. Maybe he won't tell anyone. I mean, he left without sayin' goodbye, so I can only assume that I wasn't anything to write home about."

"Seth's not like that. He won't stay quiet. I don't want to hurt your feelings, but you need to be prepared, just in case. Hopefully it will all blow over in a couple of days."

Just as I started to reply I heard a phone ringing, and it wasn't my normal tone. I shuffled through the sheets until I found an unfamiliar cellular device. It was obviously Seth's.

"Oh shit. That's Seth's phone isn't it?"

I nodded. "What should I do? It says that it's Mike."

"Pick it up. It's probably just Seth looking for his phone."

I did as she suggested and lifted the receiver to my ear. "Hello?"

"Chris, it's Seth. Can you meet me later so I can get my phone? I left it by accident."

The elephant in the room was obvious to me, even if it wasn't meant to be. He wasn't bringing up where he'd left it, or the fact that he'd left without saying goodbye. "Yeah, I guess."

The line was quiet for a second. "Do you think maybe we could study later together?"

This caught me off guard. Did the popular man I'd just spent the night with really want to get behind a book with me? "Are you jokin'?"

"No. Listen, I'm late for something, but I'll call you later when I'm done."

"Okay," was all I could say to him. I was still in shock, too flabbergasted to think about my actions.

After the call ended I noticed that Becca was still standing in front of me. Her hands remained on her hips, while her brow was cocked. "I could hear what he asked you. Chris, you can't see him again. I mean, we all like Seth, but he's the kind of guy that's too good to be true. I can assure you that you're nothing but a rebound."

I didn't care. I hadn't been with him because it was love at first sight. Things like that only happen in novels. He'd gotten into my pants because I'd let him for selfish reasons. Love had nothing to do with our predicament. "I'm a grown woman, Becca. I'm not afraid of the competition. As for his ex, well she shouldn't have let her man go if he meant that much to her." I was risking a lot by standing up for myself, but I'd been around this girl long enough to say she appreciated a woman who stood her ground. I intended to remain in control, even when I didn't dare have a clue what I was getting myself into. "Last night Seth and I had a great time. Who knows if somethin' will come out of it. He's sexy and all, but I'm not about to get carried away like it's some fairytale. We both know the probability of us becoming a real couple is slim to none. Before you get all judgmental I want to make it clear that it was the first one-night-stand I've ever had. As much as I enjoyed it, I don't plan on making it a habit."

I watched the corner of her lip curl as a half-smile formed. "We're goin' to be great friends, you and I. It's funny because when you moved in here I thought you were lame. I'm sorry for judging you. It's quite obvious you're a woman who knows what she wants. We could all learn something from you."

I wanted to laugh. If she only knew that I was shaking as we spoke, in fear of being called a liar, or someone who didn't have a clue about standing up for herself. "I wouldn't go that far. I'm just a quiet girl tryin' to make new friends. Thanks, by the way, for taking me out last night. It was a great time."

"Amber really likes you. It's funny. She's one of Seth's go-to girls when he and his girlfriend are on the outs. I'm surprised you two hit it off so well. She's been crazy about Seth for years."

It was discerning hearing that Amber secretly had a thing for the guy I'd just spent the night with. She hadn't brought it up, but neither had he. If I wanted to be accepted by all these people I couldn't freak out, at least until Becca left the room.

Then I wondered if she was testing me. Perhaps her queries were more on an insight as to what type of friend I'd be. "I wish she would have told me that. She must be so pissed at me."

As much as I enjoyed meeting Amber, I couldn't let my guilt distract me. I also couldn't let the past night's antics set me back. "Do you think she hates me now?"

Becca shook her head. "Amber's not like that. Honestly, she's too smart to let a man get her down. Besides, you've seen how she has them lined up. Seth's just one of many that she's messed around with. Don't get me wrong, she's not a whore. She's got this seven date rule where the only play she'll give is a kiss or some shit. She says if they are good guys they'll wait it out."

"You're making it worse. So she's gone out with Seth more than seven times?"

"That I don't have a clue about. He spent the night a lot, but who knows what happened between the two of them. Amber's too proud to let someone like Seth win her over. If you learn anything from living with me it will be how to handle a man. I can't have my friends getting involved with losers."

I giggled, finding it impossible to contain how I felt about being schooled. On the other hand, hearing her call me a friend was invigorating. "I appreciate the support. Don't worry about Seth. I can handle him. Last night is in the past. I'm sure it was a one-time thing for the both of us. I'll give him his phone back and let him know that it's never goin' to happen again."

She seemed content as she pranced out of my room, leaving me to stew with everything she'd shared. While intoxicated I hadn't considered that Seth could be a man-whore. I'd also not gotten an inclination that he and Amber had hooked up more than once. They seemed like friends, but nothing more.

For someone that promised to not give a damn about Seth, I spent the next few hours going through everything in my closet in order to look my best. It occurred to me early on that I was most definitely interested in him. The problem was that I didn't want to get involved with drama just so my peers could accept me. Because I longed for real relationships, I had to be careful.

My cell phone began to ring, sending me scavenging around to locate it. Though the caller wasn't whom I'd anticipated, my heart skipped a different kind of beat seeing the name.

"Hi, mom."

"Hey, honey. Dad wants to know if you'll be home tomorrow night for Sunday dinner? Your brother and Shalan have some wedding stuff to discuss with you."

I played with my fingernails while resting the phone against my shoulder to hold it in place. "Yeah, I'll be there. Noah messaged me yesterday about it."

"Okay, well you know your brother doesn't relay that stuff to me. Also, I'd like it if you had a talk with your sister. Your dad found out she's been seeing that guy again. We're at our wit's end."

"I don't know why you think I'll be of any help. She and I have nothin' in common."

"Please, Christian. Just try."

I rolled my eyes. It was harder said than done. "Whatever. I'll attempt to talk some sense into her, but I'm not makin' any promises."

"Between the two of us, I'm worried she's going to get herself into trouble. She's promiscuous, and I'm terrified it could lead to her getting pregnant or even assaulted." I heard my mother beginning to sniffle. When it came to my sister my mom had struggled. She was defiant, and the more they tried to help her, the worse she became. "I hate watching her making bad choices. I pray every night and nothing changes."

Church had always been important to my family. The power of prayer had been proven many times through the years, but my sister's drama was self-inflicted. She didn't want to get better, because she liked her life. She should have been named trouble instead of Addison. It didn't help that she was the youngest who, for better argument, had a more lenient upbringing. My father was a strict man, who'd been brought up with old-fashioned morals. My brother had the hardest time, especially since I was so quiet. Addy just couldn't stay out of trouble. "Mom, calm down. I'll be there tomorrow and talk to her. Don't get yourself in a tizzy, because then daddy will freak out and make it worse."

She sniffled a few times before answering. "You're right. I'm sorry. I know you're tired of hearing it. It's probably why you moved out in the first place."

"I moved out because it was time to act like a grown woman. I can't keep dependin' on you and dad to take care of me forever."

"Just promise me that you'll always make good choices, Christian. I can't handle it if I fail with both of my beautiful daughters."

It pained me to hear her talking like that. My mom hadn't failed, and neither had my father for that matter. My sister needed to wake up and realize what she was doing to our family. I thought about what my mom was asking me. Last night I'd made terrible choices for a very selfish reason. I shouldn't have done it, and now I knew I'd have to live with my decision for the rest of my life. My guilty conscience would haunt me, and I was going to have to figure out how to accept it and move on.

At the end of the day one-night-stands weren't going to make me popular. My asinine idea was now like a punch to the gut.

How could I have been so foolish?

Once I'd hung up with my mother I stood in front of my mirror staring at my own reflection. Was I even going to like the person that I was trying so desperately to become?

As ridiculous as it was, I spent the rest of the afternoon washing my sheets, as if it somehow erased what had been done. When Seth called to meet up with me I told him I couldn't make it.

Determined to obliterate my obvious regretful idea, I pretended to be sick to prevent from hanging out with my roommates. By the time the sun set I was back to being alone, crying myself to sleep with less dignity than I had twenty-four hours before.

Chapter 6
Christian

Spending the day with my family was something that I always looked forward to. As much as I liked being away from them, nothing compared to how happy I felt when we were all together.

My family was huge, and I had a ton of cousins. I wish I could say that I was close to all of them, but it wasn't the case. They'd always treated me like I had the plague, especially my twin cousins Jake and Jax. I knew deep down they cared about me, but they'd never admit it. Since they lived in North Carolina, and only visited Kentucky for special occasions, I found reprieve from their constant badgering.

As I pulled my little gray Fiat down the dirt driveway I felt a sense of relief. I got this way every Sunday when I knew I was at the one place in the world where I was loved. It was funny how when I first left for college my parents would be waiting on the porch for me to arrive. As my freshmen and sophomore years passed their excitement seemed to fade.

When I walked inside of my childhood home, I immediately smelled my mother's cooking. My dad's voice could be heard from his office, located down the hall of the first floor. I dropped my keys on the side table. "Hey, I'm home."

Before anyone replied I saw my brother, Noah, rounding the corner. He leaned against the trim and crossed his arms, giving me a once over. "What's up, sis?"

I jabbed him lightly in the gut as I walked by. "Nothin' much. What're you doin' here? Don't you have some hay to bale?"

My brother had once struggled with taking over the family ranch business. It took a huge falling out with our dad, and a new love interest to change it all for him. In so many ways I envied his life. Sure, he had a hard daily routine, but he was so loved by everyone he'd ever been around. Noah never had trouble communicating with people. He spoke his mind, and was very popular with the ladies, at least he was before he met Shalan.

His girlfriend and I had a lot of similar qualities. During her teens she'd withdrawn from a lot when she lost her mother to cancer. After meeting my brother her dreams had come true. Now she was on every radio station around for her hit single, *Broken Love Darlin'*. It was written about losing my brother, and how she'd never be able to move on. It was that same song that got them back together. The rest is history.

Their wedding had been postponed because our cousin Isabella got pregnant. She wanted to be able to participate more with the wedding, so they decided to hold off on the nuptials. Now it was obviously back on, and the engaged couple wanted all the bells and whistles to make their day perfect. It was another reason I envied them.

After my one-night stand I was more ensured that a happily ever after was never going to happen for me. As much as I wanted to sit back and daydream about having a house built on the family land in order to start a family with my dream guy, I knew it was pretty far-fetched. Not only was I single, but not in any position to remotely look for Mr. Right.

"Where's Shalan?"

"She's at the house. Mom asked her to bring some vanilla and we forgot it. I thought you were her comin' back in."

"Nope. It's just your lame ass sister." I looked down at the hardwood flooring instead of straight into his eyes. My brother had a way with trying to convince me that I was some kind of precious beauty queen. I knew better.

"You need to quit that, Chris. Some guy's goin' to try and take advantage of you if you don't watch yourself. I get that you're stubborn, but there ain't nothin' ugly about you."

I finally looked up to meet his gaze. His eyes were widened and baring into me. He'd made his point, and I became overwhelmed with anger.

"Noah, please don't start this again. You're my brother, but it's no secret that I'm awkward."

"Do you own a mirror?"

Before I could answer our sister came walking down the stairs. She was wearing an all black outfit and her hair had been dyed to match. Her eyes, which were shadowed in a dark color so much that she appeared sick, peered at the both of us. I noticed immediately how heavy they looked. It had only been a week since I'd seen her last, but it was blatantly obvious she wasn't well. "Addy?"

Noah leaned forward to whisper in my ear. "You think you've got problems."

I shoved him. "Shut up," I said quietly before looking in her direction again. "What have you done to your hair?" I wasn't about to come out and say that she looked like death.

She grabbed a chunk and ran her fingers through it. "I colored it. It's more me." Even her speech seemed to have slowed down.

"Are you drunk?"

"No, of course not." She laughed at me before taking a few more steps toward the front door.

When we realized she was walking away from us, Noah and I followed. "Where are you goin'? Mom's got dinner about done."

She motioned with her hand like she didn't care. "I'm goin' out. Tell her to put a plate in the fridge for when I get home."

I took hold of her by the arm and forced her to a halt. "Wait. You can't leave. I won't let you get into a car in your condition."

"Fuck you, Miss Priss. I'm leavin' and there ain't nothin' either of you are goin' to do about it. Don't give me those looks either. I hear enough from mom and dad every day. I can't wait until I get out of here for good, so y'all can mind your own damn business."

Suddenly a car rolled down the lane. A guy with his head shaved hung out the window of the driver's side. "Come on, before your daddy gets his gun."

While Addy jumped in the passenger side, I watched Noah marching over to take matters into his own hands. He reached inside of the vehicle and the guy started driving away. Noah jerked his hand away right before he was injured.

"Son of a bitch!" He yelled.

"Who is that guy? What the hell is goin' on with our sister?" I was literally afraid for her. "What is she on?"

"Hell if I know." He pulled his cell phone from his pocket and began talking to someone. "It's me. Close the gates out front. I don't care what time it is. Close the damn gates until I get there." He hung up abruptly before walking in the direction of the house. Before he hit the first step our father was coming out.

"What's goin' on?"

"I'll be back in a minute," Noah murmured before climbing into our dad's truck and taking off down the dirt driveway.

I looked at my father, still in shock from what had taken place. "Dad, what's wrong with Addy?"

His face told me everything I wanted to know. It was obvious that he was aware of her condition. "I've been on the phone all afternoon tryin' to get her into a facility."

"A facility? Like rehab?"

"She's in bad shape, darlin'. Your mom's been a nervous wreck over this. We've tried everything. Your sister needs professional help. She's been stealin' from us. First it was blank checks for twenty dollars here and there. Last week I found out she pulled all of the money out of her savings account. She tried to access her college funds, but I'm the account holder."

We'd had savings accounts since we were born, and I knew for a fact that we kids had been given the same amounts to deposit. Addy had blown through thousands of dollars, and she clearly had nothing to show for it. I sank down on the porch steps, in attempting to come to grips with how bad off my sister was just as Noah returned. Addy was in the passenger side, waving her hands all around as she screamed at him. Our father heard the profanities coming out of her mouth and hauled ass over to the vehicle, practically pulling her out by her black gothic looking t-shirt. She froze in place as he stared her down and waited for her reaction.

"Get your ass in that house, and don't even think about pullin' a fast one, young lady. That there was the last straw. You're out of here come mornin'."

"Fine, kick me out. I don't even care," she slammed.

He shoved her forward, and I half expected him to pull her pants down and spank her like when we were little and drew all over the bathroom walls with Sharpies. Noah met our dad on the porch and they both watched as Addy marched inside, slamming the door behind her.

Just then Shalan came pulling up on a golf cart. Since their new home was built only through the woods from our parent's house, it was the easiest way of getting to and from each place without having to start up a truck or car. I think she knew from how we were all standing there that something was wrong. Noah put his head down as she climbed the first step. He spoke clearly so he wouldn't have to repeat himself a second time with the bad news. "Looks like we're goin' to have to postpone the weddin' again, darlin'."

I sighed and watched the excitement leave from her face. The two of them were never going to catch a break when it came to them tying the knot. I felt terrible for them, even though I had nothing to do with it.

"She's goin' to be gone for about a month. The program will detox her and then she'll have aggressive therapy to tame the addiction. It's a long road until she's back to her old self again."

I looked over at my brother who did his best to shoot me a half smile. I gave one back to him even though my head was in a million places. This wasn't exactly how I pictured my Sunday going, but somehow I knew I was right where I needed to be.

Chapter 7
Christian

As much as I wanted to stick around after dinner it was obvious that I was just in the way. After saying my goodbyes, I headed back to my house near college in hopes of being able to sleep without worrying about my sister.

I couldn't have anticipated that Seth would be sitting on the front railing waiting for me to arrive. He stood up slowly and approached my vehicle before I could climb out. I let him open my door while I clutched my purse that his cell phone remained in. "Hi."

Without speaking he grabbed me by the waist and pulled me close. It was so unexpected that I didn't even realize it was happening until our lips brushed. He tasted of alcohol again, which in turn made me pull back in shock. Was this guy an alcoholic?

"Sorry, I've been thinking about doing that all damn day."

I wiped my face with the back of my hand, not wanting the scent to linger for longer than it should have. "I suppose you're here for your phone."

"Well, yeah, but-."

"Please don't make this awkward, Seth. We both know last night was a mistake. I know you just got out of a relationship, and honestly I'm havin' a hard time knowing that you and Amber were involved. Friendships are hard to come by, so I'm not really at a point where I want to risk ruinin' any for some guy."

He seemed shocked before shaking his head with a gruffly smirk. "Go out with me."

"What? Did you not hear anything I said to you?"

"Yeah, I heard you. I'm choosing to ignore it. I had a great time last night, and frankly I needed it. I'm not going to lie. I think you're sexy, and being with you was a great reprieve. I get that you don't want to damage new friendships, but I can assure you that Amber and I are nothing."

"And your ex?" I had to ask, because I certainly didn't want her to come looking for me.

"We're through. That bitch has issues, and I'm done with it. Now, how about that date?"

With my hands now on my hips I peered into his eyes, desperately searching for another reason to decline his offer. "You're relentless."

"I know what I want and am confident I can have it again."

It was no exaggeration that this guy was attractive. I half expected his head to explode after his comment, but he just stood there relaxed, as if he had no care in the world. I didn't know whether to feel annoyed or impressed. "Can I think about it?"

I handed him the cell phone as I spoke.

He looked down at it noticing that I'd turned it off. "Is it dead?"

"No. I shut it off."

"Did it ring a lot?"

"I turned it off after we spoke. I had dinner with my parents, and didn't want it goin' off in my purse. If you're worried about me goin' through it, don't. I have no interest in your business." The truth was that I had morals. Snooping wasn't something I needed to do. It wouldn't bring me happiness, so it was irrelevant.

"Damn, well you might be the only chick on the planet." His face was so close to mine. "Your accent does things to me. I could listen to you talk all night."

I sighed and responded, "That's flatterin'. If you haven't noticed, I'm not like other women."

"No, you're not. That's why I'd like to see you again, and I don't mean in class. Let me take you to a movie. It's my treat. Just come out and do something normal with me. We don't even have to touch."

I don't know why I couldn't resist this man standing in front of me. My mind was saying no, but my body was eagerly begging to see where it would take me. "I don't know."

"What's your number?"

"If I give you my number will you let me think about the movie?"

"Only if I get to kiss you one more time."

I snatched his phone and plugged my number in before I could change my mind. Without wasting a single moment, my body urged forward as my lips pressed gently over his. I kept my eyes open, watching as he closed his. Pulling away became hard when I felt his hands cupping my face. In a matter of seconds his tongue entered my mouth and my kiss goodbye turned into something altogether different.

I pulled away only a few minutes in, catching my breath after someone yelled out of a car window for us to get a room. Embarrassed over my public display of affection, I took his hand, leading him inside with me.

It was wrong to want Seth after one kiss, but following the stress I'd dealt with at the ranch it was the distraction I needed. He didn't boast as we walked through the living room, saying nothing to my roommates who were watching television. My bedroom door closed and we were right back to where we were the night before.

Seth lifted my shirt over my head, highly intent on what was to come next. This time I refused to hold off the inevitable. Reaching for his pants, I opened the fly and shoved them down, including his boxer shorts. A stiff erection pressed over my stomach the next time our lips met. Seth pulled away only in as much time it took to lift the shirt over his head. Our teeth clanked as we kissed while marching backwards to my bed.

I kicked my pants off my feet and backed up on the mattress. Seth stood for a moment taking in my naked body. I licked over my bottom lip, dragging my teeth as I did it. His abs were pronounced, and I got chills imagining the way it had felt to run my hands over them the night before.

"I bet this wasn't how you saw things going," he teased. Seth's body came down overtop of mine. He rolled us over, as his hand gripped the cheeks of my ass. With his guidance I began moving my horny body over his. Low groans vibrated over his lips when we kissed again.

"Don't talk." I didn't want a reason to change my mind. This was necessary for me. I craved release and he was going to give it to me. I figured this was a win-win scenario for Seth. He wanted sex, and I was giving it to him. Plus, he didn't have to take me out to get some. In a matter of minutes we were naked in my bed.

Once he'd located a condom and put it on, we were back on the mattress tangled together. Seth reached his hand between my legs feeling how turned on I already was. In my eyes it was embarrassing. All he'd done was kiss me, and I was eager to spread open.

Seth had other ideas.

He tugged on my arms, forcing me to sit up. Our gaze met and I was resolved to go along with whatever he had in mind. As he stood, I knew right away what it implied, although I wasn't sure if I wanted to proceed. Oral sex was very personal to me, and with my not having any experience I feared that I was probably horrible at it. In all honesty it was breaking my focus, causing me to rethink having intercourse with him.

I had a better idea to break his attention, and get him to participate in something else. With no warning I flipped my body around, getting on all fours. My ass stuck high in the air, right in front of his face. His hands spread over the skin on my ass, gently caressing each side. I shimmied as he did it, teasing him with the view. Another groan sounded from behind me. At first I felt his erection pressing at the base of my asshole. I shifted so he knew I wasn't down for that. "Let me," he begged.

"No. Shut up and fuck me." Since I never talked that way it made me feel uneasy, as if I'd be punished.

"Say it again," he requested as he urged himself inside of me. I gasped feeling his length filling me. Immediate satisfaction overwhelmed my senses. My movements back and forth made slapping sounds when our bodies hit. Butterflies ran through my body, tingling every limb. I became lost in the act of being satisfied. Nothing could break my concentration.

My knees started to burn while continuing to grind forward and back. Fingernails dug into my hips, put there for control, only leaving to slap me hard on the cheek of my ass. The pain burned, also giving me goose bumps. "Harder," I called out for him to repeat.

He slapped me again, this time so close to where he was inside of me. I could feel the quivering of my muscles each time his palm made contact with my smooth skin. Clenching the covers didn't help hold me in one place. We were banging so hard against each other that we'd moved clear across the mattress. I had sweat running between my breasts and they were making sounds as they bounced. This was the definition of fucking. It was pure consummation.

I felt Seth tightening up, his sweaty chest pressing against the skin on my back, though a release didn't come. Instead I was flipped over and picked up, and I wrapped my legs around his back as he carried us over to the desk. I could feel papers beneath my ass as he lowered me down. His hot breath edged closer. Soft lips crushed over mine, sucking and licking with no pattern. He was lost in the essence of unadulterated bliss, not caring about being fantastic, but racing for ecstasy. His palms coursed over my hardened nipples causing my body to go into turmoil.

I watched as he got off on me losing control. Only moments later he stilled my body and let his head fall over my shoulder. We both stayed there for a moment to catch our breath. "Well then," he said as he backed away from me, breaking our connection.

I closed my legs and covered my chest with my arms. "Yeah, sorry."

"Don't be. It was unexpected, but nothing to apologize for." I watched him remove the rubber and toss it into my garbage can. He looked so handsome as he located his clothing and began redressing. I followed his lead, wanting to cover at least my most private parts. "So about that movie."

I lifted my shirt over my head as I answered. "You still want to take me out? I figured you got what you wanted already."

"I like you, Chris. You're different."

"Thanks, I think."

He stepped toward me breaking the distance between us. I watched his hand reach up and touch my cheek, before he tucked my hair back behind my ear. "Let me take you out. The last show is in about an hour. I'll have you home before midnight."

Since I'd just put out it wasn't like I had a good reason to steer clear of Seth. In fact, I knew if I did it would make me look like a slut. Since I was far from being promiscuous I decided that it was better if I went along with it. The brutal truth was that besides Ethan, Seth was the closest I had to a new friend. I mean, Becca and Amber seemed nice. I wanted them to accept me. Thinking I'd screwed up with Amber, I decided to give Seth a chance. At the end of the day it was obvious that we were attracted to one another. It wasn't exactly how I would have liked to start a relationship, though all of it was uncharted waters as far as my experience went.

"Fine. Let's catch a movie."

Seth waited for me to clean up a bit before we exited my room. He took my hand as we walked through the living room and even said hi to my roommates. Despite feeling uncomfortable something about being in the presence of this popular man made me giddy.

I'd thought I'd had a one-night stand. It was my impression that we'd never be friends. Seth seemed genuinely interested in me, and I had no clue what to do about it.

Chapter 8
Christian

The movie theater was dark and for the most part empty. Except for a few couples scattered throughout it was vacant. Seth held my hand as we watched in silence. Halfway into the show we began making out. I couldn't get enough of his kisses, and for some reason it didn't matter if we were in public. I actually liked knowing that I was his date.

You can imagine the shock I felt when his hand traveled down underneath my panties. His warm palm cupped my pussy, his finger circling over my clit. I looked around the dark room to see if anyone was watching us. Once a little more pressure was applied I refused to worry.

The draw of his finger entering me caused me to whimper. It was turning me on so much that I began lifting my butt off the seat to match the way his hand was working. I knew that if someone were behind me they'd know exactly why my head was bouncing. To imagine it being someone we knew was terrifying yet thrilling. We started kissing again as he continued to plunge his finger inside of me while flicking my clit with his thumb nail. I couldn't contain how amazing it felt, soon falling prey to an earth shattering orgasm.

Slowly he revoked his finger, shocking me when it was brought up to my lips and drug over them. I pulled my head away until he came forward and kissed my lips, sucking in the flavor himself.

It turned me on more. Our tongues meshed together and I immediately went searching for the fly on his pants. His stiff cock, so apparent, was there waiting once I made it inside. He stopped kissing me and whispered against my lips. "Please kiss it. Suck my dick, Chris."

For the second time he'd asked me to do something I wasn't comfortable with. The strange thing was that this time my mouth began to water. I wanted to return the favor he'd just given to me, and I was prepared to go against my better judgment to make it happen.

Crawling down on the concrete floor wasn't the hard part. It was trying not to think about being caught giving oral sex in a movie theater. If my parents ever discovered what I was doing they'd disown me.

Even with that terrible fate looming in my mind, I cupped my palm around his shaft and leaned forward, taking the tip in between my lips. His warm skin felt so soft. The taste of rubber from our sexual relations earlier still lingered. Unsure of what I was about to take part in, I loved the idea of impressing Seth. He clenched a clump of my hair as my mouth consumed his hard cock. I sucked hard while using my free hand to massage the remainder of his shaft. I could hear the little sounds escaping him. They made me work harder to please him. My cheeks began to ache just as I felt a hot gush filling them. The salty flavor caused me to gag, spewing the wad onto the floor. Seth leaned forward offering me the edge of his t-shirt to wipe my face off with. "Damn, girl. Where'd you learn how to give head like that?"

I shrugged and sat back down next to him. I couldn't tell him that I'd ever done that in my life. Ethan never asked me to do it, probably because he thought I'd never want to sleep with him again. Like I mentioned before, it was something I'd always considered intimate. My recent actions were ruining my good standards, leaving me to make bad judgment calls that literally left a bad taste in my mouth.

"I'm just going to use the ladies room." I stood up and left the room, hoping to be able to rinse my mouth out as best I could.

The well-lit bathroom was a change from the dark theater. I headed over to the sink and started washing my hands so I could use them to rinse out my mouth. I'd no sooner began to swish the water around when someone came walking in. As quickly as possible I spit the water out and used a paper towel to wipe off the excess. The reflection in the mirror displayed a beautiful blonde. Her bright blue eyes caught my attention. I smiled at her, expecting the same action in return. I certainly didn't think she'd come at me, or start shoving me into the porcelain vanity. "You bitch! Who do you think you are?"

"What are you talkin' about?" I may have been quiet, studious, and a bit peculiar at times, but nobody pushed me around. My brother taught me to defend myself if I needed to. "I don't even know you," I said as I shoved her back.

She had tears falling from her eyes. "I saw you with him. You came here with Seth."

My eyes widened. "We're friends." Were we? I didn't even know if it was the truth. Did that make me an awful person?

"Well I'm his girlfriend."

I put my hands up. "Whoa. Are you Mila?" My body began to shake. I wasn't afraid of fighting this girl. She was smaller than me, and it was clear that her emotions were all over the place.

"You know my name? Did he tell you about me?" She had hope in her eyes. Unfortunately, I didn't have good news for her.

"No. I heard that the two of you used to date. Listen, I was under the impression that Seth was single. I never would have agreed to see him otherwise."

"I don't know why he'd lie. He keeps doing this to me," she sobbed.

I reached over and placed my hand on her shoulder. It was obvious that she could have attacked me at the moment, but I got this feeling she needed support. "I'm so sorry."

"I'm in love with him. He loves me too. I know you don't see it, but he does. When we're alone he's different. We're going to get married. He promises me all the time."

"I don't understand."

She wiped her eyes and continued. "Seth likes to be popular. He considers himself some kind of leader. I'll never get why he does this shit. He says it's important to keep up the charade. That's all you are. You're just a game to him. Frankly it's pathetic that you gave in so easy."

"It's not like that." I tried to justify my actions had more meaning, but I was coming up with nothing.

"You're just another conquest. Don't think you're special." I hated her sarcasm, but understood why she was so determined to hurt me.

"I'm just goin' to go. Do me a favor and tell your boyfriend not to call me. I don't have time to deal with this drama."

I stomped out of the bathroom to find Seth waiting for me. He had his arms crossed and they fell down to his sides when Mila followed me. It took one look in his eyes to see that he knew he was screwed. "Lose the number I gave you," I said as I walked by.

Thinking he'd rush to comfort her, I was surprised when he followed me outside. "Chris, wait. It's not what you think. She's psycho. What did she say to you?"

I stopped walking and turned to face him. "For starters she said you were together. I'm basically a whore; one of your many, and that you play games like this all of the time."

He threw his hands up in the air. "What the fuck? Mila is crazy. Look, let me drive you home. I'll explain everything."

I crossed my arms, and refused to look him in the eyes. "I'd rather walk."

"It's getting late, and we're miles from your place. Just let me drive you. I swear I won't do anything."

Since I didn't have many options, I pulled out my phone and dialed the one person I knew would come to my rescue. He picked up on the first ring.

"Christian Mitchell. Long time no speak."

"Shut up, Ethan. I need a ride. Can you come pick me up from the movies?"

I looked up as I awaited his reply, seeing Seth shaking his head. For some reason I felt bad for him.

"I'll be there in ten minutes. Are you alright?"

"Yes, I'm fine. Just hurry up." I wasn't fine, but I knew Ethan's temper well enough to not want him getting into it with Seth. I'd made enough things a mess.

Once the phone was back in my purse I turned to look at Seth. He was leaning against his car watching me. "I'm not a bad guy, Chris. When I said I liked you I meant it. I asked you out because I wanted to see you again." He pulled out a flask and started drinking the contents. He obviously had a drinking problem.

"Oh, it wasn't because I put out so easy?"

"No. Of course not. I mean, I'm not going to lie. It was nice. We have good chemistry. You can't deny that."

It was true, yet I couldn't admit it at this point. "Please don't do this." I started to feel overwhelmed, used, and completely confused. It had been one day, though I felt like we did have something between us. The idea of giving up after I'd screwed him was an awful feeling. It was as if I'd slept with him for nothing. I wasn't that girl.

I couldn't be that girl.

Mila walked out of the building and I watched his posture straighten. He pointed toward her, yelling clear across the lot. "Thanks a lot! I hope you're happy, you stupid hoe."

She kept walking to her car, as if she couldn't hear him. He motioned in her direction. "See what I mean? She's full of shit, Chris. I swear."

I placed my hands over my face as I thought about how to respond. I hadn't asked for this crap to happen on top of all of the drama at my parent's house. "Seth, I've had a bad day. I'm goin' home."

"I'm sorry I ruined your day. Even though it ended terribly, I enjoyed the parts where we were together. For the record, I'm not losing your number."

"Seth, please stop. It was a mistake."

"Which part?"

"All of it. I'm not some easy lay. It never should have happened. I had a lot to drink and you kept pushin'."

"Don't give me that shit. I'd believe that if it weren't for today. What's your excuse?"

"I'm havin' family problems. You wouldn't understand. My sister's messed up on drugs. I guess I needed reprieve."

"So you used me? This is completely wrong on so many levels. I liked you, that's why I hit on you. Yeah the sex was great, but I would have been okay waiting. You're the one to make the choice. You can't take it back. I just can't believe you used me to clear your fucking head."

I was offended. "I did not!" He was right and I hated being aware of it.

"Yeah, that's not how I see it. Just because I was willing doesn't make it right."

"Screw you. I'm not a slut."

"I never said you were." He didn't have to. He obviously expected to sleep with me and when it happened he knew he could come back for more.

The sound of a car that desperately needed a new muffler pulled into the parking lot. I felt comforted knowing that Ethan had arrived to save me from myself.

I turned to walk in the direction of his car and felt Seth tug me back toward him. In an instant I was slamming against his hard chest. I tried to fight him but he pushed his lips against mine. His eyes were closed making me feel like it was personal. When I finally freed myself from his hold he seemed more content. "I always get what I want. I'll talk to you soon."

I backed away. "I'm sorry. I wish things were different. Goodnight, Seth."

"Chris, wait. Don't walk away from me."

I ignored him and headed toward the car, not wanting to look back and see the man that I was ashamed of sleeping with.

Chapter 9
Christian

"What the hell were you doing with that scrub?" It was the first question Ethan asked when I climbed into the passenger seat.

"Don't start with me, Ethan. I'm not in the mood."

"Dude, I watched him kiss you. Why am I here if you were clearly on a date?"

"I said I don't want to talk about it. Please. It's been a terrible day." I covered my face with my hands while we pulled out of the parking lot. "Sorry. I'm not tryin' to start a fight."

"How long have you been seein' that jackass?"

It wasn't Ethan's fault that I was in this predicament, but I wasn't about to give him all of the details. Some things were better left unsaid. "I'm not seein' him. Are you goin' to give me the third degree? I'd just as soon walk if you are."

"Whoa. Defensive much? Who crawled up your ass today?"

"Addy's fucked up on drugs. It's bad. My parents are sendin' her to rehab. Dinner was horrible, and now Noah's postponin' the weddin' again. Everything's a mess, and on top of that I may have just ruined my chances of ever bein' friends with my new roommates."

"How so?" He asked.

"It's a long story. Besides, we agreed not to talk about people we get involved with."

"So you're involved?" He beat his hand to the beat of the song that was playing as he spoke. With his eyes focused on the road he waited for my response.

"It doesn't matter. It's never happenin' again."

"You screwed Seth didn't you? You're such a hussy!" He teased.

I smacked him on the arm. "Shut up. You have no room to talk. How many girls have you banged in the past two years?" For a while it used to hurt me severely to think about him being with other people. I'd learned to live with the jealousy because it was the only way our friendship would survive. It was also another reminder of how much he'd always meant to me.

"That's beside the point. I'm a guy. You're a sweet woman of innocence. You can't let a guy like Seth deflower you."

"Oh my God, stop! Deflower? Did you just say that? We both know who deflowered me, and it wasn't Seth."

He patted me on the leg. "It was my pleasure by the way. Your cherry will always be mine."

"You're so sick."

"You love me. Stop bitchin'."

We pulled up in front of my house, and I looked down at my knees. "I don't even feel like talkin' to any of them."

Ethan turned away from the curb and began driving again. He reached over and took my hand, the same one I'd had down Seth's pants. As he clenched it I felt horrible. "You can spend the night with me, but no funny stuff, and you better not try somethin', because I ain't into sloppy seconds."

"I wouldn't even -."

"I might, because it's you, so make sure you don't let me. Tonight I'm your best friend with no benefits."

I laughed and looked out the window. "You're hopeless."

"There's hope for me out there somewhere. I just haven't found it yet." He paused for a second. "Oh, just to warn ya, I've got company, but I'll kick her ass out as soon as we get there."

"Who is it this week?" I had to ask. Ethan may not have been a jock, albeit his good qualities were obvious to other women. His dark blonde hair was longer, almost always hanging out of the John Deere hat he wore. His parents were also farmers, giving us a common connection both academically and with our family life. Ethan was on a scholarship, but he didn't have to work hard. His intelligence was hidden by his witty sense of humor. Though apparent in his GPA, he was always a fun person to be around. It was another reason why he never had trouble getting laid. Ethan was the whole package, and I'd never regret him being my first. "I don't have to come over and ruin your night."

"Yes you do."

I rolled my eyes. Even if I started an argument with him, he'd still insist that I stay over. In this case I needed him. He was my rock; the one person who could make all of my frustrations disappear.

It took him less than two minutes to send his new conquest on her way. She didn't exit without giving me looks of disapproval, not that I cared. Everyone on campus saw the two of us together. It was no secret that we were friends. If they wanted to imply we were a couple I wasn't going to correct them. To them Ethan was just another college guy looking for play, but to me he was so much more. Our friendship meant everything to me, and his support was my lifeline.

Once we were in his apartment with the door shut, he pulled me into his arms and kissed the top of my head. "Sorry you had a bad day."

"Is it okay to hate myself?"

"It's not okay, and I'll tell you why." He sat us down on his bed before continuing. "You're smart, and somewhat sexy, probably a little more than somewhat, but whose judgin'?"

I shoved him down flat on the bed, immediately feeling a rush of anxiousness. He must have seen how I responded and sat back up abruptly. "Be nice to me."

"I'm always nice to you, Chris. I only pick on you because I love ya."

We said those words a lot, but they weren't romantic. Our friendship was special, and we loved each other as friends, so I reminded myself on a daily basis. It was hard after being in real love with the guy. I wished things were different. Even after sleeping with Seth my heart would always defer to Ethan. He knew me like no other could, and for that I'd forever care about him.

When Ethan got up and held out his hand I was a little confused. "We just got here."

"I'm gettin' a shower. Come with me."

I gave him the stink eye. "No way. I'm not goin' to divulge details, but I can't get a shower with you. I refuse to be that girl."

"Jesus, Chris, I ain't askin' you to put out. Share some water with me. Save the environment one gallon at a time. I've seen you naked, and you've seen what God graced me with. Stop bein' a prude. You need my attention, and I need a shower."

I slowly got up and followed him into the bathroom. Even though I knew we weren't going to do anything, it was still hard for me to imagine that I'd be naked in front of two different men in a matter of only a few hours.

From the moment the water hit my body I felt a rush of relief. Ethan kept his distance shampooing his hair, while I stood there hoping the water would wash away all of the bad. With my eyes closed I got startled when two warm hands touched my shoulders. He pulled me close, running the bar of soap over my neck. Instead of letting him continue, I placed my head against his chest and started to bawl. "Don't cry, Chris. You're safe."

"I'm ashamed of what I've done. It's so easy for you to make friends. All I wanted was attention. I wanted to know what it felt liked to be wanted."

He backed away and lifted my chin, forcing me to look up at him. "I tell you I want you all the time."

"That's not what I mean. You and I are... I don't even know what you'd call it. This was different. He was interested, really interested in spendin' time with me. I thought I had a chance. I believed that my life was goin' to change. He'd introduce to me his friends, and I'd finally be able to walk across that damn campus with a smile on my face because I'd know people."

"You didn't? Please tell me you didn't screw that douche for popularity?"

He knew me so well. I looked down feeling utterly disgusted in myself. "It doesn't even matter."

My chin was being lifted again, and I knew I had to look him in the eye and face the consequences. "Don't you get it? Don't you see how special you already are?"

I pulled out of his hold and leaned against the shower wall. My knees were too weak to stand up on my own. Admitting that I'd stooped to a whole new level in order to be accepted was harsh. "I didn't just let him in my room and drop my panties, if that's what you think."

He leaned against the opposite side and crossed his arms. For a second I thought about how comfortable we were with each other, and how neither of us was staring at our obvious exposed body parts. "I'd hope not, since you made me wait for years to get some."

"That's different! Besides, I'd hardly call it years. After our first kiss it was pretty fast." I snapped. "Don't compare the two."

"Why? Because if your time with me was more special you might as well start prayin' for forgiveness for your lies."

"It was," I whispered as another bout of emotions washed over me. Ethan was giving me shit and I didn't understand why. He'd slept with other girls, and been the one to make it clear we were only friends. "Why are you bein' like this? You had a girl here tonight, but that's okay?"

He let out an air-filled laugh. "Forget it, Christian."

Hearing him say my whole name gave me butterflies. He never said that unless it was important. When Ethan began walking out of the shower I caught his arm. "Please don't be mad at me. You're all I have."

His brows remained furrowed, and I could have sworn that he was hurt, even though I knew he'd tell me if he was. "I'll sleep on the couch, you can have the bed." It was the only words out of his mouth as he exited the bathroom, leaving me vulnerable and alone.

I'd often wondered what made women break in movies and sink down to the shower floor, but as my butt hit the cold tile I finally understood their pain. Even though I could say that Seth was handsome, interesting, and someone I'd totally date, I'd made a terrible mistake, not once but twice.

Ethan left me to suffer in my own pool of misery, not coming in to check on me like I expected him to. It was obvious he was angry at me for my choices, but couldn't see how it was any different from how he made me feel when he was with one of his easy lays. I was just as human as him, and obviously nowhere near perfect. We all had skeletons in our closet, and if that was the only terrible mistake I made in my life it wasn't that horrible anyway.

I took my time finishing up in the shower. Between my sobs and the fact that even my safe place wasn't enough, I thought about going back to my house. Sure, there'd be questions and whispers behind my back, but it had to be better than looking in Ethan's eyes and seeing nothing. It was another cold reminder of how much that love I had for him still existed, even though I promised it wouldn't. The truth was that being best friends with him was one-sided. I longed for more, but knew it would never happen, so settling was the only answer, no matter how undignified it was to live with.

Chapter 10
Christian

His bed smelled of him, even though he wasn't in it. I curled my body, hugging my knees while my sniffles finally settled. Ethan was just in the next room, albeit I didn't dare seek him out. Whether he was pissed or just plain disappointed, I couldn't face him. The best thing for me was punishing myself until regret was all that remained.

According to the blinking clock an hour had passed. The room was quieter than I remembered it ever being, making me feel alone. At least if I'd gone home I could hear the whispers. This was agonizing.

Out of nowhere I heard my phone vibrating. Since the room was so quiet I jumped up to get it before it annoyed Ethan. The number was Seth's and my stomach dropped as I hit the ignore button and turned off the device. It wasn't the phone calls that were going to drive me mad as much as seeing him in class. I couldn't look him in the eye after what we'd done. I'd given him head in a movie theater for Christ sakes. If that wasn't the lowest point in my life I don't know what was.

As much as I would have liked to be strong and face that I'd made the decisions that had led me down this path, I simply couldn't shake the ill feeling they gave me. After climbing back into the bed I struggled with my emotions once more. Even though I attempted to hide my sniffles, it was obvious that if Ethan was awake he could hear me. Despite the fact that I was covered and completely warm, my body trembled. I hated my life. No matter how hard I tried I'd always be the woman that was awkward. My desperate attempt for recognition was a complete failure. I'd never be popular, or the woman that men lined up in front of for a chance to date. My aspirations of being someone else were fading away, leaving me lower than I'd ever been before. Even my own best friend hated being around me.

Knowing that I'd never be able to sleep, I climbed out of the comfortable bed and gathered my things. It was a long walk but I'd make it just fine. At this point it wouldn't even be a loss if I didn't. Sure, my parents would miss me, and Ethan would probably shed a tear, but he'd easily replace me. Hell, he probably only kept me around because he felt sorry for my struggles. It was embarrassing knowing that I'd poured my heart out to him and he hadn't returned the feelings. I should have known back then that our friendship was doomed.

Ethan would wake up and wonder where I'd gone, so I chose to leave him a note.

I went home to sulk in my own misery. Sorry I bothered you with my problems and ruined your night. It's obvious that I've somehow destroyed this friendship. I'm sorry for that. I'm sorry for falling for you and ruining everything we had. If I could take it back I would, because I couldn't wish this pain on my worst enemy. I won't call you to save me anymore. I'll figure it out on my own. I knew college would tear us apart. You're too great to stick around with a nobody like me. Thanks for everything, but I can't keep pretending I'm happy. It's best if I focus on school and nothing else for a while.

Love- Chris

I'd made it to the front door before stalling to catch my breath. My feelings for Ethan had suddenly overwhelmed me. My heart ached imagining him not being a part of my life. I knew he didn't love me the way I loved him, but was I willing to sever everything because of that?

I had to.

I couldn't keep doing all of this myself. My schoolwork would come first, and I'd stay focused on that until graduation. Once I was out of college I could start my life over somewhere else. Until then I was going to pretend that my heart was intact, and that I hadn't just lost my very best friend.

Ethan

After all this time she still didn't get it. Christian Mitchell wasn't just any girl. She was THE girl.

I'd known it from the moment she walked into my life so many years ago. Her mouth full of braces, and a big red pimple at the tip of her nose was my first impression, but I'd seen beauty.

We were paired as chemistry partners. Her voice was like an angel, and those green eyes captivated my soul. I suppose I could have told her how I felt. I could have asked her out, knowing she felt the same way, but I knew better. This girl was too special to get lost in some adolescent romance. Statistics told me it wouldn't last, and I knew I'd be the one to mess up.

There was only one way to keep her in my life forever; one way I knew I'd never lose her.

I think for a long time I assumed that she'd always stick with me until I got my shit together. In some perverted way I hoped she'd remain single so I didn't have to watch her fall for someone else. I knew she loved me, it was never a big secret since we discussed pretty much everything. I just always selfishly thought she'd wait for me.

I may have screwed around, sleeping with chicks that were willing, but they'd never hold a candle to her. They'd never be able to fill the place that I knew would always be hers.

I'd called her the night before because I was tired of waiting. Thinking she was finally coming out of her shell to get to know her new roommates, I didn't give her a hard time about it. I never could have imagined that she'd go out and be with another guy, especially Seth. I didn't think she'd find him interesting, especially enough to allow him into her bed.

I joked it off as much as I could, while inside I felt like I was being stabbed by a thousand daggers. Saving her from the bad date gave me empowerment, but it was short-lived. I should have known from that first moment that something was different. If anyone could read her it was me. All of the signs were there. I should have known she'd fucked him. It was just too hard to accept.

This woman that I'd put on a pedestal had betrayed my heart and she didn't even know it. I'm not going to lie when I say it took everything in me not to come clean. The damage was done though. She'd slept with another man, and although I had my own skeletons, I couldn't look at her the same way anymore. My perfect girl had been tainted. How was I to look at her and not feel destroyed inside? How was I supposed to look myself in the mirror and know that I could have prevented this from happening?

While in the shower I tried to be understanding. The brutal truth was that I needed her to be close to me. In other words, I needed to reclaim her in some caveman kind of way. Christian wasn't like the other girls I slept with. She'd been my first for a reason. She and I shared something that other people couldn't understand. We'd always been outcasts in school because we were smart. It was a shame that our intelligence had been the reason for failed relationships with our peers. High school is a hard place for a nerd to fit in.

Once in college we'd set out with a common goal to reinvent ourselves. It had worked so far for me, but not so much for Christian. I can't say I wasn't happy about that. Secretly I wanted her to remain untouched. It's the reason why I knew I wasn't ready to commit to her. I couldn't be selfish and keep her for myself. I had to let her live.

In all of my attempts to do the right thing I'd somehow forgotten how precious our relationship was. I comforted myself with other women to prevent her from wanting me. I'd given her every reason to seek attention from another guy.

Being in the shower with her had been a mistake. I couldn't look into those green eyes and picture them peering into another guy's eyes the way they did mine. I couldn't touch her skin and imagine that someone else had consumed every inch of it. I certainly couldn't hold her hands any longer after wondering where they'd recently been.

This was a catastrophe. I needed to be alone; to dwell in the mess that I'd made of what could have been our future. Selfishly I knew I couldn't tell her my feelings. She was too messed up over what she'd already done. Tangling more stress into the mix would be a dick move. Keeping her at a distance was all I could bring myself to do. I had to calm down before I was able to put on a brave face and pretend that she hadn't just cut me into tiny pieces.

Hearing the door open and close let me know she'd left. More than anything I wanted to run after her. I needed her to know I'd never let her go. She had to know that every moment of every single day I was thinking about when we'd have a life together. My buried feelings had been forced free and now I struggled with the outcome. We still had two years of college; two years to make mistakes and find ourselves again. If she knew I returned her feelings she'd forget about what was important. I couldn't let her lose focus. Somehow I had to get over this, and be the friend she needed, because losing her completely wasn't an option either.

When I got up to retrieve my shoes I found the note. Her words caused me more confusion. Did she really think I wanted a life without her in it?

It made me angry, so much that I crumpled up the note and tossed it across the room. My next move was to call her and tell her off until she told me where she was so I could drag her ass back to my bed. Suddenly I didn't care about Seth and what they'd done together. All I wanted was to remind her how important she was to my life.

The phone rang with no response. After a while it went straight to voicemail. I kept calling it, even when I'd gone out to look for her. I coasted every street from my place to hers with no sight of her anywhere. She obviously didn't want to be found. It was the middle of the night. She'd be able to hear my car coming down the road and hide. I slammed my fist on the steering wheel out of frustration. By the time I'd reached her front door I didn't care who was sleeping. I banged on it hard, waiting to be let in.

Becca answered in her pajamas. She was clearly not happy that I was standing on the porch. Instead of asking me what I wanted she simply opened the door and motioned for me to come inside. I burst through Christian's bedroom door only to find the room vacant. After looking around for a piece of paper I noticed the used rubber in the trash can.

Sitting down was inevitable as another wave of jealousy hit me. Then I looked down noticing the messed up sheets and became enraged. I couldn't take it. The image of that dude fucking her on the same bed that I sat on was like a kick in the balls. The reminder still so apparent, I reached down and began ripping the linens from the bed. Once I'd stripped everything off, I flipped the mattress completely over. I had to rid it of any reminder of Seth.

Since Christian obviously wasn't home, I grabbed the sheets and blankets and left with them. After tossing everything in a local dumpster, I drove home still heated from everything that had transpired. With no sign of her back at my place I was left to sit awake all night, both annoyed and worried at the same time.

One way or another I'd have to get over my anger. I needed her more than she knew, and the fact that there was a chance that our friendship was over was making me sick. I wouldn't stop until she knew the truth.

I couldn't.

Chapter 11
Christian

I was a blubbering mess when I left Ethan's house. My hair was still damp, making the shivering worse. When I heard his car coming my way I ducked behind a hedgerow to prevent being discovered. He couldn't know how much he'd hurt me. Ethan had made it clear that our friendship couldn't be anything more, and since I'd screwed up and slept with Seth, someone he clearly hated, I knew I'd damaged our already strained bond.

My phone rang until I shut it off, but not before seeing I had more messages from Seth. He was begging to explain everything to me, going on and on about how he and Mila were not together. To be honest it didn't even matter to me. I couldn't trust him, or his lunatic girlfriend. Drama wasn't something I was used to, so it was important to stay out of it.

Once I'd shot him a quick text simply telling him to leave me alone, I continued walking back to my house. It was still dark out, even though I knew the early morning sunrise was only hours from showing its face. While the town slept, I was left to sob alone, without a single friend to call.

When I heard another car heading in my direction I ducked back behind a vehicle in case it was Ethan again. This time the driver didn't keep going. They stopped and I heard the sound of the door shutting and footsteps heading in my direction. I peered around the car only to come face to face with Seth. The shock of him being the one person to find me made me uneasy. "What are you doin' here?"

"I might ask you the same. What the hell are you doing out in the middle of the night? I thought you were with a friend."

I shook my head. "I was. It's a long story." Frankly, I didn't even want to explain it, especially with him.

"Come with me. I'll take you home." He held out his hand to motion for me to join him.

I wrapped my arms across my chest and stood still. "That's not a good idea. I told you that we had nothin' left to talk about."

He seemed frustrated, gritting his teeth to hold back a boast of something he'd regret. "Look, just let me take you home. It's dark, and who knows what could happen to someone who looks like you."

I rolled my eyes and walked toward his car. "Sayin' that won't get you back in my pants."

Once we were both inside I appreciated the heat being on. My frigid fingers started to warm up as we took off down the road, except we weren't headed in the direction of my house.

It was too early to panic, so I simply asked. "Where are you takin' me? Did you already forget where I live?"

"I know where you live, but you're coming back to my place until you listen to me."

"No, I'm not. Turn this car around and take me back, Seth. I mean it. I'm not in the mood."

He drove faster, ignoring my demands. He even locked the doors to prevent me from opening them. I think that's when I started to freak out a little bit. The only thing keeping me from screaming was the fact that he'd been wonderful when we were together. I had to take a second to think about his feelings.

"Why couldn't you just hear me out?"

"I'll listen, Seth. I will. Just stop drivin' so fast. You're scarin' me. Why can't we talk at my place?"

"It's too late for that. We're here." He pulled into the driveway of a dark house. It most definitely wasn't decorated with letters like a frat house.

"Where are we?" I asked.

"Come with me. You'll be fine."

While leery I followed Seth into the house. As soon as we got inside I began to worry. This house wasn't lived in. He grabbed me by the arm and pulled me into another dark room. He let go of it and illuminated the room with a lighter. I got one quick look before it became dark again. The stairs were falling apart, and the paint was peeling off the walls. In the middle of the floor was a mattress covered with bunched up blankets. "Oh my God," I started backing up. "Tell me you're homeless and you're not here to kill me."

The sudden fear of being in terrible danger hit me like a ton of bricks. Before my eyes were able to adjust to the darkness enough to find my way to the front door, he was taking hold of my hand again, jerking me into his chest. "I'm not going to kill you. I said we're going to talk, and then you'll see that I wasn't lying. You'll see how much I want you, Christian."

"Don't call me that!"

"Why? It's your name?"

"Please turn on a light. You're scaring the shit out of me, Seth. This ain't funny at all. I promise to listen to you, but get me out of here first." I knew I was starting to beg, but this wasn't normal. People didn't go to abandoned buildings to have serious talks. It wasn't right, and the longer we stood there the more upset I was getting.

Seth took me by the waist and pulled me forward. He tugged me down on the mattress and sat next to me. The outside light finally gave me a little visibility. He was staring at me, and I felt uncomfortable being alone with him. "You're so beautiful. I've watched you come into class for weeks, waiting for the day that you noticed me. I knew I'd have you if I was patient. Girls like you are worth the wait."

That was enough for me to hear to become terrified.

"Why are you doin' this?" I was getting choked up with my words. There was no explanation to the ill feeling that I had. This guy had never put me in harm's way until this moment. If this was some sick joke it was working. I was afraid. "Please take me home. I promise I'll forgive you."

Seth pinched my cheeks with one hand and forced me to look in his direction. His widened eyes sent chills over my spine. The trembling was no longer from being chilly. I was shaking in fear of losing my life to a psychopath. "Is that how you talk to the guy who you slept with a few hours ago? Do you know how good it felt when you wrapped your lips around my cock in that movie theater? I could have fucked you right there in those seats. I can't stop thinking of the way your pussy tastes. I knew you'd be sweet." His fingers trailed between my legs, dragging over my pussy. I shuddered, repulsed by his touch.

"Get off of me."

Seth's strength came into play after that first rejection. He clenched my wrist, preventing me from freeing. When I felt the force of his hold I immediately started to try and push him away from me. This only angered him more. He grabbed my other wrist and pinned me down on my back. I turned my head to the side, still trying to wriggle away. "Calm down. Stop teasing me."

"Teasin' you?" Was he crazy? "I want to get away from you. This ain't funny, Seth. Let me go. Get the fuck off of me."

He started laughing. Then I felt his tongue licking over my cheek. The smell of alcohol became apparent, and I wondered how much he could have consumed in the time since I'd seen him last. I closed my eyes and flipped my head around to make him stop. He pinned my thighs with his legs, pressing all of his weight over me.

My cries were unheard, but I still continued. He attempted to kiss me and I moved my head, determined to fight him off. When my sobs remained he brought both hands together and held them with one of his, while using his other to reach into my pants. I felt him there, touching me without permission. "Why are you fighting me? You know you like it. You gave me this pussy without a fight earlier today." He entered me with more than one finger. I gasped in between screams then felt his mouth covering mine. I tightened my lips to keep his tongue out. When he relaxed his own I bit down and pulled. He tightened his grip on my wrists and shoved his fingers as far inside of me as he could. The gentle guy I'd slept with was gone. This person didn't care if I was begging him to stop. He was on a mission to sleep with me, and I was going to fight until I was free.

"What the fuck did you do that for?" He yelled.

"Get off of me." I spit in his face, waiting and prepared for him to hit me.

Instead he leaned forward wiping my own fluids over my cheek while whispering in my ear. "I like it when you fight. It's almost as sexy as watching your lips devouring my dick."

The bile rose to the back of my throat as he adjusted once more, removing his finger only to shove it in my mouth. I tried to fight it, but he thrust it in so fast I began to gag, not from the taste, but from it being forced halfway down my throat. When he removed it I coughed and turned to the side in case I had to throw up.

Seth used those seconds to flip me around and hold me down with the weight of his body. He tugged on my pants, pulling them off of my ass. I scream and yelled, begging for him to stop what he was doing. The taste of my tears filled my mouth as I cried out feeling him entering me. Time froze, and in that instant I knew he wasn't going to let me go until he finished what he started. The pain, feeling wretched and dirty, followed by the sounds of him getting off on ripping the skin of my asshole as he continued pumping his hard shaft inside of it caused me to lose sense of what was actually happening. I don't know if I was in denial, or the whole thing was just too tragic for me to be able to accept. No matter which way I tried to understand how I'd gotten to this point it all kept coming back to the fact that I'd let this man sleep with me. I'd let him have his way. I'd given him false hope, and now I was getting the brunt of his brutal display of anger. If Seth couldn't have me he wanted to make sure that nobody else would ever want me again.

While crying hysterically, I waited until he slowed down. The moment he pulled out of me I twisted around, sending him down next to me. With my pants at my knees I got up and started to run in the direction of the door. I refused to look back in fear of him being right behind me. My hand made contact with the doorknob the exact second that I was being spun around.

"Please, don't. Just let me go. You don't have to do this. I'll listen to you, I swear. I'll do anything. Seth, please don't," I repeated over and over.

He grabbed my face hard and pushed his lips over mine. I continued crying silently begging that someone would come to my rescue. He was too big to overpower, and I was honestly afraid of what would happen if I fought him too much.

Once he pulled away from his kiss, he put his lips up to my ear. "Stop fighting me. I know you want this, just like you let me have it earlier. Spread your fucking legs like a good girl. My dick's been craving you since we left the theater."

I was bawling. Snot ran down over my lips. I couldn't see anything but his shadow in front of me, but knew I was trapped. "Please don't hurt me, Seth. I'll do what you want." He shoved me harder against the wooden door, lifting me up against it. When I refused to wrap my legs around his waist he pulled me away and then slammed me back against it harder. The back of my head immediately began to throb. I dug my hands into his shoulders, feeling him placing my legs behind his back. I raised one hand and slapped him hard across his face, dragging my nails from his cheek to his ear.

He yelled out loudly and shoved himself inside of me before leaning his head down and biting the skin under my chin. The new waves of pain were agonizing, so much that I wished I'd just pass out. He pressed his lips over mine again, and this time I refused to fight him. I'd done my best to break free, but he was double my size.

The time that passed in the house all seemed to blur. Seth forced himself on me for hours until he couldn't get hard anymore.

I don't remember him leaving. Had I blacked out? How could I not recall his releasing me from his hold?

The sun was just beginning to rise when I became coherent again. My pants were clinging onto one ankle, and my shirt was torn and tattered. With shaking hands I managed to pull up my underwear first. After getting both legs back in my pants, I pulled them up and did the best I could covering myself with the fabric of my ruined shirt.

My purse, which had somehow ended up across the room, was left untouched. I found my phone inside, but stared at it wondering who I should call. My parents would never understand. My roommates weren't close enough for me to trust them, and there was no way I could call Ethan, not about this.

Before exiting the house, I found an old bathroom. The plumbing was off, but I managed to wipe off a mirror enough to take a look at my face. The person that stared back at me was unrecognizable.

Chapter 12
Christian

When I crept out of the bathroom I was able to get a better look around the old house. It was obviously used as a fraternity house at one time. Posters still hung in the rooms, and there was even leftover furniture in some.

Even though I knew I was alone, I took my time going down the stairs. My body ached with each step, and a metallic taste reminded me that I was pretty beat up, on the inside and out.

A few pictures were left on the walls, and where the mattress was left on the floor was a large area rug that had seen better days. Part of the ceiling had caved in where the dining room was, but I decided not to look any further. The less I knew about this house the better, because I knew it was going to haunt me.

After doing my best to hide my ripped shirt, I began to trek in the direction of my house. Students jogged by me, and some were on bicycles. None of them noticed my condition, and if they had they never stopped to ask if I was okay. I kept my head down low as I marched down the sidewalk, focusing on every part that hurt.

When I arrived at my house I'd gotten lucky that no one was around. I entered my room and locked the door. The first thing I noticed was that the blankets were off of my bed. I searched the room, not finding them anywhere. Since they were the last of my priorities I started removing my clothes.

While standing in front of the mirror I peered at the reflection looking back at me. Tears filled my eyes as I touched each injured sore area, reliving how that particular ailment had occurred. Vomit rose to my mouth, and I hauled into the bathroom to puke. After throwing up for a few minutes I turned on the shower and climbed in. Much like the one I'd taken at Ethan's house, I sunk down to the floor and held my knees up to my chest. Bawling wasn't the answer, even if I was unable to control my emotions.

It was still unbelievable. How could someone that seemed harmless do what he did to me? It was clear that this certainly wasn't a dream, therefore I'd been assaulted sexually, and I had no idea how to go about seeking help. I was ashamed of my actions, so much that I couldn't admit to ever being with him in the first place.

Time got away from me again after my shower, in which I scrubbed every inch of my body hoping to rid myself of any remaining hints of his scent. After dressing I laid on my mattress and thought about calling my parents, but they were already dealing with my sister's latest catastrophe. I couldn't call them with this information, not after I'd let the guy in my pants the same day it happened.

While blaming myself for everything that occurred, I fell asleep crying.

I awoke to someone knocking on my bedroom door. I climbed off of my bed and walked over to the door, hesitating just before opening it. "Who is it?"

"It's me. We need to talk." His voice caused me to cringe. I placed my hand over my mouth so he couldn't hear me freaking out. "Chris, let me in."

Seth's voice vibrated off of my door as if he were leaning against the opposite side. I backed away, fearful that he'd bust it open and hurt me worse. "Go away! Just leave me alone!"

"I know you're mad. Please let me in. I need to talk to you about it. I was drunk. When I woke up I remembered what happened. Chris, please-."

"Get the hell out of my house. I have nothin' to say to you."

"I'm not leaving until we work this out. I know what happened was wrong, but it's not a big deal. You need to forget it."

I thought about what he was asking me. Of course I wanted nothing more than to forget it ever happened, but as the constant ache of my body reminded me of how he'd held me down, I refused to let him off the hook. "This wasn't an accident. You knew what you were doin' when you took me there. I'm not stayin' quiet, Seth. You raped me, and I'm goin' to tell the whole fuckin' world what kind of guy you are." He may have thought I was weak, but he had another thing coming to him. Nobody was going to hurt me and get away with it.

"What the hell? I didn't rape you. Don't even go there. Don't you dare fucking tell that to anyone."

"Why, it's the truth? You held me down and forced yourself on me over and over again." I was crying through my words, struggling the whole time.

"You little cunt. Nobody will believe you, do you hear me? They'd never believe I could do that to someone, besides, good luck trying to prove that when everyone around you knows we fucked. You were ready and willing, baby. They all saw you."

I was so angry that if I had a pole I'd beat him with it. "If you don't leave I'm callin' nine-one-one. You have two seconds to get out."

I heard footsteps and then the front door slamming shut. When I knew I was home alone again, I opened my door and went out to the front to lock the deadbolt. My roommates had keys so they'd be able to get in.

I spent the rest of the night locked in my room while the people I lived with went about their evening as if nothing terrible had happened. I wasn't even positive that they were aware I was home. Not one of them checked on me.

I picked up my phone to call my parents a few times, losing my nerve at the last second. When it got dark outside Ethan started blowing up my cell. I ended up turning it off so that I wouldn't have to hear it anymore. I knew none of this was his fault, but somehow I felt that if he hadn't overreacted I never would have been out on the street alone. I think I was so desperate to put the blame on anyone but myself.

After hours of being a hermit, I walked out into the kitchen to grab a glass of water. Amber sat at the counter sipping on a bottle of soda. Her eyebrows rose when I entered the room. "Hey, girl. What's new?" She asked.

I shrugged and grabbed a glass, holding it under the running faucet. Since I couldn't exactly explain my situation I chose to lie. "Nothin'."

"How did it go with Seth? I heard he took you to the movies." Was she insane? He wasn't great. He was the devil.

"I won't be seein' him anymore if that's what you're wonderin'."

"Why? Don't tell me it's because of Mila. She's such a bitch." Even though I wanted to go back to my quiet room, I knew she wasn't at fault. Amber was a nice person, and I could use a friend once all of this mess was resolved.

"She's part of it. Can you believe that she followed us to the movies and confronted me in the bathroom?" I had to keep the blame on this girl until I could figure out what I was going to do. I didn't want too many people talking to Seth if I was going to go to the police with his assault on me. This type of situation required me to be especially careful. Either direction I took could ruin my life worse than it already was.

"I'm sorry. She did that when we went out once. I'm glad she did though. I don't have room in my life for guys like him."

"Yeah," I was losing my patience. Seth was the last person on earth I wanted to discuss, and hearing her talk about him made me cringe. "I need to get back to my studies. I'll see you later, Amber."

She clutched my arm as I tried to walk by. It hurt and I pulled back, grabbing it.

"Are you alright?"

"I fell when I was out last night. I tripped over a curb," I lied.

"Was Seth with you?" She inquired.

"Look, I don't want to talk about Seth, okay? If I never saw him it would be too soon. He's a drunk, and I know you think he's great, but he's not."

I stormed in my room leaving her to assume whatever she wanted. Just hearing his name was causing me to lose my shit. There was no way I'd be able to go to class in the morning knowing he was sitting only feet behind me.

I spent the next couple of hours researching sexual assault on the computer, wondering if I even had means to go to the authorities. Sure, he'd taken me to an abandoned building and had his way, but just hours before I'd given him oral in a movie theater. I'd already given him my body earlier in the day. If this was some kind of sick fetish I didn't want any part of it. Not to mention that telling anyone this happened to me would make me look like a trouble maker. Seth was on a scholarship, he'd lose everything. As much as I hated the fucker, I was unsure of what I wanted to do. The idea of my parents finding out made my skin crawl. They'd never look at me as being the daughter they were proud of again.

Then there was Ethan.

Not only did I walk away from our friendship, but I knew he'd never be able to see me the same. This was devastating, and the more time I gave myself to think about it, the more confused I became. I needed help and advice, or someone that could help me through this terrible time. The problem was that I didn't have anyone that I could turn to. It was yet another reminder of what I was lacking in my life.

Since I knew I wouldn't be going to class in the morning I decided to drive back to the ranch. My grandmother's mansion had a whole wing that nobody used. Until I could calm down and make important decisions I needed to hide out there.

After the drive that seemed to take forever I pulled through the main entrance to my family's ranch. Thankfully I didn't see any sign of either of my parents, or my brother. I wasn't that fortunate when I stepped inside the house and saw Shalan and my Gram standing at the kitchen counter.

"Christian, what are you doing here?" Gram asked.

"I'm, um...I'm havin' a tough day. I was hopin' I could sleep here tonight to clear my head."

"Is everything alright, love?" I appreciated her concern, but she couldn't help me.

"I'll be fine, Gram. I'm just goin' to head up to one of the rooms and lay down. I'll see you in the mornin'."

After making my announcement I walked out of the room, realizing that I hadn't said anything to my soon-to-be sister-in-law. In the morning I'll get up the courage to call her and apologize. What I needed was to relax and get my mind on track.

The first thing I did was get into the large soaking tub. I filled it with boiling hot water, hoping it would rid me of the dirty feeling I couldn't seem to wash off.

When I retreated back to the bedroom and plopped down on the large fluffy bed it felt nice. This wasn't like being back at college in my room. This was serenity, and exactly the kind of solitude I needed in my current situation. I was safe, loved, and going to get through this, no matter what I had to do.

This wouldn't break me forever. I wasn't going to let it.

Chapter 13
Ethan

After searching for Chris, and then calling her repeatedly I felt like she needed time to get over whatever was bothering her. Since it wasn't like her to fly off the bat like she had, I knew I'd hear from her once she calmed down.

It was difficult to fall asleep knowing she was out there somewhere thinking I was an asshole. Honestly, I didn't even get why she'd gotten so bent out of shape. We'd had disagreements in the past, and she'd never overreacted like this time.

It was two in the morning when my cell phone started blowing up. I ignored the first few rings on account of being asleep. When it continued I rolled over to see who the caller was. That's all it took for me know it was important.

"Chris?"

She was sniffling.

"Talk to me. I've been tryin' to call your ass all day. What's goin' on with you? If you like Seth that much just tell me."

She began to sob on the other end of the call. "Trust me it's not that at all."

"Then you need to tell me what's wrong. How am I supposed to be your best friend when you won't talk to me about it?"

"Do you think I'm weak?" She questioned.

"What?" I scratched my head and checked the time on my alarm clock again. "Woman, what's gotten into you?"

"I just need to know. Do you think I'm weak? Do I have a sign on my head that tells people to take me for granted? I don't understand why I can't be like everyone else."

"You're not weak. You're pretty damn strong if you ask me. I don't get why you want to be like everyone else when the person you are is perfect. They're the ones that need to take notice of you."

"I'm not askin' for you to flatter me. I need the truth, Ethan. For once can you be serious."

"I am," I argued. "Chris, you're awesome. Any guy would be lucky to be with someone like you."

"No they wouldn't." She cried harder, making it impossible for me to understand the rest of what she was saying. I felt so bad, but didn't know a way to convince her that I thought she was amazing. I never should have kept it from her, but I sure as shit wasn't about to tell her my true feelings over the phone.

"What's wrong, babe?"

"I don't understand why life is so hard for me. I can't catch a break. Every time I try to change, things take a turn for the worse."

"I'm lost."

"Take you for instance. I never should have told you I was in love with you, because nothin's been the same since that happened. You say things haven't changed, but we're not as close. It's like I pushed you away."

I wiped the sleep from my eyes and sat up completely, trying to figure out how to manage this kind of conversation without being there with her. "You know that's not true. I care about you too."

"It's not the same." She let out an air-filled laugh. "It doesn't even matter. Nothin's ever goin' to be the same. We can't be together anyway, even if you changed your mind. I'm damaged goods."

"You're not makin' any sense, Chris. In fact, you're worryin' me. Stop bein' all cryptic and tell me what the hell is your problem. Don't make me come over there in the middle of the night and force it out of you."

When she began to bawl I wondered what I'd said to make her so upset. Nothing was making sense. She obviously called me to comfort her, but I had absolutely no idea what was going on.

"Christian, please say somethin', or else I'm gettin' in my car and comin' for ya."

"Don't come near me. I'm not there anyway. I had to get away from all of it. I can't be there, Ethan. Why can't you get that?"

"I'm tryin' to. Is this because of me, or that douche you were with last night?"

"This call was a mistake. I won't bother you anymore. I think I just wanted to hear your voice one more time before you hated me. Goodbye, Ethan. For what it's worth, you're the only guy I've ever loved. I'm glad I got to experience that feelin' before all of this happened; otherwise I'd never know what it was like. I'm sorry for ruinin' our friendship."

"Wait, you didn't-."

The line was dead.

I tried to redial her number, but it went straight to voicemail.

Out of desperation I threw on some clothes and drove over to her house, hoping to make sense over all of this.

First I beat on the door, hoping she'd hear it first. When no one answered, I rang the bell. A girl who I didn't know answered. I could tell she was sleeping. "What?"

"I need to see Chris. Let me in."

"She's not here." She started to close the door.

I put my hand up preventing her. "Hold up. What do you mean she's not here?"

"She left earlier, dude. Go home."

"Did she say where she was goin'?" I asked.

"How the hell would I know? She doesn't say shit to me. Go on now before I kick you in the balls for wakin' me up."

This time the door closed in my face, but I remained standing there wondering why Chris would leave campus. This couldn't be about me and our last conversation. Something must have happened to her, and I was going to get to the bottom of it.

My first class on Tuesday's wasn't until the afternoon, and since I hadn't gotten but a few hours of sleep I knew I had to find Chris and get things worked out with her. After trying to call her several times, I climbed in my car and headed to her parent's house. If she wasn't with me, and she wasn't at the campus house, that was the only other place she'd go.

I guess it slipped my mind that her family would be dealing with her sister's latest bouts of trouble. When I pulled into the driveway I saw them climbing out of their SUV. They recognized me right away, and from the shocked look on their faces I knew they were confused about my visit.

"Ethan, what brings you by this late?" Christian's father, Colt asked.

"Sorry, sir. I was hopin' Chris was here, but I can see that she's not. Our messages must have gotten mixed up that's all. I'll just head on back to campus and see her in the mornin'."

I started to turn to climb back in my car when I heard him respond. "Hold on a minute. Why would Christian say she was comin' home? Is she alright?"

I threw him the most convincing smile I could. "Sure. Like I said, it's probably a miscommunication. I'm certain she's probably back at her place by now. Come to think of it, I'm sure she said she was catchin' a movie with some friends."

He cocked his brow, as if he didn't believe a word coming out of my mouth. This was a man that people didn't lie to. He was powerful and a force to be reckoned with if he was crossed. I was lying to him about his daughter; someone he'd most definitely protect with his life.

"Colt, your mom called earlier. She said Christian is spending the night at the main house. She didn't give me specifics." Christian's mom turned to look at me after addressing her husband. "Ethan, did something happen at school? Is that why you drove out here tonight? Were you worried about our daughter?"

Since I'd just been caught in a lie I didn't know how to reply. "Honestly, I don't know. We had a fight yesterday and she hasn't talked to me since. I stopped by the house earlier and they said she wasn't there. You know I always look out for her, so I came here to make sure she was safe." That part wasn't a lie. "If somethin' happened she didn't tell me."

"You best be gettin' back to school now." His stern order wasn't meant to be a suggestion. I nodded and climbed into my car, only to be stopped from starting it by Christian's mother.

"Ethan, you should stay on the ranch tonight. It's late, and the deer are going crazy lately. I'd hate for you to hit one and get stranded or worse. We've got plenty of room. It's no trouble, right, Colt?"

I refused to look his way, because I knew what he was thinking. He was under the assumption that I'd not only lied about his daughter once, but also about why she'd come to the ranch. He couldn't understand that I'd driven all this way because I was ready to confess my love to his daughter.

"Just make sure you have your ass back to school in the mornin'."

I often wondered if the man liked me at all. His stern demeanor left little to the imagination. "Yes, sir."

I followed the two of them inside the house and let Miss Savanna show me the guest room. The whole time I wondered if I could sneak out and make my way to the main house, even though it was a terrible idea. Just as her mother was stepping out of the room she turned to me and smiled. "I'm glad she has you, Ethan. I've never understood why she struggles. That girl is beautiful inside and out. I just wish she'd see that."

"She'll always have me."

She walked out of the room after I'd said it, and I wondered if somehow she knew my feelings for her daughter were stronger than I'd admitted. I was resolved to hoping that by morning Christian would get over whatever was bothering her. The anticipation of coming out to her was killing me.

Lying in a bed in her parent's house made me feel close to her. I knew she wasn't there, but it still gave me that connected feeling I longed for. I'd lied for too long, and feared it had cost me my chance of being with her. There was still concern about screwing it up, but I couldn't sit back and watch her seeing other people. I'd learned my lesson feeling the pain of knowing she'd been with another guy besides me.

I'd experienced what it felt like to be jealous of another person, and was hell-bent on making sure it never happened again.

Chapter 14
Christian

It would have been nice to be able to sleep without interference. God knows I needed the rest. What I required more than sleep was to find resolution to my current situation.

In the middle of the night I got up and headed to the kitchen for a glass of water. While standing alone in the dark room I took notice of all the little sounds the old house made. Each time something creaked I felt the need to jump and look around, making sure there wasn't anyone there. Finally when I knew it was my nerves I headed back up to the bedroom and locked the door behind me.

Never in my life had I felt more alone. This wasn't about having friends anymore. I'd been violated and couldn't comprehend what I was supposed to do next.

For the rest of the night I sat there in that room with a small light on, crying, fighting with my reservations, and struggling to understand what was to come.

In the morning I heard my mother's voice even before she knocked. I sat up realizing that I'd dozed off. The sun was beaming through the light colored curtains as I climbed out of the bed to unlock the door.

From the moment I looked into my mother's eyes I knew I had to lie to her. It was impossible to look that woman in the eyes and tell her that someone had hurt me in a way that I wasn't sure could be repaired. As determined as I became to keep it a secret, the moment her arms reached around me I lost it. She held me tight, never asking me a single question until I let it all out.

After time had passed she handed me some tissues from the nightstand. "I wanted to come over last night, but dad and I didn't get home until late. Then Ethan showed up and-."

"What? Ethan was here?"

"I thought you knew he'd come looking for you. Honey, please tell me he isn't the reason for all of this."

I shook my head and looked down at my legs, covering an obvious bruise before she could spot it. "He's not. Ethan had nothin' to do with my problems. Trust me, if he did you'd be the first to know."

She moved the hair away from my face, but I still refused to look in her direction. "Please talk to me. I can't have both of my girls miserable like this. It's killing me. Your dad and I are here for you, no matter what you're going through. I hope you know that. Nothing is more important to us than you kids."

"I know, mom. I'm not ready to talk about it yet."

"Are you sure? You know, I had a terrible time in college. It's when I was dating your uncle Ty, and he had his accident. I had one friend, who ended up not being that great after all. Anyway, I just want you to know that I get what it's like for you. You're not alone, Christian. I've seen the way Ethan looks at you. He was worried last night."

"Mom, Ethan and I are just friends, if we're even that now. It's a long story and I can't think about it. Please tell me he left already."

"He did. Your father made sure of it. He's convinced that Ethan was the reason you came home last night." My mother giggled to herself. "Sorry, it's funny how your father gets about you girls. I feel sorry for the men that ask for your hands in marriage. They're going to have to go through hell for him to approve."

I wanted to smile, but my pent up emotions wouldn't allow it. "If we even find men that want to be with us."

"Don't say that. You may not want to indulge me with what's going on in your life, but I'll always be here, Christian. God didn't give me you kids if he thought I couldn't handle it. Whatever it is, you'll get through it."

This made me so upset. Desperately I needed to tell someone what had happened to me, but for the life of me I wasn't able to spit it out. The pain inflicted on me both emotional and physical was draining to think about. Even though I'd come home for comfort, I knew it was time for me to leave before my mother pried the information out of me, forcing me to relive what occurred. "I have class soon so I better get goin'. Thanks for checkin' on me, mom. I appreciate it."

She leaned over and kissed me before standing up. "I love you with all of my heart. No matter where you are, you need to remember I'm only a phone call away."

"Thanks."

After she'd left the room I got up and dressed. My intentions were to go back to my house and sleep the day away. For the second time I was skipping my classes. I sent an email to professors telling them that I'd encountered a family emergency. Luckily, since my grades were always good, they offered my assignments through the internet, allowing me to submit my work online. I still didn't know how I'd be able to keep focused, but at least I had the opportunity to not fall behind.

As I was leaving the ranch I spotted my dad in his truck. He pulled up next to my car and his window slowly rolled down. "Good Mornin', darlin'. You alright?"

"Yeah, dad. I'm fine."

"You sure?" I could tell he was giving me a once over. "Your mom and I are worried. Next time you come home instead of goin' to gram's."

"Okay."

"Tell that boy to treat ya better so he doesn't have to chase you down again." Even though my dad was speaking about Ethan, I thought of Seth chasing me down.

Without explaining my bout of shock I pulled off of the property and took off down the road. My dad would go to my mother and together they'd try to fix me. I wish it were that easy to make all of this pain vanish, but I wasn't going to kid myself. This would haunt me for the rest of my life, and no matter how hard I tried I'd never be able to forget it.

I'd stopped crying about a mile from the house, and as I pulled in I was determined to get some rest and then make a few calls to find a professional to talk with. As ashamed as I was, I knew I couldn't go through it alone.

I'd no sooner stepped inside of my bedroom when I saw him sitting there. His hands were on his knees, but his focus was on me. Slowly I backed out of the bedroom, praying he wouldn't stand up too fast.

"Chris, wait. Let me just talk to you."

After locking myself in the bathroom, I pressed my hands against the wooden door, praying he couldn't get through it.

I could feel him knocking on it as the warm rush of tears poured out of my eyes. I wasn't just afraid of seeing him again. I was petrified that he was here to do what he'd done before.

"Why won't you return my calls? I don't know why you're being such a bitch. Come out and talk to me. You can't push me away forever."

"I told you before that I didn't want to see you, Seth. You need to leave."

"I can't stop thinking about you; the way you taste, and how good it feels to be inside of you. You probably don't know this, but I've wanted you for a while now. I sit behind you and watch you chewing your pens, imagining those teeth biting into my skin as I'm fucking you."

I cringed, closing my eyes and praying for this to be another nightmare. "Please stop it."

"I can't. I won't let you walk away from this. We're so good together."

"I hate you. Don't you get that? I'm scared of you, Seth." I cried harder. "Please leave me alone. Why are you doin' this to me?"

"To you? You're the one being a damn dick-tease, putting out then pretending it never happened. You came on to me you little closet slut." He punched the wood right at my face, making me jump out of my skin. "Open the fucking door."

I backed away, while reaching into my pocket to retrieve my cell phone. I had one bar of battery left, and knew it was just enough to call Ethan. As mad as he probably was at me, I knew he'd come to my rescue.

It rang once before he answered. "It took you long enough."

"Shut up and listen to me. I need you to come to my house and help me."

"With what? You said we were done, Chris. What the hell is going on with you?"

"Who are you talking to?" Seth yelled from outside of the room.

"Please," I begged. "I'm so scared."

Just then I heard someone on the other side of the door. Becca spoke and I started to relax. "What are you doin'?"

"I came to talk to Chris, but she won't open the door."

"Make him leave, Becca. I don't want to talk to him."

I heard her ordering him out of our house. When the front door slammed she knocked. "Chris, honey, it's just me now. Seth's gone."

"I have to go," I told Ethan.

"Wait!" I hung up on him without responding.

Slowly I cracked open the door until I saw Becca waiting on the other side. "Hey."

Her eyes widened when she looked me in the eyes. "Oh my God. What's goin' on?"

She pulled me into her arms and comforted me while I sobbed. Becca was kind, getting me a glass of water and some tissues while I let it all out. Once I'd finally calmed down I knew I had to explain. After taking a deep breath I began to tell her what happened.

"It started the other night when we all went out. I met Seth and he started hittin' on me. I thought he was nice, and easy on the eyes. When he came back to the house we hung out some more, and then one thing led to another. We ended up in bed, which is somethin' I've never done before. Then it happened again the next day."

"He obviously likes you."

"Yeah, if that's what you call it."

"What do you mean? You can tell me."

I sighed, hoping I was making the right decision. "He took me to an abandoned house and forced himself on me, Becca. Seth raped me," I admitted.

"What?" She stood up and put her hands on her hips. "Seth may be a lot of things, but he's no rapist. I don't know what your problem is, but callin' someone out like that is pretty fucked up."

I couldn't believe it. She didn't believe me. I'd spent the better part of the day holding it all in and when I finally want to come clean the person listening tells me I'm lying. "It's true. I wouldn't lie."

"I'll tell you what I know, Chris." She pointed to the exterior door. "That guy you had me kick out is one of the nicest guys I know. His ex would do anything to get back with him, no matter how many times he screws up. Do you honestly mean to tell me that he'd rape you when he could be with any girl he wanted? You're pretty, but you ain't worth that kind of trouble."

"I wouldn't lie about somethin' like this. I swear."

"We just met, so forgive me for not bein' able to trust your word. I've known Seth for years, and he's never been accused of such madness. I think you've had a hard time makin' friends because you can't keep your stories straight. People don't want to be around someone who starts drama where it's not needed. I was here when you took him into your room and let him stay overnight. I know you fucked him more than once because we could hear you. Obviously you liked it. He'd have no reason to rape you."

I was a blubbering mess. I'd struggled with making friends for so long, and now I regretted it, because obviously they were never going to accept me. "I have bruises from where he held me down."

"You could have done that to yourself. Please get out of my face before I say somethin' I might regret later. If I were you I'd keep this story to yourself and do your best to get back into Seth's good graces. Otherwise you'll end up looking for another place to stay for the rest of the semester."

With that she walked out of my room, leaving me all alone.

Chapter 15
Ethan

It wasn't just the phone call that had me worried. Her voice was raspy and I could tell she was upset. Since I still had no idea what was going on, I left my class and rushed over to her house.

I don't know how many times I beat on the door before Becca finally answered. She gave me a dirty look after seeing it was me. "She's pretty popular today. I should warn you to be careful around that one. She's liable to ruin your life too."

I furrowed my brow while wondering what she was talking about. "Whatever," I said as I moved by her toward Christian's room.

I tapped on the door after realizing it was locked. "Chris, it's me. Open up."

I could hear her walking across the floor and stopping a few feet on the other side. "Ethan?"

"Yeah." It was upsetting she had to ask, as if she was expecting another guy.

Finally the latch unfastened and I walked inside, finding her hiding behind the closing door. She looked so bad, worse than I'd ever seen before.

I reached my hand out to touch her face and she quickly retracted. "Don't."

I threw up my hands, surrendering to her order. "Okay, I won't touch you. What gives? When you called you begged me to come save you, now I can't even touch you."

"It's not you, I swear." She headed over to her bed and plopped down on the mattress. "No one can save me."

I headed in her direction, sitting down right beside her. "Why do you keep sayin' that?"

"Because it's true. Please don't make me talk about it."

"Should I go?"

"No!" She replied quickly. "I need you to stay."

For the second time I moved my hand over to touch her. She shoved it away, distancing how close we were sitting to one another. "I'm not goin' to hurt you, Chris. Why are you pushin' me away?"

She covered her face and began to sob. I didn't get it. She wasn't a crier, yet for the past couple days it seemed like all she was doing. I'd obviously missed some significant happening in her life, because I couldn't figure out what could possibly cause her to become so distraught.

I made a third attempt to touch her, this time on her shoulder. At first she jerked, but I refused to pull away. "I'll never hurt you," I reminded her.

Despite the fact that I still had no inkling of what was going on, I accepted her body when it fell

145

against mine, and I held her tight when she lost control.

Christian never mentioned her bedding being gone, so I refused to talk about it. For two days I'd struggled with finding the words to say to her. With her in my arms, in such a terrible condition, I knew my revelation was going to have to wait. This wasn't the time to confess that I'd been lying about my feelings for years. Right now she needed her best friend.

After some time had passed she'd gotten quiet. I moved my arms away to reveal that she'd fallen asleep. It was another suspicion to warn me that something was very wrong. Then I started thinking about what it could be. She'd left that note out of nowhere, and now she was running away, and avoiding my calls. It was like she was having a hormonal imbalance.

That could only mean one thing.

She was pregnant.

A part of me that wasn't feeling terrible for my friend became overwhelmed with hope; hope that this could be a new beginning for us. Sure, a child would change things, and we'd have to figure out how to finish school and care for a child, but we had huge families, and our union would be celebrated; maybe not by her father at first, but I'd change his mind.

I'd come to the conclusion that she'd been afraid to tell me, and that's why she was freaking out so much. After she rested we'd be able to talk about it, and I'd finally let her know that she'd always had my heart. I was prepared to nourish her, to prove that I'd do anything to take back all of the times I'd pushed her away.

Shortly after I'd dozed off myself I felt her stirring. It caused me to tighten my hold on her, and that's when she jolted out of my arms. I sat up on the bed watching her head to the far side of the room, while hugging the front of her own body. "What is it?"

"Just stay away from me, Ethan. Please. You can't touch me right now."

"I get it, okay? I understand now. I don't know why you couldn't tell me before, but I get it. Now, please come over here and calm down. I promise I won't touch you."

Her eyes widened, "What did you say?" She asked in just a whisper.

"I said I won't touch you," I repeated.

Christian sank down on the floor, and began to bawl again. I rushed to her side, more concerned for her latest breakdown than what was actually freaking her out so much.

"Talk to me, babe."

"I can't. I can't talk to anyone. I tried. It's no use."

"You can tell me anything."

She shook her head, refusing to look in my direction. "That's where you're wrong. Trust me when I say that you don't want to know this. It's my burden, and I'll take care of it on my own."

Imagining her aborting our child made my blood boil. "Why would you even say that? How could you think I wouldn't want to help you through it?"

"It's none of your business, Ethan. You should just go. Talkin' about it only makes it real. You don't understand how much I wish it never happened. I should have known somethin' like this would happen. I should have seen it comin'."

I'd never heard her talk to me like she was. In all of the times where I knew her true feelings for me, this was a shock. She was pushing me away when we finally had a reason to move forward together. It all ripped through me like a knife, dull enough to make the pain last inevitably longer than it should.

"I won't let you go through this alone, no matter how much you fight me. I know you're pregnant, Chris. That's what this is about. You think I don't want -."

"Pregnant?" She interrupted. "You think that's what this is about?"

I was shocked. "What else could it be?"

Her lips quivered as she looked up at me with desperate eyes. "I'm not pregnant Ethan, and now I don't even know if I'll ever want to become a mother. I wouldn't want to watch my child go through somethin' like this."

"If you're not pregnant, than what is it, because I'm not leavin' this room until you tell me the God damn truth. We've been friends for too long. Of all the people in this world you know you can trust me. I know I've hurt you in the past, and for that I'm sorry, but I'd never let you go through this kind of pain on my watch. It's my job to protect you. I promised your father I would. Tell me now. Tell me what in the hell happened in the past twenty-four hours. Are you upset because of me? Did I do something to cause this?"

She finally shook her head. "No. It's not you." There was a long pause, and I wondered if she was even going to divulge anything else. "It's Seth."

"Did he say something to hurt your feelin's? Did he call you a whore, because if he did…"

"He raped me." The words came out so sudden, yet I froze in place, unable to grasp the meaning of them. It was as if time stood still to give me a moment to take it all in.

In that exact moment I'd lost all sense of hope. This wasn't something I could fix. She was broken, and there was nothing I could do to take the pain away.

Chapter 16
Christian

My words vibrated off my lips, but I wasn't in control of them coming out of my mouth. Something else was forcing me to confess my tragedy to Ethan. One look in his eyes told me everything I'd feared. He'd never look at me the same again, because I was damaged. If I'd listened to him more often none of this would have happened. I knew he blamed me. Why else would he be speechless?

"Chris," my name was spoken so smoothly.

"Like I said before. You can't help me. There's nothin' anyone can do to help me."

"You've got to call the police."

"Why?" I questioned. "What good will it do? I slept with him twice right before this happened. People saw us together. We went to the movies. No one will believe that I changed my mind."

"They have rape kits. There's plenty of people that know you wouldn't lie."

This was unbearable; seeing the pain washing over him as he desperately searched for a way to console me. I understood that he meant well, but after my talk with Becca had gone terribly wrong I knew that making a formal report would deem more difficult. This was where Ethan wasn't going to understand. He wouldn't get that I'd rather bury this secret than have the whole world knowing my business. He couldn't understand that I wouldn't be able to handle the ridicule that I'd receive from everyone if this came out.

I'd had long enough time to debate on what I wanted to do. Becca had helped me make that decision with her response. I knew that if I couldn't even convince her, than I didn't have a chance at winning the respect of the rest of my peers, not when Seth was such a popular person on campus.

"I don't expect you to find a resolution for me. What's done can't be erased." My body began to shake, and when I looked up into Ethan's eyes all I saw was pain.

They were glossed over, so much that I swore tears were about to fall. The only time I'd ever seen Ethan cry was when his grandfather passed away suddenly. He'd had a heart attack at the state fair in front of hundreds of town's people. We'd been at the mall when he got the news, and was able to keep it together until we reached his truck in the parking lot. It was there that I watched my tough friend break.

While thinking about that moment I hadn't noticed Ethan reaching his hand out to touch mine. Even though it startled me, his warm embrace was much needed, although it wasn't going to go any further. "I can't make the decisions for you, Chris, but I sure as hell know I can find that son-of-a-bitch and beat the shit out of him."

I pulled my hand away and put both up to my face. "It won't help. It won't make me forget what happened."

"I get that you don't want to tell anyone, but can you at least tell me why? Why can't we call your parents? Why can't we call the police? You can't hide out in your room for the rest of your life. This guy needs to pay for what he's done, and the longer you wait the harder it's goin' to get."

Turning in his direction was a mistake. I was overcome with guilt. "What if it's my fault? What if I led him on? We weren't strangers, Ethan. I already told you this. Whatever you're tryin' to do it's not goin' to help. Besides, I'm pretty sure that goin' to the authorities will somehow make me lose my scholarship, which in turn would destroy my parents."

"Listen to yourself. Do you really think they care about college when your life was in danger? You're obviously not thinkin' clearly."

"You know what? Just go. I don't need someone sittin' here tellin' me what I should and shouldn't do. I'm the one that got raped. I'm the one who was held down while that retched piece of shit had his way with me over and over again."

He turned away. "Don't."

"Don't what? Talk about it? Isn't that why you're here; to force me to go over every single detail again, makin' me have to relive it so I won't be able to even contemplate havin' closure?"

"I would never want you to hurt. You know that." He reached for my face, watching as I suddenly jerked away before he was able to touch me. "This never should have happened. If I'd just agreed to be with you before, you never would have gone out with him in the first place. You think it's your fault, but it's not. It's mine."

I couldn't hear this; not because I didn't want to, because that would be a lie. I couldn't let him take the blame. One thing I'd never want was for him to have been with me out of pity. I got that he didn't have the same feelings for me as I had for him. As far as I was concerned it was water under the bridge compared to what I was going through. That's why I knew him being around was probably a bad idea. Ethan was grasping at straws, looking for some kind of resolution to heal me. "We both know that's not the truth."

"I love you, Chris."

I couldn't believe it. In all of the times that I needed his friendship, my stomach knotted when he'd said those three words. I knew we were best friends and he loved me in a special way, but right now it wasn't enough. He was my only friend, and he could either sit here or let me figure things out, or go home and let me do it alone. Feelings or lack thereof weren't going to save me. I honestly didn't even know what would. "I need you to go."

"Why?"

"Because I don't want company. It's nothin' against you. I just need to be alone right now. I need to handle this on my own."

"If you don't go to the police I will. I'm sorry, but I can't sit around knowin' what that fucker did to you, and you better hope I don't see him, because I'm liable to kill him."

I turned and looked at the one man I trusted with my life. I peered into his eyes, pleading with myself to be gentle as I possibly could without ruining what we shared together. "Ethan, as much as I appreciate that you're tryin' to help, I need you to back off. I don't want to call the police, and honestly I don't know if I ever will. This is my life, not yours. It's my decision."

"It's the wrong decision," he argued. I could tell he wasn't going to let up about it. Ethan was adamant about retribution. I could tell he wanted Seth to go down for what he'd done no matter if it happened legally or not. My fear was that he'd go after him, putting his own future in jeopardy. I wasn't willing to allow him to put himself out there like that.

"It's my decision," I reiterated.

I knew he was pissed, but as he stood up I knew he would abide with my request. If I knew anything about my friend it was that he'd do anything I asked him. "You're makin' a mistake if you do nothin'."

"It's my mistake to make. Why can't you see that? Why can't you see that this has to stay buried?"

Before opening the door to leave he turned around and faced me. "I'm not goin' anywhere, Chris. I won't back down."

"I wouldn't expect you to."

"If you need anything call me. I can be here in five minutes. Keep your door locked, and monitor your calls. I'll stop by in the mornin'."

I watched him walk out, leaving me all alone in my room. Crying wasn't the answer to my problems, but I found some kind of release every time I did it. After putting my spare set of sheets on my bed I climbed in and covered up, burying my head in my pillow so nobody would hear me. I refused to go out of my room until I knew my roommates were all asleep. Knowing Becca, she'd probably already told the girls what I'd suggested happened between me and Seth. I was certain they'd have the same opinions of me, and soon I'd be asked to leave the house.

The longer I thought about it the more I was okay with that happening. Far be it from me to live with three women that thought I was a trouble-making liar.

I couldn't be sure about anything except the fact that telling others what happened would only cause me more pain. Had Ethan not pushed my buttons I would have kept it from him too.

After twenty-four hours I was sure about one thing. What happened to me was getting buried, and somehow, someway I'd figured out how to get past it.

I had to, because I wouldn't be able to wake up every day and know I'd been violated in the worst way possible. What happened to me was vial and disgusting. There was no perpetual end to what it was going to do to me emotionally. I'd read stories, and seen documentaries on assaulted women. I knew the battle for salvation hadn't yet begun for me. In fact, I couldn't even see a light at the end of the tunnel. Right now there was no tunnel in view.

Chapter 17
Ethan

Did she really think I'd walk out the door and forget all about what was going on? If I didn't know any better I'd say she was in denial, but I knew that wasn't the case. Chris was in a bad way, but it was fear that was preventing her from taking this to the authorities.

She was afraid of losing her new fake friends.

She was also afraid of losing her chance at being accepted by our peers.

It was stupid, tremendously ridiculous that her priorities were so out of whack that she'd put her own health at risk. Just because she'd been with Seth before didn't mean he couldn't have hurt her much worse than he had. He could have killed her, leaving her body where it wouldn't be found. I cringed at the thought of never seeing her again, and that's why I knew I wasn't going to stop pushing, even if she shut me out for a little while. Her future was worth the risk. I'd rather that woman hate me forever and have some sense of security in her life, rather than living with the fear of it happening again.

It took a good part of the day to settle down, and even when I felt like I could be around people it was obvious that I wasn't good company. This chick Mariah that I'd been seeing stopped by for a quick fuck between her classes. As much as I needed release, my mind was in other places, making it impossible to stay focused. Each time she kissed me I not only thought about Christian, which was normal, but I also thought about her kissing Seth. The mere image caused me to force the easy lay to leave my room.

It was pathetic that Chris being assaulted had finally broke me. It had caused me to realize that my plan had been shit. Procrastinating my feelings for her was the worst mistake I'd ever made. There was no denying that I'd always assumed we'd end up together. For the first time since recognizing how strong my feelings were, I feared that it was no longer going to happen, and I didn't know how to cope.

After several hours of sitting alone in my room, drinking and researching survivors of rape I had a better understanding of everything she was going through. Despite the fact that every case was different, I knew Chris better than anyone, which also allowed me to read her actions.

Right now she was in denial. She knew what had happened, but was determined to act like it never did, because it gave her a false sense of security. She also thought that if nobody knew about it, she didn't have to dwell on what she couldn't change. Chris wouldn't have to worry about what people were saying behind her back.

Pretending was not the answer though. I knew it was only a matter of time before she literally lost it, succumbing to the fact that some things in life can't be resolved on their own.

I shot her a text message after I couldn't hold out any longer. It took a long time for her to respond, but I was able to convince her to get out of the house. I picked her up a short while later with hopes to get something in her stomach. When Chris was upset she'd forget to eat, which wasn't healthy in her current condition.

I could tell she was uncomfortable in her own skin when she came outside with a huge sweater wrapped around her body. She hugged it close to her chest, only letting go to open the car door and climb in.

When I reached over to greet her like I normally did with a kiss on her cheek she lurched away, and widened her eyes as if I'd just violated her. It offended me, but I immediately understood. "Sorry. It's a habit."

"I know. I'm not mad."

"Do you know where you want to eat?" I asked, hoping to change the subject.

"Actually, can we stop somewhere first?"

I agreed, and followed the directions she gave me until we pulled up at the dilapidated home. From the street view I could see where caution tape had been removed from the door. It blew with the wind, catching my attention as Chris climbed out of the vehicle. "This is where it happened."

I turned off the ignition and ran after her, praying she wouldn't make it up the first step before I caught her. "Chris, wait!" I hurried, grabbing her by the arm at the last second. She jerked herself out of my hold.

"It needs to be done. I have to do this, Ethan. You can either come with me or wait outside."

While I watched her speaking it was apparent that she was already a nervous wreck. Her lips trembled and her hands were shaking profusely. Her eyes, always so green, were filled with tears that were ready to drop down her cheeks at any second.

"Don't go in there. You don't have to cope this way. I read all about it."

Out of nowhere she shoved me. "You don't know how I feel. Don't try to put yourself in my position, Ethan. You don't want this."

"I may not want it, but I'll be damned if I sit back and watch you inflict more pain on yourself."

She pointed toward the house, gritting her teeth as she spoke to me. "I'm goin' inside. You can either come with me, or stay outside. Either way I'd appreciate it if you kept your opinions to yourself."

She and I liked to disagree. On usual terms it would lead us to sleeping together. As much as I was trying to be supportive, I couldn't condone her decisions. "You're being a stupid bitch!"

She stormed inside of the old home, leaving me standing there alone. It took me a few seconds to calm down enough to face her again. When I had I journeyed toward the condemned property, praying that when I found her in the house, she wasn't worse off.

My worst fears were revealed when I stepped inside of a large living room. At the far end was a mattress on the floor. Chris stood over it, peering down speechless. I approached her, reaching my hand out touching her shoulder. She jumped, turning around with frightened eyes. "Sorry, I wanted you to know I was in here." I paused and looked back down at the bed. "This is the dumbest idea you've ever had. Please can we go now?"

Her body stiffened. "I can't."

It took everything in me not to pick her ass up and carry her out of the decrepit building. Instead of causing a huge scene, I leaped in front of her, standing on the mattress, and turning to face her. She looked so distraught, so weak.

"This is where he did it."

I reached for her chin, pulling it up until she was looking me in the eyes. "It's over, Chris. There's no need to rehash it. Let me take you out of here."

She shook her head, never allowing her gaze to linger from mine. "I left your place, and I was so mad at myself. All I wanted to do was get home. I was bein' so careful, hidin' behind things when cars would drive past. I knew the risks of bein' out alone in the middle of the night."

"One of those cars was mine. I looked everywhere for you."

"I know," she said sadly.

"I was ashamed of the letter I'd written. It wasn't what I wanted. It was what I felt needed to happen."

"Forget about it. I knew you'd come around. You can't get rid of me that easy," I reassured her.

"It doesn't matter. Everything's changed now."

I opened my mouth to argue, but she cut me off.

"He must have seen me duckin' behind that car. I tried to hide, but there he was, tellin' me it wasn't safe to walk the rest of the way. As mad as I was at what happened earlier at the movies, I knew I'd get home quicker. From the moment I got into the car I could smell the alcohol on his breath. I should have jumped out."

She finally looked down at our feet. It made me feel awful. "This ain't your fault, Chris. None of it."

"Why did I agree to follow him inside this place? I should have known from the outside that it was shady? I should have known what would happen!" She began to weep, so hard that I had to catch her when her knees gave way. I could hear the pain in her sobs, and felt as if the world was crashing down around us. Her pain radiated through me, and all I wished was that I could somehow make it all go away.

"Tell me what to do, babe. Tell me how to help you?"

"Why?" She cried out. "Why did he do it? How could he hold me and get off on hurtin' me? How could he think that I'd be okay about it? He took everything from me, Ethan. He took everything," she repeated.

I held all of her weight as she broke down even more pleading with me over things I had no way of answering. The sheer emotions that weakened my ability to respond were heart wrenching. I pulled her close to my chest, allowing her to let it out. She needed to know I wasn't going anywhere.

Suddenly she backed away, spinning around so that I couldn't see her face. "I just want it to go away. I can't stop thinkin' about him bein' inside of me. I can feel the pain every time I close my eyes. He violated me so many times. He took me like I was rag doll. He said I wanted it." While she sobbed, covering her face with her hands, I walked up behind her, pulling her arms down to thread our fingers together. When she didn't pull away I kissed the top of her head. "Why would I want to be violated? I told him to stop. I begged him to stop hurtin' me. Why didn't he? Why didn't he stop hurtin' me?"

Though I didn't exactly know what to say, I knew she was safe now. "You're goin' to be okay, because I won't let this destroy you. We'll figure it out together, no matter how long it takes."

The most reassuring thing happened after I'd made that claim. Chris turned around and wrapped her arms around me, placing her head on my chest. "I can't do this without you. I thought I could, but you know it's not true. I feel so lost."

"Don't worry, I've got you now, and I'm goin' to make sure you find yourself again if it's the last damn thing I ever do."

Chapter 18
Christian

I don't even remember the drive to that old abandoned house, and for me to unconsciously want to revisit that place made me cringe. Had Ethan not been there I don't know what would have happened. Due to my recent ordeal, I was unable to make rational decisions. I couldn't care less about returning to my classes, or keeping up with my studies, even though I'd requested my work from my professors.

All I wanted to do was lay around and dwell in my own misery, waiting for the day I woke up and the pain ceased to exist. Imagining that day was the only hope that I had left, and as the minutes passed I was starting to become increasingly concerned that it may never happen.

Ethan didn't have to drag me out of that house. I walked in front of him, hoping to never visit it again. He was adamant about me staying at his place, but I declined. I knew I'd be crying all night long, and he'd feel obligated to stay up with me even though he knew he had class in the morning.

Just because my life was going to shit, didn't mean his had to as well.

When Ethan dropped me off at my house I felt scared about walking inside and seeing Becca. Somehow I was going to have to pretend that we'd never talked about my experience with Seth. It irked me that she couldn't give me the benefit of the doubt and believe that I'd been assaulted by one of her so-called friends.

Even with the world closing in around me, I still longed to be accepted. I wanted normalcy, however I was able to get it.

I hadn't expected the house to be filled with people, and I certainly didn't expect a bunch of dirty looks as soon as I stepped foot through the threshold.

"Chris. We've been waitin' for you to get back," Becca said.

I hugged my sweater around the front of me feeling like everyone in the room was watching me. "What's up?" I pretended to be calm, even though I was trembling.

"After speaking to everyone in the house we think it would be best if you moved out. It's just not workin' havin' you here. We need a roommate that we can trust."

"You can trust me," I said in almost a whisper.

"Did you really tell Becca that Seth raped you?" The question came from across the room, and I was shocked to see that it was Mila.

I headed in the direction of my room, only getting halfway there before she was up in my face. "What's wrong? Cat got your tongue you fuckin' skank?"

I shoved her out of the way, getting inside of my room before she could catch me. Once my door was shut the yelling and banging began. "Open the door you little slut. Why can't you talk to me face to face? Come out and look me in the eye and tell me that my boyfriend raped you. We both know it's not true. You're nothin' but a trick he messed around with. When you found out he was spoken for you thought you could fuck with his life, didn't you? You thought you could turn everyone against him?"

I sank down to the floor, covering my ears, but it still didn't keep me from hearing her bashing me.

I hadn't even noticed that all of my belongings had been tossed around the room. My clothes were ripped out of my dresser, and even my laptop was shattered in the far corner.

The more they yelled the more the room started spinning. I got nauseous, swearing that at any second I was going to fall unconscious. As quickly as I was able, I pulled out my cell phone and called Ethan. He'd just be arriving back to his place, but I knew he'd turn around to come get me.

With the loud slamming still going on in the background he picked up the call. "Hey, you okay?"

I was crying, but able to get out a few words. "I need you to come back and get me."

"What's that noise?"

"They went through my things. They broke my computer with all of my school work. They're forcin' me to move out, Ethan. They said they want me gone."

"What the fuck? I'll be there in five minutes."

"What did I ever do to deserve this?" I literally began to bawl. They were laughing from the other side of the door, becoming enthused that they'd gotten to me in such a way.

"We'll grab your stuff and you don't ever have to go back there. Hang tight. I'm already in my car."

All of a sudden I felt beating against the door my back was against. "Open up, whore. Someone's here to give you a good time."

I closed my eyes and prayed that they'd stop.

"Kick it in. I'll record it and put it on YouTube," I heard a female voice saying.

I quickly backed away from the door, watching as it opened without being kicked. "These doors are easy to jimmy open," someone giggled.

Appearing in the doorway was the devil himself. Seth stood there, a big smile on his face as if he knew he was God's greatest gift to the world.

I backed away further, distancing myself from the monster he was. "Please don't."

He moved forward, rushing toward me. I closed my eyes, burying my head between my legs. I could literally feel the floor vibrating with each of his steps. He leaned down until his hot, familiar, alcohol breath was near my face. "Are we having fun yet?"

I couldn't speak. I couldn't even move.

"Did you really think anyone would believe a nobody like you? Did you think they'd help you take me down? You're nothing but an easy fuck. I took what I wanted and you're pissed it's over. Get that through your head and walk away. I won't let a little bitch like you ruin my life, do you hear me?"

I nodded my head, not even knowing if he noticed. I couldn't open my eyes and see him so close to me. The pain of rehashing the awful event was making me dizzy again.

The loud taunting from the living room was feeding the atmosphere around me. The negativity was preventing me from standing up for myself. I was outnumbered, and belittled, lost in an environment set out to destroy me.

Seth grabbed me by the hair, pulling it back and forcing me to look at him. My lips trembled as I kept my gaze on him. I was petrified of this guy, and people were laughing at that. "Check this crazy bitch out."

They were laughing more; laughing at me, making me want to close my eyes and never wake up. They were awful people, feeding off his essence while they cut me down and ripped me apart. Everything I ever thought I wanted was hidden behind a sick façade of evil people.

Then I heard his voice; my knight in shining armor. It got louder as he came into the room. Suddenly Seth's hold was released. He backed away from me, holding his hands up when he saw the size of Ethan; though both muscular, years of working on a ranch had given Ethan more definition. It was very clear who'd win a fight.

"You have one second to get the fuck away from her before I kill you."

Seth kept his hands up. "We were just talking, dude. You can have her all to yourself now. I've already had my fill."

I heard the sound of the punch before looking in their direction. It was apparent who'd thrown the punch. While Seth covered his face with his hands, blood was pouring out between his fingers. Ethan reached his hand out, pulling me up and leading me out of the house. We didn't take time to gather my things, and honestly I wasn't worried about them. All I wanted to do was get as far away from those people as I possibly could.

I'd like to say that I calmed down once I was in the security of his vehicle, but it was impossible to settle myself. Too much had been said for me to sit back and relax. I was the laughing stock of everyone, and soon they'd probably share the video with fellow peers from school.

I felt Ethan's hand lacing with mine. He squeezed, giving me a silent reminder that he was there with me. I refused to pull away, knowing for certain that he was the only real person in my life that I could turn to. I'd wanted to die back in that room until I heard his voice. In that moment of despair I knew he was there to save me.

"Thank you," I managed to get out.

"Don't you dare thank me. It's takin' everything in me not to go back there and kill every one of them."

"They aren't worth it."

"Yeah, but they deserve worse. I heard what he said to you. Our call never disconnected. I heard that bastard tauntin' you. If I could reach through that phone and choke him I would have."

I wanted to smile. I needed to. It just wouldn't happen. I'd been through too much, and though I'd tried to be strong, they'd broken through my temporary wall of solitude and gotten straight to what I had left. I was nothing, and the idea of being whole again was so far out of reach it was impossible to imagine.

"I wish he'd killed me in that house, Ethan. I don't want to feel this anymore. Please make it stop. Make it go away."

I don't remember talking after that statement was made. The next thing I knew I was being carried inside and laid down on top of his bed. He didn't bother removing anything but my shoes before covering me up. I didn't let myself fall asleep until I felt him climbing on the mattress. When Ethan took my hand I knew I was safe. That's when I finally let myself go.

When I woke up to the sound of a rooster I realized I was back at the ranch. My bedding, a black and white tree theme, let me know I was in my own room. A warm body was nestled next to me. His hair was shabby making me think it was

Ethan's. I reached my hand over to touch him, and when I did I got the shock of my life. It wasn't Ethan in my bed, but Seth. I screamed and opened my eyes realizing I was in a dark room.

The figure beside me pulled me close and kissed my left temple. "You're havin' a nightmare, babe. Go back to sleep. No one can hurt you now. I promise," he said in a groggy voice.With my heart still feeling like it was beating out of my chest I lay there awake, in the pitch black room. Had it not been for Ethan's hold on me I may have gotten up to get a glass of water, but I knew feeling protected was more important than being a bit parched.

There was a time so recent that I would have loved being this close to him, knowing it always lead to intimacy. It pained me to imagine ever doing that again. The thought of sex made me queasy, and I didn't see it going away anytime soon. For the most part I needed exactly what Ethan was giving me. He was my hero; the one person that would ride through the gates of purgatory to save me.While wide awake, I replayed the events of the day in my head. It was revolting how my peers had believed a liar over me. Seth may have been popular, but he was a known cheater. For them to gang up against me was surprising, to say the least. My mind wandered, sending me to consider my options. With no one willing to collaborate my story, I was left to either go to extremes to save my dignity, or surrender to the fact that he was never going to be punished for what was done to me.

172

Ethan stirred and woke to find me staring at him. It would have been nice to conjure up a half-smile, though I found it impossible. "What are you doin' awake?"

"I can't sleep," I confessed.

He moved the hair away from my face. "Are you frightened?"

"Not when I'm with you." I didn't have to be embarrassed when it came to Ethan. I'd spent years opening up to him. Even in my current state I knew he wouldn't dare hurt me.

"That's a step in the right direction."

"All of my stuff is probably ruined. How am I goin' to explain that to my parents?"

"Say the house got robbed."

"Where am I supposed to live? It's too far into the semester to apply for housing."

"You're stayin' here with me. It's small, but we'll make it work."

Chapter 19
Christian

Was he crazy? Did he really think I'd be able to stay with him when I knew it was because I had nowhere else to go except back to the ranch? Did I think that I'd be alright with him pitying me?

I wasn't going to let him do that, no matter how desperate I was. "Ethan, as much as I appreciate the offer, I think it's best if I make other arrangements. I can't be a burden to you."

He chuckled. "Seriously? You a burden? That's not possible. Besides, I could use the company."

I rolled my eyes. "You have plenty of company. I hear all about them."

He cleared his throat and looked away. "Yeah, well that's different. It's just sex with them, Chris. We're not even on a last name basis when they leave in the mornin'. Havin' you around will be good for me."

If he was trying to convince me to stay he was doing a horrible job at it. Reminding me of his lifestyle made me want to grab my purse and run out of there, before I'd have to tolerate any more pain.

"It's not goin' to happen. You'll end up blamin' me for your failing sex life. The next thing you know we'll be partin' ways as friends, and if you haven't noticed I don't have many other people linin' up to hang out with me."

"We've been friends for a long time. Do you honestly think I'd let some chick come between us?"

I shrugged. "I have no idea what goes through your head in a single day."

"I'm tellin' you right now, I want you to stick around." I got this weird vibe like he was getting agitated with me. Since I knew how much he liked having late night visitors it made no sense.

Secretly I felt like me staying with him could help with my jealousy issues; if no woman could come around to steal him away from me then I'd have nothin' to worry about.

Then I came to the realization that it was going to be a long time before I could trust even my best friend in a sexual way. Every time I imagined being touched it felt like tiny pins were being jabbed into my skin. Closing my eyes only made it worse, because I envisioned my attack repeatedly. "I'm hungry." I changed the subject, feeling like our conversation was getting us nowhere, and requiring me to use too much of my energy, when I knew I needed to conserve it.

"Do you want to go out?"

I nodded. "No." I didn't want to go out in public, because I knew that if I ran into anyone I'd have to rehash the events again. I couldn't face them, not now, and probably not ever.

"Chris, you know you're goin' to have to talk to someone about this. It's obvious that you're scared, and I'm not goin' to push, but it's crucial to seek professional help. You're not the only woman that this has happened to. I've been readin' up on this, and there are support groups in the area we could go to."

"Stop it!" He said he wasn't pushing, but that's exactly what was happening. "You want me to go out in public and tell my story to a bunch of strangers? Are you out of your mind?" I could feel my body shaking as I spoke, reminding me how upset the mere mention of it made me.

"I never said that. You don't have to share your story. A lot of people go there to listen. Maybe it would help to hear other people that have gone through similar circumstances."

I got up and walked out of the room, refusing to hear him out. He didn't understand that I needed to bury it. I wasn't like those other women. Talking about it made everything come back full-force. I couldn't continue to dwell on what Seth did to me, and I sure as hell wasn't going to broadcast it to a room full of strangers.

Ethan found me a couple minutes later. He was eating a small bag of chips and offered me one. "I know you're pissed, and you think you know what's best for you, but you're wrong. Let's go to one meetin'. We can sit in the back and listen to one story. If you want to leave after that I won't fight you. We've got to do somethin', Chris. If you're not willin' to call the damn police at least come to a meetin' with me, because I can't sit here and watch my friend witherin' away. Don't you get it? This isn't just hurtin' you. It's tearin' me apart to see you this way. It kills me to see you wantin' to give up. That asshole did somethin' horrible to you, and it can't be forgiven, but you can learn to move forward despite what's happened. It ain't goin' to occur overnight, and I'm certainly not expectin' a miracle, but dammit you've got to keep going. You've got to want to overcome this. Please, if not for me then do it for yourself."

I stood there completely dumbfounded, staring into his lost eyes. I'd been too annoyed to hear that he too was suffering. "You're right."

He stepped forward and grasped my hands, keeping his gaze on me. "I just want you to be happy again. We'll figure it out. I promise you we will."

When he let go of my hands I wrapped mine around his back, burying my head against his chest. "I'm afraid."

Feeling him kissing me on the top of my head was always his trademark, except for this time. I knew it was assurance that he was going to see this through, no matter what he had to do to make it happen. "Don't be."

An hour later we were walking out to his vehicle to head to the closest meeting. I got about four feet from his car door before noticing something was written all over his passenger side window.

The words LIAR and WHORE were capitalized in what looked like white paint. I froze in place, watching as Ethan circled around the car. "What the fuck?"

This was all my fault, but yet he marched over, took my hand and got me inside before even admitting that he'd have to clean it all off in order to drive anywhere.

After locking the doors and running back in the house he came out with cleaner and some rags. I started to climb out to help him, but he suggested I stay locked inside to keep warm. I was pretty sure he was more concerned about where the vandals were, and if they'd been waiting to verbally attack me again. Either way, I felt safer being locked inside.

We'd gotten lucky by coming outside when we had, because the paint was still wet, and came off with little effort on Ethan's part. After tossing all of the rags, he finally got inside the car and put his head on the steering wheel while beginning to speak. "If I find out who did this shit I'm goin' to hurt someone."

I turned away to hide the new tears falling down my cheeks. They weren't for me this time, but for my friend, who was now right in the middle of my battle.

The meeting was to be held at a local church. Once we'd pulled in the parking lot Ethan turned off the ignition and looked over at me. "How are we doin'?"

"You probably shouldn't ask me that right now. Better yet, maybe we should head back to your place and forget about this."

"We're goin' inside. I'm not goin' to let those assholes come between you and recovery. Fuck them all."

I faked a smile, wanting so much to be as hopeful as he was. "Yeah, fuck em'."

We both let out a laugh before I watched him getting out of the vehicle. My stomach turned as he sauntered over to my side, opening the door for me. "See, I can be a gentleman."

He offered his arm for me to hold as we walked, but I leaned my head on his shoulder instead. "You were a gentleman at prom. You bought me flowers, and opened the door for me."

"Then I took you to a hotel and had my wa-. Oh shit, Chris. I didn't mean..."

"It's okay. I'd never compare the two." The truth was that I couldn't do that if I wanted. My prom night was amazing, all because of the man standing beside me. We'd spent the night in each other's arms, after he'd satiated my every desire. It didn't hurt that I was infatuated with him. That night I could have sworn that we were both in the same place as far as feelings. Everything was in sync, and he'd made me feel like the only female on the planet.

"Still, I need to be careful what I say around you."

"I'm not a sheet of glass, Ethan. You don't have to walk on eggshells to be around me. If you start actin' weird I might have to punch you."

He laughed. "I wouldn't want that. You might damage my sexy face."

"I'd aim for that first," I teased.

"No doubt."

It was nice to be able to joke just before opening the doors to enter the meeting. I was so nervous that I'd become sick to my stomach. As the bile rose to my throat Ethan led us inside. Sitting in a circle was a group of men and women. I wanted nothing more than to turn around and run, but Ethan took my hand and squeezed it, reminding me that no matter what, I wasn't going at this by myself. He was going to protect me, and if I couldn't handle it, he'd get me out of there as fast as he could.

Since I was desperate, it was important to try. I couldn't go to the police, and I sure as hell couldn't call my parents. They were dealing with my sister's problems. They didn't need mine to boot. I'd handle this, because I was out of options.

Chapter 20
Christian

"Good evening. I'm Eve. Come on in and have a seat."

My lips felt dry, and I swore that I'd just eaten a cup of sand, because my mouth refused to open to address the woman.

Ethan reached out his hand. "I'm E-."

"No names, except for mine," she interrupted. "These meetings are confidential. What we say here stays here."

In that instant my uptight body relaxed.

We pulled up two chairs, watching as people made room for us to scoot in. I avoided making eye contact with everyone, in fear that they would all want to know my story. Thankfully, Eve settled my mind.

"Who would like to share tonight?"

A young blonde raised her hand and waited for Eve to acknowledge her. She folded her hands together, but constantly kept moving her fingers around. She peered down at the floor in the center

181

of the circle, instantly reminding me how I would be if I had to share my story in front of all these people.

"I, um, I came here tonight because my doctor thinks it's a good idea. Since the attack I've become agoraphobic. I dropped out of school six months ago, and pushed all of my friends away. It's taken me a long time to realize that none of this was my fault."

I stared down at my own hands, praying that she wasn't going to go into detail. Unfortunately, it didn't go the way I wanted it to.

"It was a Friday night on campus, and I looked forward to a big bonfire that was takin' place. I lived in the dorms, and felt like I was pretty popular with everyone on my floor. Most of us partied together on the weekends, and we became this huge click. It was nice to always have someone to buddy around with, especially after dark." She fidgeted more with her hands. "Anyway, we got all dolled up and headed out to party and meet guys. I wasn't exactly what you'd call promiscuous, but I wasn't a virgin either. A bunch of us started doin' keg stands and actin' silly to get attention. We were dancin' around, grindin' all over one another. My best friend, Nikki and I started actin' like we were together. A couple times we even kissed to get the crowd to react." She started to sniffle. I refused to look her way. "We were just havin' fun. We were out for the night not really wantin' to hook up with anyone. In our eyes we thought it was the best way to keep the creeps from hittin' on us."

She had to pause again, this time because she'd gotten choked up. Eve chimed in that very moment. "Take a few breaths before continuing. Remember that you're in a safe place. If you need to stop it's okay."

"No. I can do this. I've practiced it for a couple days. I can't hold it in any longer, because it's tearin' me apart."

"That's good. Stay positive," Eve suggested.

"I'm not really sure how long we were there that night. After all the alcohol we'd consumed neither one of us was in any condition to process something as silly as time." She wiped her nose with a tissue that Eve offered her. "Things started to get fuzzy, and all of a sudden Nikki was gone. I didn't panic, figurin' she'd probably had to pee or somethin'. There was this guy there. He pulled me off to the side and whispered in my ear that he knew where my friend had gone. He told me she wanted me to join her. It was stupid. I shouldn't have believed him, but I did. He led me down this long path in the woods, and when we got far enough away that we couldn't hear the music he pressed me up against a tree and started kissing me. I brought my knee up high enough to make contact with his junk. The moment he sunk down in pain I darted in the direction we'd come from." This time she began to sob. "I thought we were alone. I never saw the other guys there until they'd surrounded me. I could smell the dirt before they shoved me down onto it. As much as I tried to fight them, I knew I was no match for the group of them.

I kept telling myself that I'd live if I didn't fight. I closed my eyes and tried to leave my body in my mind. I prayed to God to help me, but they just kept raping me, over and over, all of them. Each one of them took turns over and over, filling me with their vile releases. They violated every orifice, while telling me how much they knew I wanted it." She cried into her tissue, so much that I thought she was done with her story. "When I thought that it was finally over, when my fragile body was left on the cold hard ground, it started to rain. As the drops hit my face I opened my eyes to see all of them standing over me. They drug me through the thickets in the woods, naked and exposed. Even though I knew I was bruised and bleeding I'd stopped feeling the pain. I begged them to kill me; to end my life so I didn't have to remember."

The girl covered her face with her hands for a minute. We all sat there speechless, frozen in our seats. I didn't know about the rest of the group, but for me it made me finally see that I wasn't alone. I felt like I needed to walk over and wrap my arms around this girl, because she needed it so much more than I did. Then she finished the rest of the story.

"The campus police found me the next morning. I was still fastened to the tree, naked and freezing to death. Before they'd left me there to rot they used a tree limb to assault me from behind. The doctors had to give me stitches to stop the bleeding. I didn't speak for the next eleven days. I couldn't. It was like it didn't happen if I didn't tell anyone about it. They put me into an institution because my parents feared I'd end my life. Most days I still want to. My friends, well the people I thought were my friends, they couldn't understand. They didn't know how to be my friends anymore. Needless to say I dropped out of school, and left everything behind. I moved back to Kentucky where my parents still lived, and I've been living with them ever since. The doctors tell me that it's time to move on; that I can't dwell on my attack, but it's all I ever think about. Each morning I wake up and relive every single second of my rape. I can still taste the dirt in my mouth. I can still see them passing me around like a ragdoll. The only difference is that I'm finally tired of punishing myself. I don't want to live like this anymore, but I also don't want to give up. For the first time in forever I have hope."

Eve got up and rushed over to the female while starting to clap. We all followed suit, giving appreciation to this woman who'd somehow gained the strength to tell her story. Eve kneeled down in front of her and took her hands. "You are brave and beautiful. You're here because you want to live again. It's the reason that I'm here too. Rape is an ugly, horrible, devastating thing. It cripples us, strips us of our life, and leaves us alone and vulnerable, but it's not the end. I was repeatedly raped ten years ago by my step-father. My mother worked nights and he'd hold me down in my bed and have his way with me, threatening to kill my mom if I told anyone. When I was old enough to call social services she believed him insisting that I didn't want her to be happy. I ran away after that, ending up in a woman's shelter. It was there that I met a woman who took me under her wing and showed me how to break free of that anguish. I've heard hundreds of stories from men and women that have both experienced this type of abuse. These meetings are for us to come together and share so that we can finally see we aren't alone. Our stories may be different, but we've all survived. Thank you for sharing your story with us tonight."

I grabbed Ethan's hand and pulled him out of there before anyone could notice us. I felt like I couldn't breathe, and didn't stop walking until we'd reached his car. "Are you okay?" He asked.

"Get me out of here."

Ethan didn't speak on the ride back to his place; even if he had I didn't hear him. My mind was too fixed on that woman's story. It was wretched and disturbing, making me sick to hear it told. I found myself comparing hers with mine, and feeling like my circumstance didn't deserve the acknowledgement.

By the time we'd made it inside I was already crying. I felt sorry for the woman, and for myself, because at the end of the day Eve was right. It was up to me to get through this, and I had to be ready for it to happen or it never would.

Chapter 20
Ethan

I couldn't stand seeing her this way. The meeting had only made things worse it seemed. It was taking everything in me not to go after those bastards for hurting her. I felt sick after hearing that woman tell her tragic story to the group. How she'd survived that ordeal was beyond me. I could tell it had gotten to Chris, but what I didn't know was if it was in a positive or negative way.

We were both exhausted after the long day we'd had. Since I knew she was safe it was easier to get some rest, but she was crazy if she thought for one second I was going to let go of her. If she was feeling anything that the woman had, I knew she was going require more than me keeping her close. She would need to rely on her parents, and the help of a real professional.

One thing I wished I could do was tell her how much I loved her. She needed to know that she wasn't a burden to me. I wanted to be able to tell her she was my future.

It might not have been the time to profess my true feelings to her, but I understood. In enough time she'd know.

Chris cried for a while in my arms. Knowing that she needed time to herself I remained silent. When her breathing settled I felt like she was in a peaceful place.

By morning we'd both gotten at least a few hours of sleep. Since there was so much going on I didn't push her to stay in bed, plus I could tell that being close to even me made her feel uncomfortable. I'd now seen and read enough to know that her road to recovery was going to be long and at times extremely frustrating. I'd decided that no matter how long it took her, I'd be her shoulder to cry on. My only concern was that her parents needed to know what was going on.

They were a tight knit group, and something like this had to be dealt with properly. I knew she was against telling them anything, but it was for her own good. She might not be in her right mind, but I was going to make sure everything was handled to benefit her.

When she first woke, Chris was calmer, seemingly relaxed. She sat down on the couch and managed to eat a piece of toast that I'd given her. Despite the fact that her eyes were bloodshot, with bags under them, she seemed in good spirits.

The key was not to bring it up, albeit it couldn't be buried forever.

By noon we'd watched several movies. She was adamant about me going to class, so I decided it was best to keep her within arm's length. Like a small child, Chris needed constant supervision. This wasn't like a bad breakup; I feared she'd try to hurt herself if left alone for a long period of time.

After I'd made us some cheese sandwiches, because it was all I could find in the refrigerator, I decided to have a talk with her about the next steps, knowing it wasn't going to go over well.

"Christian, we need to make some decisions."

"Don't call me that. When you call me that it's somethin' serious, and I can't go there right now."

"You're going to have to. This ain't goin' to disappear. Now I get that you're scared, but we've got to report this guy. It's important he's charged for this crime. I'm not willin' to sit around watching you fall apart while he's out there somewhere enjoyin' his freedom."

"Please don't do this to me. I went to that place with you last night and it left me more messed up."

I slid my cell phone across the table. "Call your parents. Tell them we're comin' to see them."

She shoved it back in my direction. "No way. They can't ever find out."

I rolled it back toward her. "If you don't do it, I will."

"I hate you right now." I knew she didn't. For some reason I knew she couldn't. I hated being the only friend she had, but appreciated that she needed me.

"Please, Chris. You're my best friend and I love you. Please trust that this is the right choice. Seth needs to go down, and I think with the right amount of legal assistance your roommates should be held accountable for destroyin' your belongings."

"You expect me to press charges against all of them? Are you crazy? I'll be the laughing stock of the campus."

"Then we'll switch schools."

She cocked her brow and shook her head. "You're on a scholarship. Your family will have a shit fit."

I wanted to tell her right then and there how I felt about her. I wanted her to know that my love wasn't in a friendship kind of way. "You're also on a scholarship. Besides, once the dean hears about Seth's involvement I'm pretty certain he'll be expelled."

"And what about everyone else? You were there last night, Ethan. Stop pretendin' things will be the same. Those girls will never let me live this down. As long as I attend this school I'll have to see them, and know what they've done to me."

Before she started crying, I reached my hand over and placed it gently on her knee. At first she began to move it away, until our eyes met. I don't know what she saw in mine, but she froze in place. "You're stronger than they are. Remember that."

She picked up the phone and played with it for a second before sighing and dialing a number. "Hey, mom, it's me. Yeah, I'm okay. Listen, I need to come home and talk to you and dad about somethin' important. Ethan's goin' to drive me."

Once she'd hung up she let out an air-filled laugh. "I think she's under the impression that I'm pregnant too."

I picked up her hand and kissed the back of it. "You know, life wouldn't suck if we had a kid together. I'm just puttin' it out there."

"I don't think havin' a kid with my best friend is how my parents saw my future going."

"Maybe you need to step out of the box for a second and accept that this is your life. It doesn't matter what anyone wants for you. What matters is if you're happy."

Chris looked down and shook her head. "Yeah, well I'm not. Honestly, I don't know if I can be after this."

"I told you this already, but I'll repeat it again. You're not alone. This will get resolved, and no matter how long it takes, you will get through this. I promise you."

Twenty minutes later we were driving to the Mitchell ranch. As much as Mr. Mitchell made me nervous, all I could hope was that he appreciated what I'd done for his daughter.

Her mother, Savanna, was waiting at the door for us to arrive. Chris looked over at me before I could turn off the ignition. "I'm scared."

"You're loved. This is the one place in the world where everyone loves you. Sure, they may freak out at first, but my hand will be laced with yours, and if you get nervous just squeeze it. It will remind you that you're never goin' to be alone."

When we stepped inside of the warm home the first thing I noticed was her father and brother sitting on the couch; my heart beat rapidly as I worried about them attacking me, before hearing the real reason we'd come to visit.

It wasn't surprising when Chris let go of my hand and approached her parents. I could tell she was trying to smile, but was unable to do it properly. They already knew this was bad news, and the sooner they found out that I wasn't the bad guy, the faster I could focus all of my energy on her.

After a few minutes of greets we all sat down facing each other at the dining room table. Noah, her brother, watched me like a hawk, as if he were ready to pounce. I folded my hands under the table to appear calm.

Her father, Colt, cleared his throat. "Christian, I think it's time you tell us why you're here."

She placed her hands flat on the table. "I'm not pregnant. Let me just say that since I can tell you're all freakin' out."

Noah got up from the table. "Well since that's the case I'm gettin' back to work. I only came to make sure I didn't have to kick some ass."

In a low murmur Chris spoke. "You might want to wait actually."

Noah looked at me as he sat back down.

Her mother smiled. "Honey, just tell us what's going on. Is it school? Is it your grades? Do you and Ethan want to move in together?"

"I was raped."

Her words were finally clear as the people at the table gasped for air. As shocked as they were, I couldn't take my eyes off of Chris, who'd covered her face and started to cry.

Her mother rushed to her side, wrapping her arms around her daughter. "Oh my God. How did this happen? Who did this to you? Colt, call the lawyer."

Noah raised his brow, directing all of his attention toward me. "When did it happen?" He knew his sister was in no condition to go on as both of their parents now crowded over her.

"A couple days ago. She didn't even want to tell me, man. It took everything I had to drag her here. She thinks it will only make things worse."

Noah pulled out his phone, and right away I could tell he was on the phone with an attorney. He walked into another room but kept on talking.

Chris finally calmed enough to begin explaining what had happened to her parents. All I could do was sit there and listen as the story ripped through me yet again. There came a point when I knew they needed to be alone with their daughter. I stepped outside on the porch and found her brother leaning against the railing. "Thanks for takin' care of my sister." He spit something out into the grass then put his head back down. "Do you know who this asshole is?"

193

"Yeah, I know him. He's on a sport's scholarship. He's a senior. He's popular, and accordin' to Chris' roommates, he's not capable of somethin' so heinous."

He let out an air-filled laugh. "Of course he isn't. Just tell me where to find him. I'll take care of the rest."

"No you won't, Noah." Her father walked out to keep his son from doing any further damage. "From this moment on we're handlin' it the right way. Uncle John's on his way over. We're goin' to get a police report, and have the boy picked up for rape. Once he's in custody we can meet with the attorney and figure out what has to be done to protect your sister. She filled us in on the roommate situation, and from here on out she's stayin' with us. I'll be damned if I let a bunch of idiot kids brake my daughter's heart. She ain't never done nothin' to deserve this."

The man was full of pain, so much that it made me think about having my own kids. Even though he seemed calm, I could tell he was determined to get justice for his child.

"She can stay with me and remain in school. I have no contact with those people, Mr. Mitchell."

"Ethan, as much as Savanna and I appreciate you helping Christian, I'm going to have to ask you to head back to school. We can take care of our daughter here. If you want to come and visit I'm sure she'd appreciate it. For right now she needs to get medical attention, not just physically, but mentally."

194

"Yes, sir." Even though I hated it, I knew I had to be mindful that this was now a family matter. I may have been her best friend, but this was definitely a private situation. "Do you mind if I see her before I go?"

"Not at all." He motioned for me to go back inside of the house. Right before I reached the front door he said something that made me stop in my tracks. "Thanks again for bein' there, Ethan. I know you care a great deal about my daughter. Make sure she knows you'll be stoppin' by to visit. I think she needs to hear that."

When I walked inside I felt a part of me feeling defeated. I don't know why I assumed they'd want me to stick around. I suppose I hadn't thought that far ahead. The moment our eyes met I knew it was going to be hard to say goodbye to her, especially where there was so much left unsaid.

Chapter 21
Christian

Ethan had pushed me to tell my parents, and even though I hated the idea, nothing could have prepared me for the emotions that I'd go through when I saw the looks on their faces.

I'd thought it was hard telling Ethan all of the brutal details of my attack, but looking into my dad's eyes and seeing pure pain was unimaginable. My mother broke down after only a few minutes, and though he'd said he wouldn't leave my side, eventually Ethan had to leave the room.

I couldn't blame him for needing air. He hadn't experienced what I did, but I knew after hearing other stories from victims he'd been affected. The horrors of what had occurred to other people were shocking. It made me want to lock myself away and never come out into society again.

My uncle John was the sheriff. Since his retirement he'd been traveling all over the place with my aunt Karen. When they arrived neither knew what they were walking into. It was a Godsend when I realized I wasn't the one who had to fill them in on all of the gory details. It was one thing to put on a strong face, but it was another to actually feel like I could conquer this large mountain of despair.

It only took my aunt and uncle a couple minutes to come rushing to my side offering some sort of condolences for my gruesome encounter. As much as I loved my family, I didn't want this kind of treatment. I wanted to forget, albeit every time I saw them I'd be reminded that they were thinking about what happened to me. In many ways it was going to make it more difficult to forget.

While sitting down at my parent's large, dining room table I listened to my uncle telling them what needed to be done. Hearing him go on and on about police involvement sent me into an apprehensive state.

"Don't fret," my uncle reassured me. "We're goin' to get this figured out."

He didn't get it. In fact none of them did. I couldn't sit back and watch my whole life be destroyed worse than it was. Didn't they see that going to the authorities was only causing me more grief? Couldn't they tell that I just wanted to run away and never look back, praying I'd never see any of those people again for the rest of my life?

"Please, dad, I'm not ready to go public with this."

"Darlin', this ain't your decision any longer. I won't allow a vicious man to do this to another woman. He needs to be punished for his crimes."

I shook my head. "No. You don't understand. Punishin' him will only hurt me more. I already can't go back to that school. If you press charges and start this huge investigation I'll leave town, daddy. I'll have to, because no place will be safe for me."

I'd never threatened my father, and his stern gaze let me know that he wasn't going to stand there and take it lightly.

He looked over toward my uncle John. "Get someone to meet us at the hospital."

I stood up, barely able to contain my emotions. I could feel the tears running down my cheeks, but wasn't yet in a state of weeping yet. "No. I'm not goin'!"

I placed my shaky hands on my hips and stood my ground. "I'm a grown woman, and though I appreciate you helpin', I won't let you do this. Don't you all get it? Don't you see that I want to put this behind me? I don't want to be poked by doctors. I don't want to be judged by the media, and don't think for a second that it won't happen. Our family is too well-known for it not to. Is that the kind of publicity you want?"

I was going after my dad with whatever I could come up with. He had to see that this was a terrible idea.

When my brother and Ethan came back in the room, probably because of the raised voices, they could tell the shit had hit the fan. My mother was beside herself, while my father and I stood over the table in a staring match. In the midst of it all I was more thankful for the argument, because although it was regarding my attack, it had taken my mind off of the little details I couldn't stop thinking about.

Finally I sat down and folded my hands on the table. My sniffles let everyone know that I was crying, even if they refused to look in my direction. "Please don't make me do this. I'm not ready, daddy." I played the daddy card, hoping to get to his heart. My father could be strict, but he always melted for us girls.

He covered his face with his hands and rubbed it. I turned to my mom, watching her wiping away a fresh set of tears.

"You need to worry about Addy. I'm goin' to recover from this. She needs your attention. All I require is a quiet place to rest, and a break from school. I don't want to talk about what happened, and I surely don't want the whole family findin' out. They already think I'm weak, and this only verifies those accusations."

"You're not weak," Noah said loudly.

"It doesn't matter. Don't you all see that I just want to forget?"

My mother led my father into another room, followed by my aunt and uncle. That left Noah and Ethan in the dining room with me. Noah sat down across from me, while Ethan leaned against the door frame. "You're not weak," Noah repeated.

"Thank you. I keep thinkin' about what else I could have done. If I'd only kicked him, or poked his eyes out. I keep rehashin' it, as if it makes a damn bit of difference."

"You know dad's not goin' to stop until that asshole is behind bars?"

"Yeah, I know. I just hope that mom changes his mind."

"If you were my daughter nothin' would make me stop fightin' for justice. You have to look at it that way."

I kept quiet after my brother's assumption. It wasn't that I didn't have anything else to say, I just didn't have the energy to keep going on and on about it. I knew where he stood, and from the look on Ethan's face I could tell he agreed. That left me the minority.

When my parents came back in the room they didn't sit down. My father crossed his arms as he spoke. "We're goin' to the hospital, Christian. We know you're scared, but it's for the best. As far as this ranch is concerned, I don't care about the publicity. Nothin's more important than my family, not even this ground we live on. You can fight me on this, but at the end of the day we've got your best interest at heart. I need you to get well, and this is the first step in makin' that happen. Your mother and I will be by your side the whole time, and if you want your friend Ethan along, he's more than welcome. This ain't a punishment; it's the path to resolution."

Knowing that I couldn't cross this man, I looked away from him, settled on the fact there was no other way.

Then I knew what I had to do.

I got up and excused myself to go to the bathroom, taking my purse with me; and in a matter of seconds after closing the door, I'd text Ethan to meet me at his car. He'd fight me, but we were getting out of there before I was taken to hospital and treated like a lab rat. The idea of a stranger touching me was making me ill.

I darted for the front door a few seconds later, seeing Ethan in the driver's seat. I could hear someone calling my name, but ran as fast I could. "Floor it. I'll tell you how to get out of here without using the front gates." My dad was probably already on the phone getting them to lock down the main entrance to the ranch. It was a good thing I knew my way around. My mom's parents had built a little house on the outskirts of the property, and they had their own entrance from an adjacent road. We made it down the dirt entrance in no time, arriving on a country highway where I knew we were in the clear.

"Do you mind tellin' me why I feel like a damn criminal?"

"Goin' there was a mistake, Ethan. I can't let them take me to a hospital. I won't be like the girl we met last night. I can't let myself."

"Chris, you need help."

"No. I just need some time to get over it. My attack was nothin' like those other women. They had it so much worse. I can handle this on my own. As much as I appreciate your two-cents, I'd appreciate it if you let me make the decisions from now on." I was adamant to be in charge, because no one knew me better than I knew myself.

After a few minutes of driving I finally answer my phone. My mother was on the other end begging me to reconsider.

"Honey, we're just worried about you. You need help."

"Mom, I have to do this on my own. I feel terrible for involvin' you. I never wanted you and dad to look at me as the victim. I couldn't sit there anymore."

"Come home, Christian. We can talk about all of this after we know you're safe."

"I am safe. Ethan will protect me. I'm stayin' with him for a while until I can figure out everything." That was a lie. I knew I wasn't returning to school. Hiding out at Ethan's was only temporary. There was a lot more than dropping out of school that I needed to worry about.

"I hope you change your mind, sweetie. We're here, and you know you're welcome to come home. If you don't want to stay with us, Gram has plenty of room. You can recover on the ranch, where we know you'll be safe."

"I need time, mom. I'll call you soon, I promise."

When we hung up I clenched the phone in my hand, staring down at it, as if it somehow held answers I desperately needed. I'd walked away from my family, leaving me pretty much alone to fend for myself. I longed for resolution; my dad was right about that. Only I wasn't sure how to go about getting it without making it a media frenzy. I refused to be the talk of the town.

I already knew I was the laughing stock at my old house. When the whole campus found out the news they'd come after me for attacking their beloved popular role model. It made me cringe.

There had to be another way out of this mess, and I just needed time to figure it all out.

Chapter 22
Ethan

I thought that going to her parents was the best decision. They could help guide their daughter to the healing that she needed.

Chris had other plans.

As much as I wanted to keep my promise to her, I knew that being her safety net wasn't without regret. Her parents were going to hate me for sneaking her out of their house. It was only a matter of time before they were knocking at my door. It didn't take a genius to guess that they'd already contacted my parents to obtain my address on campus.

I didn't say much in the car on the ride back to my place. Chris wouldn't have liked to hear my opinion. As much as I understood that this was her problem, I also knew that she had the best family I'd ever known. She had to know that.

Once we were inside of my apartment she headed back to my bedroom, closing the door behind her. I don't think she meant for it to be rude, but I took offense since it was my neck I was sticking out for her. Still, I let her have some time to herself, to maybe realize she'd made a mistake.

I sat down at my computer to get some school-work done while everything was quiet. I headed to my email, hoping to have a response from some of my classmates about assignments I'd missed. I didn't expect to have a message in my inbox from Seth. Any student could obtain addresses for other classmates. The directory was out there on the main website. I clenched my jaws as I opened the message, not really knowing what to expect.

First there was a written message.

Ethan,

We don't know each other well, but we do share a common friend. Christian Mitchell and I hooked up last Friday night and then again on Saturday. To be honest she was an easy lay. She came on to me in a strip club, and then later on after she'd invited me back to her house. We're both guys, so you can imagine how she was easy on the eyes. I didn't hesitate when she asked me to follow her to her room.

I won't go into details about how she was all over my dick. I think you see where this is going. I'm reaching out to you because she's all of a sudden gone psycho. The bitch is accusing me of rape. I've got a ton of people who can back my story of her being all over me. I'm not looking for another witness. I'm writing to ask that you convince your friend to back off. She doesn't know who she's messing with. My friends are pissed this is happening, and I'm afraid they're going to make sure this story gets buried.

Please pass this on to your friend. Make sure she knows that I want this shit to be forgotten about. I get that women change their minds, but I never attacked your friend. We slept together on three different occasions, all of which she was a willing participant. For Christ sakes, she blew me in the movie theater. Does that sound like someone who was forced to have sex?

Think about it, man. I'm not the bad guy. Your friend needs help, but not from being attacked. She needs mental assistance.

Thanks for your time,
Seth

If I didn't need the computer for school I would have thrown it across the room at that very moment. Just before closing out the message I saw the attachment. A ten second video sat waiting to be played. Against better judgment I clicked on the link. It was dark, but light enough to see what was going on. Chris was on her knees with a cock in her mouth. I could hear the sound coming from the person recording it, and how his voice changed when she took his load. As much as I wanted to stop watching I couldn't take my eyes off the screen. When the video ended, I played it again, somehow in denial that it was my Christian on her knees.

I had to get up and walk away.

I knew she'd been with the guy, but this was a kick to the balls. Never in my wildest dreams did I think I'd have a visual of her doing something like that to another man.

After heading out to my balcony I looked at the horizon, praying it would distract my mind from the permanent image I couldn't shake. She'd been so into it, making it impossible for me to comprehend how on that same day she'd claimed to be raped by this guy.

Chris and I had talked about oral sex. I liked giving it to her, and I'd been doing it for a long time. She was never willing, but promised to save it for me. We had this pact that we'd experience all of our firsts together, that way we would never regret it. I couldn't fathom that she'd give this guy something that should have been mine. It didn't only disturb me, it ripped me apart. In the twenty seconds it took to watch the video, I'd felt like everything I'd ever wanted for my future had been flushed down the drain. She may as well have ripped out my heart with her bare hands.

It didn't matter that this guy hadn't a clue what we were to each other. People could assume what they wanted, not that I ever cared when it came to Christian. If they wanted to think we were a couple I didn't correct them. I knew one day we would be. It had been planned out perfectly for years.

In just a few days my aspirations were suddenly beginning to change. The woman inside, that had my heart for so long, had betrayed the sanctity of our friendship. She'd destroyed me.

I knew why she hadn't told me, but it hurt more knowing she carried that secret. Did she think about blowing that guy while she was around me? What did he have that I didn't?

I couldn't rationalize with myself over it. Something had to give.

When I heard the sliding door opening I didn't turn around to greet her. I couldn't look into those green eyes and feel anything but betrayal. I'd thought I was the one hurting her all this time, but had the girl I'd always known to be so pure changed without me noticing? She was determined to do whatever it took to come out of her shell. Had she danced with the devil on her own will, only to regret it enough to act out this terrible scenario? I hated doubting her, but there was some truth in that video. He wasn't forcing her to perform. As the image repeated in my mind I finally turned around.

"It's cold out here. Why are you standin' around without a jacket?" She asked as she wrapped her arm into mine. I closed my eyes and looked in another direction. As much as I wanted a reason to be close to her, I couldn't stand her touch.

"Are you goin' to be alright if I have to run out for a bit?"

She pulled away, seemingly shocked at my question. "I thought you didn't want to let me out of your sight?"

"I forgot I made plans I can't break."

"Yeah, I guess. I'll keep the doors locked and try to get some rest." She was unaffected by my question, leading me to believe that this really could be some kind of act.

I needed to get out of there; to think about what my mind was telling me. I couldn't doubt her, not after the way I felt about her. This was the woman I loved. Was I really considering that she could be lying to me? Had she betrayed my trust so much that I couldn't believe her?

"Okay." Where I'd normally kiss the top of her head I turned and walked away. Maybe she'd assume something was wrong. At this point I didn't even care. Watching those lips around another man's dick had me messed up. I had to release my anger, my hurt, and everything else I didn't want to be feeling.

I knew I'd hate myself for doing it, but I picked up my phone and dialed the number anyway. There was only one thing that could take my mind off of what she'd done to me. She answered on the second ring, and the sound of her voice was already helping my mood.

"Hey, I tried to call you last night." Star wasn't just on my jock tonight, she'd been clear that she'd drop everything if I'd give her the time of day. She saw me as her meal ticket out of this town, thinking that my intelligence would get me far in life. She saw dollar signs. Little did she know that my place was back at home. Sure, I'd like to have an engineering degree, but it wasn't where my heart was.

"Sorry. I was helpin' a friend. What are you doin' now?"

"Why? Do you want to come over?"

"I'm already on the way."

"I don't have anything to eat. If you're hungry you might want to grab something out."

"I'm hungry for something else. Be naked. I'll see you in five minutes."

Determined to wash my mind of Christian, I planned to bury myself in someone else. It was the wrong choice, but the only way. She'd hurt me, forcing me to seek reprieve. I'd have to address the problem, but until I was able to do that, I had to get some release.

Chapter 23
Christian

I didn't get why all of a sudden he was leaving me alone. Out of nowhere he'd recalled something that was more important than being my shoulder to cry on. I waited until I heard the front door shut before walking inside. The first thing I noticed was that he'd left his laptop, meaning this wasn't about school. Whatever my dear friend was doing had nothing to do with catching up on assignments.

I sat down as his computer and started researching sites about rape victims. It helped to read the stories and relate to each experience. In some ways it was more support than anyone I knew could have given me. The women, and even men, lost themselves because of vicious acts done to them. They knew what I was going through, having the knowledge of it happening to them. We all had a common goal of recovering, and no matter how many stories I read they all ended the same.

The victims wanted justice.

I closed my eyes and thought about Seth. I imagined how wonderful he'd been the night we first met, and how good of a time we'd had playing drinking games and retreating back to my room. I recalled all of his innuendos, which creeped me out. He was so gentle that first time, making sure he satisfied me first. How could one day have changed him so much? It was like he'd become a monster. Had me walking away from him, rejecting him, caused Seth so much rage that he'd found it necessary to rip me apart, leaving me like some piece of trash?

I tried to shake off my scenarios, but nothing would work. I felt abandoned by Ethan, and he hadn't even provided me with an explanation. What bothered me the most was that he didn't even kiss me goodbye. It was his brand, yet why in my most emotional state had he done that?

After going into a crying fit I closed out my internet box, leaving only his email left open. When I saw the name of the last sender my heart jumped. It didn't take me but a second to click on it and see what it was about.

I think after the first sentence my mouth hung open. He'd taken everything and turned it around on me, making me seem like a liar. I got up and ran to the bathroom vomiting out the little amount of food I'd consumed. While I lingered there on the bathroom floor I cried out for God to help me through this, because without Ethan I'd have no one else I could trust. Sure, my parents were wonderful, but they only saw one way out of all this, and I wasn't ready to let that be my only option.

Feeling discontent, I dialed Ethan's number, prepared to do whatever it took to plead my case. Yes, I'd gone against our stupid little pact that we'd made years ago, but it wasn't like he hadn't been with a slew of women. He knew how I felt about him and went about flaunting his perversions to me every chance he got. He's lucky I stuck around and tolerated it, because many other women in my situation would have wised up and moved on.

After it rang several times his voicemail picked up. I knew for a fact that he never listened to his messages, so I hung up and redialed the number. I continued repeating those steps until he finally answered the call, out of breath. "What?"

"I know why you left, Ethan. I saw the video and I can explain. I swear I can. Please just hear me out before you make any assumptions."

"Like what, Chris? Like assuming that you weren't really attacked at all? I can't stop seein' you with your lips wrapping around his -."

"Stop it! Please don't even talk about it."

"Why? It looked like you were pretty into it. It's why I'm havin' trouble believin' that a few hours later you were raped. Tell me how that works. Do you agree to give oral, but not ass?"

His words hurt me. "Why is it such a big deal to you? We made that pact years ago. It's not like you want to be with me anyway. You've done nothin' but tell me we're just friends."

"Don't you dare change the subject." He wanted explanations that I wasn't willing to think about. I had no excuse for why I did that to Seth. I also couldn't explain how in just a little amount of time I'd changed my mind about him completely. The man that picked me up and took me to that abandoned house wasn't the same person I'd been intimate with. He was intoxicated, and had become violent.

"Well, don't you dare walk out on me when I need you the most."

"I'm hangin' up now. Maybe I need some time to unwind before I come home. It's best that I calm down so I won't say somethin' I could regret later. Right now I feel like I can't trust you, and to be honest, it fuckin' hurts. I always thought that pact meant somethin'. It was put into place for a reason."

All of a sudden I heard a female talking to him in the background. "Who's that?"

"She's a friend, which is more than I can say for you at the moment." It stabbed me right through my heart. Never in my life had I ever felt so broken. This was the man I loved, and I'd pushed him into another woman's arms. If my life wasn't over before, it certainly was now.

"Ethan, please don't hang up. I need you."

The line went dead, and I was left to suffer the consequences of yet another poor decision. Ethan was so angry with me, and I wasn't used to that. He'd always been my rock. The idea of him not trusting me was almost as serious as everything else I was going through.

My crying fit was short-lived. A knock on the door startled me, sending me to peek out the tiny peep hole. Seeing my parents standing on the opposite side of the door made me nauseous. There was no way out of this. I had to go with them, and seek assistance, because my best friend wanted nothing to do with me.

When I opened the door I didn't speak. There were no words I could say to make this any less awkward. I'd run away like a child, and now I'd been caught. "Where's Ethan?"

"He had to run out." As much as I wanted him by my side, I couldn't tell my father where he'd really gone. My parents always assumed that he was it for me. In my eyes they were right, even when Ethan only wanted to be my friend.

"Get your things. We're goin' home." My dad ordered.

"I don't have much, dad. My roommates destroyed it the other day when this all came out. Nobody believes me." I watched my dad clenching his jaw. It was obvious that he was pissed at this new information. He picked up his phone and was immediately connected to the nine-one-one operator. "Yeah, I need an officer to come to a residence so that my daughter can retrieve some personal items."

He waited for a moment and then gave the address to the house I'd been living at for a short time. My mother hugged me, probably seeing that I was ready to jump out of a window and call it the end.

215

Five minutes later we were heading to the house, and with the little amount of talking my dad did in the car I knew he was about to go off the deep end.

Once we pulled up at the residence I was ordered to stay in the vehicle. My parents walked up to the arriving officer and they all went inside together. A few minutes later I spotted Becca walking outside on the front porch. I tried to duck down on the backseat to prevent her from spotting me, but it was too late. I saw her heading in my direction and she looked pissed.

She knocked on the window. "You had to get your parents involved? Bitch, you barked up the wrong tree. You're lucky I don't bust in there and beat your ass. Why don't you get out and face me?"

"I'm not afraid of you, Becca."

She opened her arms wide. "Come on, slut."

"I'm not a slut!" I yelled from the other side of the glass.

"You're just a liar. We've all seen the video. He showed everyone. You blew him in the movie theater, in public. There's no way he raped you. He said he rejected you, and you got pissed."

"He's lyin'! I swear it. He took me to that abandoned house and forced himself on me. I begged him to stop."

She shooed my comment away. "Just get your shit and leave us all alone. I should have known you were nothin' but trouble."

Before I could say anything another officer pulled up. He walked inside of the house, coming

216

back out with my parents, who had their hands full of my belongings. I sat quietly in the car, stewing on Becca's threats. She didn't have to threaten me to leave campus, because it was the last place I ever wanted to visit again. Without the support from Ethan I was left to go through this alone. My parents would do as much as they could, but they'd never understand what it felt like to be lost.

Right before they climbed into the vehicle I heard Becca getting loud. She was up in my mother's face, pointing at me. "She's trouble. You ought to lock her up and throw away the key. That girl tried to take down my friend." She pulled out her phone, and before I could react I saw my mom's eyes widening. She covered her mouth with her hand and froze. "You still think she's the victim?" Becca asked.

I jumped from my seat, running over toward them, but my dad stopped me. "I don't know what this is about, but we're leavin' right now!"

I didn't fight as he led me back to the car. There was no use. The damage was irrefutable. My mother couldn't look at me as she joined us, and I knew why. She'd just seen my lips around my rapist's cock.

I buried my head between my knees and cried the whole way home, feeling like there was no way they'd ever believe my version of the story again. I knew they'd protect me, but seeing their disappointment would literally kill me. Death had to feel better than this fate. As I considered that option I knew I'd given up hope.

The time of me wanting to fit in; to be popular and loved, was over. I didn't deserve this result however it was exactly what I'd been left with. I was nothing, a loner who'd lost her faith in everything positive. Though I knew I didn't deserve it, I'd been labeled as an outcast; who'd live out the rest of my days in solitude, because I'd rather be alone than face what else the world had in store for me.

Chapter 24
Ethan

Star knew what I wanted from the moment I hung up from my call. She'd unlocked her door anticipating my visit, and as I approached it, I knew she'd be able to settle me down, at least for the time being.

There was just one problem with that plan.

I wasn't hoping to stop stressing about an exam, or something mundane in life that annoyed me. I was trying to forget about Christian; the woman I'd purposely pushed away because our timing was off. I'd been a fool to think that statistics should factor into my feelings for her. What kind of idiot prolongs being with someone because there's a chance that it might last longer?

I did.

Yes, it was true that I was angry with her. A part of me wanted to ream her out for what she'd done. There was another part of me that remembered the events of the past week. Knowing her like I did, it was impossible to assume she'd been lying. Christian may have been highly intelligent, but she was a terrible actor, and horrible at lying, especially to me. I didn't know every single detail of what led to her attack, but it had happened. I'd witnessed her break down right in front of me. I'd seen her react to being back at that abandoned house. I watched her fall apart during the group session. It wasn't something she could fake. Her actions were heartfelt, painful to watch in fact. There was no way in hell she could make that up.

Star pulled me inside of her apartment and I immediately regretted being there. Her naked body pressed against me while her lips found mine. I closed my eyes and tried to respond to her initiation, but it was impossible. I'd abandoned my best friend, and it was crucial that I go back there and console her.

My mind went into a whirl as Star reached down my pants, gently caressing my limp dick. Within seconds I'd become hard, needing a release I knew I wasn't going to get if I went home.

She tugged down my jeans, eagerly taking my cock between her lips. My head fell back while I persuaded myself to go along with it. The pact had been broken. Her doing this was now allowed, and I wasn't about to stop her, besides, it felt better than I could have imagined. She hungrily lapped up my cock, savoring it in her mouth while sucking vigorously. In no time at all I was ready to explode down her throat. She'd satisfy me like she always did, which in turn made me come back for more.

Just as I was about to finish I heard my phone ringing. I ignored it, hoping to find closure with my current predicament, but it just kept blowing up. Finally I pushed Star off of me and answered, annoyed. "What?"

"I know why you left, Ethan. I saw the video and I can explain. I swear I can. Please just hear me out before you make any assumptions." The last thing I wanted to talk about at the moment was her giving someone else head. It bothered me so much that I felt the need to get a few things off my chest.

"Like what, Chris? Like assuming that you weren't really attacked at all? I can't stop seein' you with your lips wrapping around his -." She didn't let me finish. I saw Star backing up, wiping off her mouth. I knew the moment was over, even as I stood fully erect.

"Stop it! Please don't even talk about it." It was funny how disgusted she sounded, when all I wanted to do was kill the fucker, and gouge out my own eyes.

"Why? It looked like you were pretty into it. It's why I'm havin' trouble believin' that a few hours later you were raped. Tell me how that works. Do you agree to give oral, but not ass?" I regretted saying it, more than she'd ever know, but I was destroyed by those actions, so much that I was lashing out.

"Why is it such a big deal to you? We made that pact years ago. It's not like you want to be with me anyway. You've done nothin' but tell me we're just friends."

Another kick to the balls, but she was right. We could have been together, and none of this would be happening. I'd been blaming myself for days. Reminding me of it wouldn't change anything. "Don't you dare change the subject."

"Well, don't you dare walk out on me when I need you the most."

"I'm hangin' up now. Maybe I need some time to unwind before I come home. It's best that I calm down so I won't say somethin' I could regret later. Right now I feel like I can't trust you, and to be honest, it fuckin' hurts. I always thought that pact meant somethin'. It was put into place for a reason."

Star said something to me, not that I was even paying attention. The next thing I know Chris is asking questions on the other end of the call. "Who's that?"

"She's a friend, which is more than I can say for you at the moment." Those words left a bad taste in my mouth.

Insert foot!

"Ethan, please don't hang up. I need you."

I had to end the call. It took everything in me not to throw the device across the room. She had me so messed up. I looked toward the naked female waiting for me to reply to her question, still not knowing what the hell she'd asked. "I need to go."

"You just got here," she argued.

"Look, I'm sorry I wasted your time. I've got shit goin' on that I can't really explain."

She walked over as I was pulling up my pants. "You could come back later. We can finish what we started."

I leaned forward and kissed her on the head, immediately feeling the connection that I'd always had to Chris. I needed to find her and apologize. She needed to know that I didn't mean those things I'd said to her. I had to prove to her that she'd never be alone.

I raced back to my apartment, the whole time practicing what I'd say to her. I had it all planned out in my head, down to sentence structure. It was time for me to convince her that she was so much more than a friend to me. I needed not only to apologize for leaving, but for what I'd done with all of the other women. All of the cards had to be laid out on the table. No more lies.

As soon as I pulled up I noticed the lights were all turned out. I walked up the stairs to my level and unlocked the door. Once I'd traveled to my bedroom I discovered she wasn't there. I called for her, looking on the balcony to see if she was outside. There was no note, and for the life of me I couldn't figure out where she'd gone.

As fast as I could make it, I drove to the abandoned house. When she wasn't there I headed over to her house. The police were pulling away. One of the girls was still outside, so I sauntered over to see if she'd seen Christian.

"You just missed her," she said before I could ask.

"Do you know where she went?"

"Look, I don't know what you are to her, but you should just walk away from that hot-mess. She's trouble."

"She's my best friend, who was raped by your friend. Listen here you little bitch, my friend wouldn't lie about what happened to her. You better check yourself, because once her family is done with that bastard, you'll be visitin' him in jail."

I turned around, ignoring her slew of comments as I climbed back in my car.

My next stop was to the location that the last meeting had been, but the parking lot was dark and vacant. After beating on my steering wheel a half-dozen times I came to the conclusion that she didn't want to be found. Even though we'd fought, a part of me worried that she might be in danger, especially after she'd been back to her old house.

I hated doing it, but I called her parents, hoping they could help me find her before something else happened. She was going to hate me even worse than she already did, but at least I'd know she was okay. I'd been an ass, and probably didn't deserve her. I knew she'd push me away, but it wouldn't stop me from trying. I'd keep at it, somehow proving that I'd be the man she needed me to be.

When her dad answered I swallowed my pride and prepared to tell him that I'd messed up and let her out of my sight. He'd go off on me, probably forbidding me to see her once we figured out where she'd gone.

"Mr. Mitchell, this is Ethan. I was wonderin' if you've heard from Christian?"

"Yes, I have. We picked her up earlier, and I'm glad we did. It seems you left her all alone."

"I can explain." Really I couldn't. Her dad didn't want to hear that I'd been jealous and left to get a piece of ass to make me feel better.

"Now's not the time, Ethan. We're in the process of gettin' Chris admitted for evaluation. She won't be able to have visitors until tomorrow since it's so late."

"Thanks for lettin' me know."

After we'd hung up I finally sat down and tried to think about everything going on. If Chris was at the hospital she had to be petrified. This was exactly what she didn't want to happen.

Against my better judgment I felt like I needed to do something to help the cause. Her parents were going to go after Seth, and nobody wanted him to suffer more than I did, except for Chris. She most likely wanted him skinned and hung for his assault on her. After obtaining my laptop off the table, I opened my email and stared at his message.

Then I replied.

Seth,
I'd like to hear your side of the story face to face. Meet me at the library at ten p.m. so we can work this out.
Ethan

There was nothing to discuss. I wanted the fucker to pay for what he'd done, and I'd make sure he got what was coming, even if I had to use my fists to get the job done.

Chapter 25
Christian

The white walls matched the floor. I didn't know if that bothered me more, or what they had me wearing. Even in the hospital bed I was annoyed by the hospital gown being open in the back.

My parents sat next to each other beside the bed. During the ride they'd asked for details, which I wasn't willing to pervade them to. Some things were better left unsaid, and in this case my sexual experiences, both good and horrible, were off limits.

I'd suffered enough in the past few days, and I knew I'd have to explain to the slew of doctors who were coming to evaluate me. I'd already been poked by a nurse who drew my blood and did vitals. An officer was on the way, but I wasn't sure why because I'd washed away any ounce of proof, besides the fact that it could be argued I had consensual sex with him hours before. I suppose they needed my formal statement, which meant this was going to get ugly. Since I'd already been threatened, I didn't want to think what else would come from this kind of publicity. In true family fashion my brother and Shalan showed up shortly after. I could tell his fiancée was reluctant to speak to me. She seemed uncomfortable, like he'd made her accompany him.

As much as I appreciated the support, I couldn't help but wonder what they were all thinking. It made me feel weak like they were afraid they couldn't leave me alone for even a few minutes.

The officer arrived, and much to my surprise it wasn't a female detective. The man asked my family to leave the room while he took my statement. Since it was so involved I knew it was important to start from the beginning. If my parents were adamant about taking Seth down than I had to make sure they had every single detail.

Starting from the strip club I accounted every single moment I'd spent with Seth. When I struggled with some parts he waited for me to get myself together in order to continue. While he wasn't a woman, I appreciated how sympathetic he was to my situation. He gave me statistics, and reminded me that it was never the victim's fault, even if they taunted their attacker, which I hadn't.

It didn't stop me from crying halfway through, or feeling like a slut explaining what we'd done and where it happened.

Just when I thought he'd changed his mind about me he smiled and put his pen down then proceeded to assure me that I wasn't the first person to fool around in a movie theater. It still embarrassed me, but at least made me feel like he was attempting to get me to feel better.

After nearly an hour of questions the officer left, and my family filled in the tiny room. They said their goodbyes, all of them leaving me to get rest. It wasn't without a fight though. My mom wanted to stay, but I convinced her that I needed to sleep. After making sure the nurse was going to provide me with some kind of medication to help me relax, she followed the rest of my family out.

The moment I knew I was alone I located the phone and dialed Ethan. I didn't expect him to answer, but I knew I wouldn't be able to close my eyes and sleep if I didn't at least leave him a message telling him how sorry I was.

If I'd known he'd react so angrily maybe I wouldn't have done it. Even though I didn't understand why it was so important to him, I appreciated that he cared enough to be upset.

Nothing surprised me more than him answering on the first ring. "Chris? Are you alright?"

"Not really."

"Are your parents still there with you?" He asked.

"No. They all left. Noah and Shalan were also here. I made them all leave so I could rest."

"You don't sound like you're restin'."

I shrugged even though he couldn't see me. "Yeah, well I have a lot on my mind."

"About earlier."

"I'm so sorry, Ethan. I didn't mean to hurt you. If I could take back everything I would."

"I hooked up with someone when I left tonight." His confession shocked me. "I know I don't have to tell you what I do, but I felt bad as soon as it started. What you did pissed me off. No, it wasn't just that. It hurt. I guess after all this time I felt like I'd always be every one of your firsts. It's stupid now, because we're both adults, but how many people can look back at their life and say that they shared everything for the first time with only one person? I wanted that with you, because no matter how mad I get at you, you'll always be my best friend. You'll always be the person I turn to; the one I can't live without."

I started to bawl. As if my life couldn't get anymore messed up, I felt devastated over hurting Ethan. Nobody meant more to me than he did. "You're my best friend too. That mistake ruined my life, Ethan. I'd do anything to take it back. I wish it never happened."

"I think the hardest part was seeing it happen. I'm sure that was the plan though. Don't cry, I've got a feelin' that Seth is about to get what's comin' to him. Don't you worry your pretty little head. We'll get through this."

"Why do you think that? Did you talk to my father? Did he tell you the police were here?"

"Your dad told me where you were. He let me know that I wouldn't be able to see you until mornin'."

"Okay. So your just bein' optimistic?" I knew Ethan well enough to know when he was keeping something from me. I didn't have to see his face. "Ethan?"

"I emailed him back, tellin' him to meet me at ten. We're goin' to have a face-to-face and get things straight. It's time that city boy learns what happens when he messes with a sweet country girl."

"Please don't, Ethan. The police are involved now. If you put yourself in the scenario it could be trouble for you. I'm beggin' you to stay out of it. Please. I need you to be there for me, not locked up for avenging. I don't need a hero."

"This ain't just about you, darlin'."

"You sound like my father." His sweet talking wasn't going to make me change my mind. I didn't want him going anywhere near Seth.

"Would you feel better if I called you once I'm back home?"

"No! I'd rather you not go and talk to me now."

"Christian, from the moment I found out what that guy did to you I wanted to hurt this guy. He needs to pay for what he did to you. He needs to be taught a lesson; one that will make sure he never hurts another woman again. Don't you get it? If I do nothin' than I'll feel like I didn't do enough. This is as much for me as it is for you. He deserves much worse than a beatin'. You can't lie in that bed and tell me that it wouldn't bring a smile to your face knowin' his pussy-ass is kissin' the concrete of some dark parkin' lot? There's got to be some part of you that wants him to pay for what he's done."

"I do, but I can't let you entertain this idea to seek out revenge. You're not a superhero, or an idiot. He could come back at you with assault charges. I don't feel like high-fiving you as we pass in a court room. Be rational."

"I can't. You can be mad if you want, but I'm goin' out there tonight. He's goin' to learn that messin' with you was the wrong choice."

I rolled my eyes feeling like nothing I said was going to change his mind. "You sound like a jealous boyfriend. You're makin' no sense."

"Yeah, well maybe that's what I was. I got to get goin', babe. I'll come see you in the mornin'."

When I realized he'd hung up I quickly redialed his number. When he failed to answer I knew there was nothing I could do to stop him. Ethan was going to do what he felt was necessary. I was so distraught, so worried he was making a mistake, that I couldn't possibly close my eyes to rest.

As much as I appreciated him going out on a limb for me, I couldn't exactly condone his actions. I continued trying to get him to answer his phone for nearly thirty-minutes. As the clock passed ten I knew it was too late. The night nurse came in and gave me medication in my IV. I could feel myself dozing. I knew Ethan's meeting was out of my hands, but as my body let go, I prayed silently that when I woke up I'd see Ethan's face smiling back at me. I didn't know what I'd do if something bad happened to him, especially because it had everything to do with me.

Chapter 26
Ethan

There was only one thing running through my mind during my drive to the library parking lot.

Retribution.

Seth needed to pay for what he'd done to my girl, and I was going to make sure I was the one doing the punching. Once I'd put a hurting on him I'd let him know that if he ever laid a hand on a woman again I'd be back to give it to him double.

Christian's pleas hadn't made me feel bad enough to go back on my plan. I wasn't going to be content with what happened until he'd felt everything he'd done to her.

When I pulled up in the dark lot I noticed I was the only vehicle. There was a chance that Seth hadn't gotten the message, but there was also a possibility that he'd chosen to not meet me in fear of getting his ass beat.

My heart rate increased the moment I watched someone approaching my car on foot. I could tell it was Seth when he got closer into view. I didn't hesitate when I jumped out of the vehicle and approached him. "I'm here, let's talk." He swung his arms open, as if to taunt me.

"I ain't here to talk. I'm here to listen to you beg for mercy, because there ain't no way my friend is lyin' about what you did to her."

Where I come from you don't wait to be taken down. You make the first and the last move. At the very last minute I watched as he saw my arm coming around and lifted his to protect his face. I didn't pause as I brought my arm back to send a second blow. His jaw cracked as my fist made contact with the skin and sent him down to the ground. "Get up!" I ordered.

He came after me, trying to take me out at my waist. "Fuck you! I didn't rape your friend."

I lifted my knee at the right moment, clipping him in the neck as his body made contact with mine. He rolled on the ground, clutching his throat.

I stepped forward, prepared to kick him while he was already down.

Seth covered his face with both hands again. "Wait! I didn't come here to fight. You've got to believe me. She wanted it. She begged me to take her to that house. She didn't want to get caught by my ex. I'll take you there and tell you everything. Come on, man. You've got to believe me."

"You've got to be fuckin' kiddin' me. Why would I want to go anywhere with you? I already know what happened. I've heard every detail." If he thought that taking me back to where it happened was going to somehow make me change my mind, he was mistaken. All I wanted to do was crush every bone in his body. I wanted him to suffer an excruciating pain, reminding him every second what he'd done to my girl.

"We're goin' to head over to where it happened. You're goin' to give me a blow by blow, and then I'm goin' to decide how to end this." I wanted to laugh, but it was very obvious this guy was scared shitless. This was his idea first, and now he was cowering over it.

"You're insane. I changed my mind. I'm not going anywhere with you." Blood ran out of his mouth as he spoke, and he kept spitting it out onto the ground. "My friends know I'm here. They'll call the police if I'm not back within the hour."

"You think I'm scared of your friends, or the police? Look around, asshole. We're out in the open. I just kicked your ass where everyone could watch. I ain't scared of the cops, and I sure as hell ain't scared of your threats. Now, if you know what's good for you you'll get in that car and drive us over to the abandoned house you raped my friend in. You can make this hard, or you can cooperate. It's your choice."

"Why would I be stupid enough to let you take me to that house now, when I know you're planning to hurt me more? You think I want to die? Forget it. I'm not going. You can suck my fat dick."

I grabbed him by the arm, pulling him to a standing position. "You're going to explain your side of the story. Then I'll leave. You have my word." What I left out was yet to be determined.

This part of my attack was unnerving because I was acting on pure rage. I wasn't being rational, and I didn't know if I'd be spending the night in a cell for assault on this douche. I needed to teach him a lesson, and since I knew he was scared of what I could do to him, I had his undivided attention.

"Your word is shit." He spit his blood at my feet. "Get the fuck away from me."

I don't know why he didn't notice my fist coming around again. This time I got a good portion of his head near the ear. He went down again, this time covering his whole head from fear of another blow. "I'm not done."

This second attack had been provoked. I knew I wanted to beat him to a pulp, and with each punch I felt a little better about my actions. He'd destroyed my friend, leaving her with a lifetime of fear. He deserved so much worse.

Seth finally followed my directions without a fight. He insisted we walk there instead of driving, and since it was only a couple blocks I didn't protest.

Halfway there he started talking about Christian. "I should have known she was trouble when I met her. It was obvious she didn't belong in that club. For what it's worth she didn't tell me she had a boyfriend."

As much as I liked hearing someone call me that, I knew I couldn't correct him. "Shut up."

"No, you need to hear that it wasn't all me. She invited me into her room. She knew what was going to happen. We talked about it first. I gave her time to back out."

When we were both standing in front of the condemned house I knew I could have taken him inside and killed him. I was that angry. A part of me wanted to keep busting him up. Just as I was about to move inside, I froze. This could cost me Christian forever. If I took this guy inside and inflicted more pain on him, there was a good chance I'd go to jail. I'd be no different than this loser and his lies.

It was difficult to do, but I turned around and shocked the hell out of him. "We're done here."

"What? You believe me?"

"No! I won't stoop to your level. If we go in that house one of us ain't comin' back out. I hate you that much. I know what you did to her in that room, on that dirty mattress. She told me every single detail. She begged you to stop."

"I was drunk, man. If she said that I don't recall it. We had a great day together. You saw what happened at the movies. I liked her." He honestly triggered more anger. Finally he was coming clean, but it was too late.

"You need to leave now. If you ever lay a hand on another girl I'll make sure you end up in a house like this one. Do you understand?"

I waited until I was a block away to call the police and report a possible rape. After giving them the description of what Seth was wearing and his full name, it would be easy for officials to pick him up. Even though they wouldn't find any sign of an attack, I knew for a fact that he was always wanted for Christian's assault. I was just pushing it along faster. This time they didn't need a warrant for arrest. While that was being created and signed by a judge, I was getting that prick off the street. It was very satisfying.

I waited nearly twenty minutes before deciding to pull out of the parking lot to head back to my place. About halfway there I noticed three police cars pulled over and one wasn't campus security. Handcuffed and being pushed into the back of a sedan was Seth. I recognized him immediately, and grew a smile while continuing on. It wasn't until I'd passed my apartment that I realized where I was going. Nothing could stop me, not even the hospital guidelines. She needed to know she was safe, and I had to see her face when I told her.

When I reached the emergency room entrance I made a beeline for the security guard, quickly putting on a concerned face so he'd give me his attention. "Help me, please. My wife was brought in earlier with contractions. Can you tell me how to get to maternity?"

He handed me a visitor's badge and pointed toward the elevator, announcing the floor number I'd need to get to.

Little did he know that I had no intentions of going to that floor, because I didn't even know anyone who was pregnant. The directory was located at the main entrance, so once I'd gotten out of his view, I headed there first.

Once I'd located the floor she'd be on, I made it to the stairs, taking them instead of alerting the nurses on duty when the elevator doors opened. I stood and waited patiently for someone to walk through the double doors so that I could sneak into the restricted area. They'd dimmed the lights, making it difficult for me to see the room numbers; but luckily I knew where the room number was located and also the last digits of the phone number she'd called me from earlier.

I sneaked inside, closing the door behind me so they wouldn't hear us talking. Then I saw her lying there on the bed. When she turned to see me standing there I watched her frown turn into a welcoming smile. "What are you doin' here?" She whispered.

I rushed over to the bed, wanting to break the distance between us. "I had to sneak here to tell you somethin."

"Why are your fists bloody?" She asked.

I stuck my hand in my pocket and smiled. "Let's just say that I showed Seth how us cowboys handle someone hurtin' our women."

She raised her brow. "You didn't?"

"I did, and I'd do it again in a heartbeat for you. Don't you get it, Christian? Can't you feel it?"

She shook her head. "What? Feel what?"

"That I've been lyin' to you for a long damn time."

She let out an air-filled laugh. "Yeah right. I'm on too many drugs to find your jokes remotely entertaining."

I straightened my face and grabbed her hand. "It's true, and it's time I came clean about everything."

Chapter 27
Christian

"Came clean?" I was so lost. Had it not been for the valium I'd been given through an IV perhaps I would have been able to follow him better. All I was sure of was that I needed to know every detail of what happened with Seth. "First tell me about your hand. What did you do?"

"We met. We talked. I shoved him around a bit. Then I called the police and told them where they could find him. All in a day's work, babe."

Since I felt so woozy it was difficult for me to react the way I should have. Normally I would have freaked out, but because of the meds I was able to simply smile and feel proud that Ethan had done something so brave in my honor. "Thank you."

"Like I said, I'd do anything for you. Now, are you goin' to let me finish what I came here to tell you?"

"I don't know what you lied about, Ethan. Right now I don't even care. All that matters is that you're here, which means you forgive me for what I did on that video, at least enough to be here with me. I was so afraid that I lost you. I swore our friendship was over."

He smiled, leaned forward and kissed me softly on the forehead. Then as he was pulling away, he found my lips. He didn't push it and try to make it more. Only his lips pressed over mine; no tongue involved or groping hands. I wasn't ready for that, not even with Ethan. His gentle embrace was short-lived, but enough to tell me that he wasn't going anywhere. It was enough reassurance for one night.

The next morning the same officer stopped by the hospital to see me. Since my parents hadn't yet arrived, I urged Ethan to stay with me. He held my hand as the officer explained to me what was going on with my case. "The truth is that the prosecution doesn't have enough evidence to take this case. Without DNA or a witness, or someone else that can attest to being a victim of this guy, it's your word against his."

"So what does this mean?"

The man looked down as he spoke. "It means that he'll be released sometime today."

I sat up, immediately gasping for air. Ethan had gone after him, thinking he'd be locked up where he couldn't get to me. Now the officer was telling me that he'd be released. "What if he comes after me?" My question was more for Ethan, but the officer answered for him.

"We don't think he will. He's going to lay low, in fear of us digging up new information. In the meantime I'm going to take a trip out to that house.

We'll take the mattress back to the lab and run it for DNA. I've got a feeling we're going to have a lot of strains to go through, so be patient. It can take weeks, sometimes even months for that kind of extensive research."

Everything out of his mouth was making me lose hope. "I understand."

Ethan didn't though. "What if you match their DNA. Can you arrest him then?"

"Again it's a he said she said. With the video of their consensual encounter it will be difficult to prove she was assaulted only a little while later. I'm sorry I don't have better news."

I shook my head and wiped away residual tears. "I get it. In order to take him down I either have to be brutally left for dead, or have recorded the whole attack."

"The key is collecting evidence. Had you come into the hospital on the night of the attack, we could have done the rape kit. It would have helped, but again, this case relies on hard evidence. There are a lot of fraudulent cases out there with women who only want to cause men problems. We have to consider each one to be real until we can prove otherwise. I believe that you were attacked that night, but unfortunately we have nothing solid to use."

When the officer started to leave my parents were just walking in. He talked to them out in the hallway. Ethan and I watched through the glass as they were given the bad news. I knew they were pissed at me for not going straight to the authorities. They didn't need to remind me of my mistakes. I had to live with them just as much as they did.

Ethan squeezed my hand. "We need to talk about somethin', babe."

"I can't right now. They're goin' to come in and tell me they'll be able to help me, but the truth is that we both know I won't be goin' back to school, not that one at least. I can't face those people, and know what they're sayin' behind my back. I know the campus is huge, but I'm liable to run into one of them. I can't handle it.

I think it's best if I transfer to another school. Maybe I can take the semester off, get into counseling, and then start somewhere fresh. The only way I'm goin' to get through this is if I start gettin' help. I can't live like this. It hasn't even been a week and I've been through every emotion possible. I'm so tired."

"I know. I get it." He looked away, and I could tell he was upset. We'd made plans to go to school together, and now I had to break another one of our pacts. I couldn't hate myself more.

"I'm sorry, Ethan."

"It's not your fault. I'm not mad, not at you at least. I get why you can't go back, and as hard as it is to hear, I know it's for the best."

I tried to make him lighten up with a joke. "At least now you won't have to hide me from your late night visitors."

He peered at me, his brows furrowed and eyes were frustrated. "I don't give a shit about them."

"Ethan, it's time that we stopped pretendin'. The promises we made, the pact, we were children when we did that. We've grown together, and experienced so many things, but let's be realistic. I only agreed to all of that stuff because I thought you'd one day change your mind and want to be with me. I thought that if I went along with that plan it would make you love me the way I loved you. I didn't just want you to be my first. Back then I wanted you to be my forever."

Ethan was a tough guy. Since he didn't get emotional very often, I could tell that what I'd said had hurt him. It was extremely confusing, especially after he'd told me he'd gone out to get ass the night before. I couldn't begin to fathom how breaking our pact could hurt him. He was mature enough to understand that what I was saying was true.

My parents walked in, making our current conversation too inappropriate to talk about. I think what really shocked me was right after that he'd got up and left. I figured he walked outside to give me time with my parents, but he never returned.

A few hours later I was discharged. My parents had changed their minds and decided to take me home where I could rest comfortably.

I slept a little on the ride home, and was welcomed by my family when we reached the ranch. After everyone made sure I was in one piece, they went off to go about their day. Even though she

246

checked on me a little too often, my mom was the only person to check on me.

Throughout the day I checked my cell phone, hoping for a call or message from Ethan. I tried to reach him several times with no response. It hurt my feelings, but I knew I couldn't focus on him being immature about our little teenage pact.

Every minute of every hour I'd been thinking about my attack. I'd thought about other women and what they'd gone through, and even considered going back to meetings until I felt comfortable enough to share my own story. I knew mine didn't compare to some, but I'd been told that it didn't matter. When a women says no it should be final. There is no maybe, or probably if you push me to it.

No is no!

Twenty-four hours went by and I still hadn't heard anything from Ethan. My mom had made an appointment for me to meet with a new psychiatrist. Even as nervous as I was to talk about it all again, I somehow knew that each time was helping me cope. I wasn't as shaken up as I was those first couple nights. I still didn't like the idea of being touched, but being able to comfortably be in the room with a stranger was a step in the right direction.

The doctor looked to her paperwork before asking me the daunting questions that she was required to ask every new patient.

"Tell me how you're feeling today, Christian. What was it like for you when you woke up this morning?"

This was an easy question, and I immediately felt less uncomfortable since she wasn't jumping right into my attack. "Well for starters I woke up on the ranch. I could hear the sounds of the birds and nature. The smell of bacon and coffee filled the room. I felt at home. I felt safe," I explained.

"Good." She wrote down something. "How did you feel about coming to see me?"

"Reluctant. Worried. Afraid."

"Can you tell me what you're afraid of specifically?"

"I'm not sure if I'm ready to go over the details again. I had to tell my best friend, my family, and everyone at the hospital. I know it's helpin', but it makes me uneasy. I want to forget that it happened, not keep it fresh in my mind."

"What if I told you that you'll never be able to forget? How would that make you feel?"

"Angry."

She seemed intrigued by my answer as she made another notation. "Angry with me or -?"

I cut her off. "Not you. Angry with life. Maybe with God. Just angry in general. It's not fair. Why do I have to live that moment forever? What did I ever do to deserve that to happen to me?"

"That's a good question. The answer is nothing. You're a victim."

"If I'm never goin' to forget, how do you expect me to heal? I don't see it bein' feasible."

"It takes time, acceptance, and even forgiveness in some cases."

248

"I'll never forgive the person that did this to me."

"You have to forgive yourself, Christian." It was easy for her say. I didn't exactly understand what she meant, to be honest. I hadn't done anything wrong, except for sleeping with Seth. That was the biggest mistake of my life. I didn't know if I'd ever forgive myself for that.

When I didn't respond she took it upon herself to ask another question. "How do you feel about yourself?"

"Today, or in general?"

"Both. How would you describe yourself before all of this happened, and then now."

After she explained I took a deep breath and thought for a second on how I'd answer. All of my life I had to overcome obstacles just to fit in. I'd never felt like I did, which made me even more awkward. If it wasn't for Ethan, I don't know how I would have survived high school. In fact, I didn't know how I would have gotten through anything.

"Weak. I've always been weak."

She jotted something down. "How so?"

"Well, for as long as I can remember I've been an outcast. No matter what was happenin' I never seemed to fit in. I was never cool enough. My clothes were never the right style. I didn't like the same things as the other kids. I wasn't as pretty as the other girls."

"You're basing your answer on how you assume people think about you. Styles change, children grow up to be adults. What's cool one day isn't the next."

"I'm weak because I can't seem to find my in. It's that exact reason that landed me here today."

"I see." The doctor tapped her pen on her cheek as she thought. "So today you feel weak as well?"

I shrugged. "I don't know. Maybe."

"Has anyone ever told you that life was what you make of it?"

"Sure. People say a lot of things to make me feel better."

"It's the truth. In order to get past your demons, and what happened to you, it's important that you learn to love yourself. You have to love that you're different, eccentric is a better word. I don't know much about you, which will change in time, but from what I can tell you're beautiful, intelligent, and looking for something you already have."

"Which is what?"

"That's for you to figure out. Until we meet again next week I'd like you to start a journal. Each night I'd like for you to write ten things you did that made you happy. It doesn't matter if it was in the past or something you've just experienced. Underneath the ten items I'd like you to write about two things that make you sad. We'll go over everything at our next appointment."

I don't know what I expected out of my doctor's visit. I certainly didn't think I'd walk out of there feeling confused. Despite feeling overwhelmed, I picked up a journal and promised myself that I'd write in it.

That night before bed, after another full day and no word from Ethan, I sat down on my bed and wrote down the ten things that I was happy about.

Things that make me happy:

1. My mom and dad. I'd been blessed with two parents that would do anything for me.

2. My siblings. Like my parents I knew I could count on them always being around.

3. My huge extended family. My cousins were annoying at times, but I was lucky enough to have a bunch of them. Some people didn't get to have the kind of holidays that the Mitchell-Healy clan did.

4. My first horse. There were many times that I spent my day out in the woods with him. Up until the day he died he'd only brought me joy.

5. Getting good grades. Of course that made me and my parents happy.

6. My ability to care for others. Each year I volunteered at local soup kitchens and homeless facilities. Helping people made me happy.

7. My eyes. Even though I always felt awkward, people loved my eyes. It never got old hearing how beautiful they were.

8. The ranch. It represented home. Nothing could make a girl happier than the safest place on earth.

9. My gram's smile. No matter how sad I felt, she'd always cheer me up with only a smile, and maybe an occasional cookie.

When I got to ten it felt like my whole world was crashing down on me.

10. My best friend Ethan.

Things that make me sad.

1.   My attack
2.   Losing my best friend Ethan.

I stared at the piece of paper, realizing that my two sad things didn't involve me fitting in with my peers. I read over the list, thinking of a bunch of other happy moments I'd missed. I began to smile, thinking about all of my firsts with Ethan, and even though I couldn't change the past, there were still a lot of firsts that hadn't been done yet.

I had hope.

It wasn't pertaining to the attack, but more about having a new future. It was going to be a long road, I wasn't an idiot. I'd probably never forget that night in the abandoned house with Seth, but I'd survived, and that was also something I should be happy about.

Chapter 28
Ethan

As impossible as I thought it would be, staying away from Christian wasn't just painful. Every moment of every day I regretted walking away from her.

Despite the fact that I knew she was just a phone call away it hurt too much to imagine hearing her voice, and being drawn to someone that had pushed me away.

It was my fault. I'd been an asshole and let one mistake dictate my own selfish actions. Chris needed positivity in her life, and it was clear that I was only bringing her down. I didn't blame her, but I certainly couldn't agree with it, not when I knew that my love had always existed.

Two days turned into two weeks. I spent my time focusing on finals, and tutoring other's so they could pass their courses. When I went home alone at night I was reminded of all of the times she'd sat on my couch, or laid in my bed. I pictured the way her hair felt between my fingers, and how her eyes captivated me, even after all these years.

I'd started running in the middle of the night to make myself tired enough to rest. If it hadn't been for that then I probably never would have come face to face with the angel who would change everything for us.

It was after midnight, and I'd been lying down for nearly two hours, staring at the ceiling, counting sheep, and doing everything the internet said to help me sleep. Nothing worked.

I hated doing it, because it was pretty cold out, but I put on a jacket and a pair of shoes and headed out. Usually I ran this one course, but since they were decorating the campus for the homecoming I took another route around the older side of the property.

The brisk air hit my face, making me regret the decision to come outside in the first place. It almost hurt as the wind ripped through the air and slapped against my face. I kept my eyes squinted to prevent them from burning.

As I made it past another row of houses I came to the corner of where the abandoned one sat. An instant reminder of Chris was standing right in front of me. The last time I'd been there was with Seth, and thankfully I hadn't seen him since the incident. Even if we passed by each other I wouldn't have noticed. My mind was fixed on staying focused when I was out and about. I hardly ever made eye contact with people when I walked around in fear of what they might be thinking.

Since it was late, and I was alone, I felt like it would be okay if I stopped for a moment and ventured inside. I don't know why I wanted to drudge up the past. I suppose a part of me wanted to feel some kind of connection to Chris, as messed up as that seemed.

Once inside I noticed the mattress was gone. The police had taken it a long time ago. Though still drafty, I felt warmer once I'd made it into the large living room.

"I don't know what I was thinkin'," I said to myself.

Right before I could turn around to head back out I heard someone sniffling. The room was dark, but I knew I wasn't imagining it. "Hello? Is someone in here?"

I heard something clank, and then it repeated again and again. Finally my vision adjusted and I saw someone slowly coming down the stairs. I could tell it was a female, but that's about it.

"Please don't go." I could hear that she'd been crying.

"Are you okay?" I went to walk toward her, but she froze in place. I halted and put my hands up in the air. "Whoa! I won't hurt ya. I was takin' a run and stopped for a minute. Somethin' bad happened to a friend of mine here. I don't know why I came inside. I guess I was curious."

"She's not the only one he brought here. I guess what I heard was true. How could I have been so stupid?"

She started to collapse so I ran to catch her before she fell down the last two steps. Once I had her in my arms I carried her outside, looking up and down the road for a car. She was in high heels, and there wasn't a house or a vehicle in sight. She had to have been left there by someone. Since it was the middle of the night, and I couldn't carry her all the way back to my apartment, I pulled out my phone and dialed for an ambulance.

While sitting there on the curb waiting for them to show up I felt something wet going through my clothes. That's when I saw where the liquid was coming from. This female had slit her wrists, and she was bleeding out.

As my heart rate thumped like it was shooting out of my chest I looked down the road hoping to see the emergency vehicle headed in our direction. Finally, in what seemed like forever, I saw the lights and stood up to wave them in. They jumped out, immediately asking questions I had no answers to. An officer showed up as she was being lifted onto the stretcher. I greeted him and explained that I'd been out running and found her. I didn't mention that I'd gone in the abandoned house.

I watched as they drove away, trying hard to save the poor girl's life. I wasn't thinking about the blood, or the fact that I'd discovered a dying woman in a condemned home. All that kept repeating in my mind was the fact that she'd said other women had been taken there and that intrigued me. Was she talking about Seth? Was this a place where other guys from that frat brought girls for ass? I had to know the answer, and the only way I was going to find it was if I was able to talk to her again.

I ran back to my apartment as soon as the officer pulled away. While shaking profusely I managed to change my clothes and get in my car almost as fast as the speed of light.

I lied to the ER nurse, telling her I was the brother of the victim. She was reluctant, but finally led me back to the waiting room. I was told that 'my sister' was being worked on, and that as soon as I was able to see her, they'd come and get me. Lucky for me I had a triage nurse that didn't ask any questions, like what 'my sister's' name was, because I didn't have a clue.

The waiting room was empty, and unlike at home I fell asleep sitting up in a chair. A nurse shouted out a name, Amber Borella, and it took me a second to realize that she assumed it was my last name too. "That's me. I'm her brother."

"You can come back to see your sister now, but only for a second. Visiting hours are over, and she'll need to be observed for the next seventy-two hours."

I knew well enough to be aware that the seventy-two hours pertained to the mental ward. This girl had tried to commit suicide, and I needed to know why.

I thanked the nurse and went into the room, finally seeing the female in the light for the first time. She was blonde with a pretty face, even though she'd been through hell. At first I thought she was sleeping, but as I was about to sit down and wait, she opened her eyes. "You saved me."

"I suppose I did."

Her eyes filled with fresh tears. "I'm sorry I got you involved in this."

I didn't know what the girl was talking about, but something told me I needed to find out. "Do you know me? Did you know my friend? Her name is Chr-."

"Christian." She nodded. "I met her once. We hung out one night after my shift at the club." She paused for another moment, and I could tell she was very weak. "I'm a dancer." She started sniffling again. "Your friend is a really nice girl. I could tell she didn't like bein' there."

"She's the best person I've ever known. I miss her bein' around."

"Did she leave town?"

"Yeah. She had to. Nobody believed her, and she's not real good about bein' bullied."

"I should have warned her, I just didn't think he'd do it to someone else."

"He? Warned her? You're losin' me here, darlin'."

"Seth," she whispered. "I used to do anything to get his attention. I knew he had a girlfriend, but I didn't care. All I wanted to do was be with him."

I handed her a tissue so she could wipe her face.

"We used to meet up at the old house in secret. I didn't tell anyone, because I knew we'd have to stop if more people found out. I was okay with being the secret girlfriend for a while, but it started to get to me. I'd see them out together and they'd be all over each other. Then he'd meet me and tell me she was nothin'. The lies went on until I couldn't stand it anymore. One night I met him at the house and told him I was done. As much as it hurt me I knew I couldn't take bein' second anymore. I deserved better."

"Did he attack you that night?" I had to ask.

"No. We parted ways for a month, until one night he got drunk off his ass. He kept callin' me, beggin' me to meet up with him. He told me that he'd finally broke it off with Mila, and wanted a chance to prove to me that I was his number one. I caved and agreed to meet him. Seth may have been a cheater, but he'd never laid a hand on me. One thing I loved about him was his compassion. Anyway, he's different when he drinks. Somethin' happened to him that night. He started taunting me, tellin' me he was lyin' about the breakup. He said that he could fuck me whenever he wanted, and I wouldn't be able to fight him. That night he forced himself on me. I kept tellin' myself that he was drunk, and he didn't mean it. The next mornin' he didn't even remember. He'd forgotten about the whole thing and called me because he'd seen on his phone that we'd talked."

She wiped her face again. I couldn't help but notice her bandaged wrists. "Five weeks later I found out I was pregnant. At the same time Seth kept comin' around bein' all buddy-buddy with my roommates to get to me. I moved out, knowin' I couldn't tell anyone what happened, and I didn't want anyone knowin' I was carryin' his child. I managed to get a nice place, and take on another shift to pay for everything."

She had to stop talking for a moment, because she literally started weeping, as if she were in excruciating pain. "It was a little girl. I felt her movin' inside of me. I had a sonogram that determined the sex. I felt like out of somethin' ugly was goin' to be my most beautiful miracle. I miscarried at twenty-four weeks. The doctors couldn't tell me why. I had to deliver my dead baby. I got to hold her in my arms that night, and it broke me. It took everything I loved in life and ruined it."

"I'm so sorry for your loss." It was the truth. I didn't like hearing tragic stories.

"Maybe it was for the best. I wasn't ready to be a mother, and I certainly didn't want anything to do with Seth."

"So you didn't report the attack?"

"I never told anyone."

"Can I ask why you tried to end your life tonight? I know it's not my business, but nothin's that bad to kill yourself."

"I recently found out about your friend, but not how you might think. Seth asked me to meet him. He was crying, begging me to talk to him about somethin'. When I got to the old house I asked him where the mattress had gone. He laughed and joked that the police had taken it. I asked him if it was because he forced someone else and he lost it. He shoved me down and started screaming. I'd never seen him so angry. He told me that it was my fault. He said I'd ran my mouth and told Christian to go after him. I didn't know what he was talking about. I ran out of there, hopin' he'd leave me alone."

"He didn't?"

She shook her head. "No." She started sobbing while trying to speak. "He showed up at my place, called my phone constantly, and waited for me outside the club. I had to change my shift to get away from him. I felt like no matter where I went he was there waitin' for me."

"Why didn't you get a restrainin' order?"

"I went to talk to Becca. We'd always been close, and I thought that if I came clean she'd help me. Instead she called me a liar, sayin' I'd talked to Christian and because I couldn't be with Seth I was tryin' to ruin his life. Last week I got an eviction notice, because I had to stop dancin'. I can't afford the place with no job. I've got nowhere to go, and no friends to help me out. Lovin' Seth ruined my life. I hate myself, and I don't know if I want to go on."

In those last words I watched as she lost it. It was that very moment where I felt like I was standing there with my best friend. I placed one of my hands over hers. "Don't give up because a scum bag like Seth made you feel like you weren't anything. He's a narcissistic asshole, who doesn't deserve your compassion."

She managed to form a half-smile across her face. "When I was lying there bleedin' out I regretted it. I started prayin' to God, beggin' him to save me. Then you were there. I'll never be able to repay you."

I thought for a second, wondering if I even had the right to ask this fragile girl something so sensitive. "I lost the love of my life from all of this. I'd never make you feel obligated, but if you went to the police I think you might be able to get the closure you seek. He can't hurt you if he's behind bars."

"I can't. I'm sorry. His family will take their money and make sure they bury the truth. I don't have the means to take them on."

I grabbed the paper off the nightstand and wrote down my number. "If you change your mind, here's my cell."

I had to get out of there. After everything, she wasn't goin' to help me. All she'd given me was hope, just to tear me back down again. This guy was a real piece of work. He had everyone thinking he was such a nice guy, when in fact he was the damn devil.

The sun was coming up when I headed out to my car. As tired as I was, my mind was fixed on one thing. Though we'd never gone this long without talking, I hoped she'd at least take my call.

As I scrolled down to find her name, I made a new pact to myself that no matter what she said I wouldn't give up. I was nothing without her in my life, and it was time she knew the truth.

Chapter 29
Christian

I'd gone weeks without a single returned call from Ethan. As much as I hated admitting it, worrying about losing him was helping me cope with everything else. I also needed to thank my psychiatrist. After the first two visits I could feel things changing for me. There was a long road ahead, but I felt more determined than I'd ever been. She was also helping me accept the things I couldn't change. I needed to love myself before I could begin to heal.

My parents were overprotective at first, driving me to my appointments, and waiting on me hand and foot. I tried to explain to them that I wasn't fragile. I wouldn't shatter if I fell down, though they still insisted.

Driving to my next appointment made it seem like I was gaining some of my independence back. I made sure to obey all of the road signs, and speed limits, always checking my mirrors, for not only incoming traffic, but also the chance that my attacker was hiding out in my parent's backseat.

Yes, I had a long road ahead of me. Accepting that was the biggest challenge so far.

When I arrived in the parking lot I checked outside of my vehicle several times before unlocking the door and climbing out. I knew I was being overly cautious, and maybe even taking a step backwards, but I'd rather look like a mental patient than be assaulted again. Cautious people were always aware of their surroundings. They made sure they were out of harm's way.

Last week the doctor and I discussed carrying pepper spray and possibly taking a self-defense class. I felt like if I'd been able to defend myself in any way I would have been able to fight him off and run.

Since I arrived on time I was sent right in to meet with the doctor. She was sitting at her desk writing in a folder. As soon as she spotted me strolling in, she stopped to greet me. "Good afternoon, Christian. How's my favorite southern girl feeling today?"

I liked how she treated me like a friend. I'm sure she was trained to know how to handle each case. For me, the personal connection was important. I needed to feel like I could trust her. After all, I was telling her all of my secrets, some of which I would never want my parents knowing about.

"I'm doing okay, maybe even good. I have moments."

"That's understandable. Did you bring your list for the week?" She asked.

I nodded and reached inside my purse, pulling out the journal.

"Things that make me happy:
1. Pancakes in the mornin'.
2. Lyin' under a willow tree and listenin' to nature.
3. Dreamin' of makin' love in the rain.
4. Learnin' how to make my Gram's apple pie.
5. Swimmin' with my cousin's at their pond.
6. Watchin' my brother lovin' all over his fiancée.
7. Hearin' that my sister is comin' home from rehab.
8. Watchin' those romance channels where you cry because it's so beautiful.
9. Going to church and hearin' my momma sing her heart out.
10. Daydreamin' about a life where Ethan and I are married and happy."

"Things I don't like:
1. Seein' my mother cry.
2. Not hearing from my best friend for weeks."

I put my head down when I finished, knowing she was going to ask a ton of questions that I may or may not be ready for.

"I would like to discuss Ethan. Would that be okay?"

I shrugged. "I guess. There's really nothin' to tell. I don't even think we're friends anymore." It hurt to admit that, especially after being friends for so long.

"You care deeply for this man, yet you say he hasn't contacted you. What happened?"

I twiddled my fingers, focusing on them moving as I spoke, as if it shut my emotions off. "We had a fight."

"What did you fight about?"

This was already getting annoying. We weren't talking. End of story.

"In high school we made this pact. It's probably stupid, but we promised to share every single first with each other. Ethan was my first kiss. He was the first person that I had sex with. You get the idea. Anyway, when I went out with Seth we messed around in a movie theater. He recorded me givin' him oral and sent it to Ethan. I didn't think it mattered. He'd been sleepin' with other girls since we entered college, and clearly didn't have any intentions of bein' with me as a couple. He'd made that blatantly clear."

"He said he didn't want to be with you?"

"Actually, he said that it would ruin our friendship and I meant too much for that to happen."

"And you don't believe him?" I was beginning to feel uncomfortable talking about

Ethan. My heart ached for the empty spot where he'd always been. This was torture.

"Can we talk about somethin' else?"

She paused and then jotted something down in her folder. "Tell me about your first sexual experience."

"It's too hard."

"Close your eyes and put yourself back in time. Remember being happy and carefree."

I did as she ordered. "It was my parent's anniversary, and they like to go to this cabin in the mountains, so me and my sister were home alone. My family was only a short walk from the house, so we were never really alone, per se. Anyway, Ethan and I had it all planned out. He drove his dad's old pickup truck into one of the barns, so my brother wouldn't suspect anything. I'd spent the day decorating the hay loft with candles. Don't worry. I used the flameless kind. I laid out blankets and brought some pillows from the house so we'd be comfortable. Despite the fact that it was our first time, I wasn't nervous. We'd made out so many times, fondling, and exploring each other. I was ready to lose my virginity. I felt like it was going to make me a real woman."

While I paused to prepare for the rest of the story I looked up to see her making more notes. "How did you feel when Ethan said you couldn't be a couple?"

"Devastated."

"Was the pain much like being assaulted?"

I hated her question. "What's that supposed to mean? Are you implyin' that they are equal?"

"No. I'm trying to grasp the emotional pull that your love for Ethan has on you. Could you try to answer?"

"Ethan means everything to me. Sometimes I feel like I can't breathe without him. When I was assaulted he pushed until I confessed what happened, and he promised he wouldn't leave my side. I get why he's upset, but I feel destroyed. My attack was ugly, and I wished it never happened, but my love for Ethan is beautiful. I could never regret that."

"Finish your story about your first time."

After talking about my love for him, it was hard to close my eyes and replay that moment in time that was so perfect. "The ambience was romantic, and Ethan took his time. He kissed me until I stopped shakin', and then made sure I was ready for every single step. I felt loved, respected, and above all consumed with confidence."

"How would you describe your time with Seth?"

I swallow the immediate lump in my throat. "Drunken, stupid, a big mistake. I was desperate, and vulnerable."

"Christian, you're very young, and with that it means that you've yet to experience so much. I'm not saying that you need to go out and find partners. I'm saying that with age comes experience. It always helps with acceptance."

"I'm tryin' to understand that. I still wake up every mornin' hopin' I won't think of my mistakes."

"We're human. We make mistakes. It's how we repent our faults that make us indifferent. I want you to go home and share your happy list with one family member. I also want you to include the two sad items. Learning to express your feelings is very important in your situation. Having a good line of communication at home will not only improve your trust with others, but also them with you."

It made sense. My parents were always trying to know my business. They'd be over the moon if I shared something so dear to my heart, especially about Ethan. Besides, I knew I was going to have to come clean about him if I ever wanted to be able to accept that he might not want to be my friend again. As much as it hurt to think about, I knew this was my only life, and I had to be thankful for having a second chance at finding myself. "I think I've always been afraid that they looked at me like I was different from my siblings. They're so outgoin', and easy to get along with. I always liked school, and playing by myself. My mom says she was like me, but I've seen her make friends easily. All she has to do is smile and they're like magnets. I don't have that gift. Maybe I have an invisible sign on my forehead that says I'm awkward."

"You're too self-conscious. You're worried about what others think of you, instead of what you think of yourself. Remember we talked about loving yourself?"

"Yes."

"When you look in the mirror what do you see?"

This was the stupidest question. Obviously I saw myself.

She reiterated her question when I didn't reply. "What kind of person do you see when you look in the mirror?"

"We've already gone over this question."

"It's important to answer again."

"I see a lonely girl who longs to be loved."

"Hmm, and what if I asked you to describe the woman you want to see in the mirror?"

This one was easy. I'd thought about this every single time I'd looked at my own reflection only to feel let down at what was really there. "I see beauty, strength, and happiness. I see a woman who isn't afraid to go after what she wants. I see a woman who conquers all struggles, leavin' no rock unturned. I see confidence. She'd have poise. She'd be skilled as a ninja so no one could ever hurt her physically."

"Let's back up a second. As much as I would like to see you become a ninja, for self defense, of course, I think it's best that we focus on one obstacle at a time. Perhaps our main focus should be on that confidence. Tell me what you don't like about your appearance."

I kept my gaze low, trying not to see her looking at me, making me more uncomfortable with the question. "I don't feel beautiful."

"So if I told you that you were a beautiful, stunning lady you wouldn't believe me?"

"I'd feel flattered, but question your judgment."

She tapped that pen to the paper again, causing me to look up. When I did I saw that she was staring at me. "When did you start to feel as if you were unbeautiful?"

I tossed my hands in the air. "I don't know. Maybe it was when my cousins started teasin' me."

"I know for a fact that you come from a very large family. It says in my notes that you have a large amount of cousins. Perhaps they were only teasing you because they knew it got to you."

"Who knows? The damage is done. If they wanted me to feel ugly they've succeeded."

"I want you to do something else for me when you go home. I'd like for you to call those cousins and ask them if you're beautiful."

"I'd say you're crazy."

"Please enlighten me here. This is my job to find the source so that I'm able to help you heal. Part of that is finding where this all stems from. Once we can determine that, you'll begin to feel differently about yourself. That's when we'll have made the most progress."

Even though I knew I'd follow through, because I was desperate for closure, I felt sickened by what she was asking me to do. I loathed my twin cousins, Jake and Jax. They'd picked on me my whole life. If I called and asked them a question so ridiculous I'd be a laughing stock.

With a new list of to-dos I left the office and headed home. I was eager to sit down with my parents and share my list. I think it was beneficial that they knew I trusted them. Calling my cousins was going to be a battle in itself.

Chapter 30
Christian

My mom was eager to get my sister home. I think she secretly hoped that both of us girls would live with her forever. Even if we built a house on the family property, I don't know if we'd be close enough in her eyes.

Being my dad had gotten the call to pick my sister, Addy, up from the hospital, he'd volunteered to drive out there to do it. It only took me a second to ask if I could ride along.

We gotten about five miles from the house before either of us said anything. I broke the ice knowing I had to share my feelings with my dad. We were alone, and of all the people on the planet his approval was most important. "Daddy," I called him that when I wanted to be on his good side. Even in my twenties, he still got a kick out of it.

"Yes, darlin'?"

"I need to talk to you about somethin'."

He reached over and grabbed my hand. I could feel how rough his skin was from years of hard work. He'd made sure we never hurt for anything, and for that I'd be forever grateful. "The doc says I need to tell you and mom about my feelin's. I was hopin' we could discuss them while we drive."

"I'm all ears."

I pulled the list out of my purse. "She thinks I need to tell you ten things that make me happy, and only two that make me sad.

Things that make me happy:
Pancakes in the mornin'.
Lyin' under a willow tree and listenin' to nature.
Dreamin' of makin' love in the rain.
Learnin' how to make my Gram's apple pie.
Swimmin' at the North Carolina pond.
Watchin' Noah lovin' all over his fiancée.
Hearin' that Addy is comin' home from rehab.
Watchin' those romance channels where you cry because it's so beautiful.
Going to church and hearin' momma sing her heart out.
Daydreamin' about a life where Ethan and I are married and happy."

"Things I don't like:
Seein' momma cry.
Not hearing from my best friend for weeks."

My father was quiet, probably because I'd just given him a lot to ponder on. I watched as his face creased. "Darlin', I've always told you how special you were. Your mom and I knew from the time you were born. We'd struggled for so long to get pregnant and just knowin' that a miracle had happened healed a broken part of your mom. Watchin' her hold you brought tears to my eyes, because she finally had that piece of the puzzle she thought was out of reach. Now you've grown into this young woman, who's not only brilliant, but also beautiful. I'm so proud of you. I'm proud to call you my daughter; to know that out of all the people I've ever known, you hold the purest heart. Now I'm not talkin' about your virginity, so don't get uncomfortable. Besides, I've known all about your little riffs with Ethan in the barn. If you're plannin' on makin' a love nest it's best that you hide the evidence when you're done."

I felt so embarrassed. I tried to pinpoint when I'd forgotten something. Had it been after our first time? The thought made me queasy. "Sorry."

"It's a part of growin' up. That bein' said your mom did have to keep me from sayin' somethin' to that boy. He's a good kid, but I wasn't sure if he was the right match for my special girl." He reached over and touched my chin.

I moved away feeling embarrassed. "Daddy, stop it. This conversation is just weird now."

"Christian, you're a woman. Remember that I loved your mother at your age. You remind me of her. . She was always timid, gettin' into trouble because she wouldn't speak up for herself. It was

276

the main reason I fell so hard for her. I felt a pull to take care of her and then it all fell into place. Now we've got you three kids, and I'm includin' your older brother, because we all know that even though he's not her biological son, she'd never love him any less than you two girls. She's a Godsend, and he couldn't have asked for a better mother."

"I know." When my brother was three social services had brought him to the ranch. My father didn't even know he existed, and my mom had just had a miscarriage. Instead of feeling like it was an omen for failure, she took Noah in her arms and never looked back. Their bond was unbreakable, and many times it made us all forget that she wasn't his birth mother. Since we still shared our father's blood, there was no trading him in for a sister. Besides, I enjoyed knowing he always had my back. "We have a fantastic family."

"We need to thank God for that, Chris."

"I know." Sadly, I hadn't thanked God enough lately. It was selfish of me, and I didn't like admitting that I'd somehow lost a little bit of faith from my experience, especially since I'd been taught that he only gives us what he knows we can handle.

"Do you mind me askin' what happened with Ethan?"

I looked out the window, hoping I wouldn't lose it in front of my father. "I guess you could say that I loved him and he didn't love me back."

"Hogwash!" He immediately spat. "That boy's been crazy about you for years."

277

"Dad, we're just friends. Well, we were. It's all changed now."

"I don't believe that. If you want somethin' you've got to work for it, you've got to fight. It's the chase that makes it better."

"Talkin' like this is uncomfortable," I admitted.

"That list you made is beautiful. It warms my heart that you see things other people your age can't yet grasp. What makes me sad is seein' you unhappy. You deserve the world at your fingertips. Now I know we didn't get justice for what happened to you, but God's got a plan. I believe that, because I've seen miracles happen."

All of a sudden I felt extremely emotional. I leaned over and let my head fall against my dad's strong shoulder. I don't know if it was the image of my mother going through her cancer treatments, or the fact that the past couple months had been hell for me. Sure, I was going out to bars and hanging with people my age, but that life wasn't for me. All I knew was that I was blessed to have the support that I did. "I love you, daddy."

He kissed the top of head, immediately reminding me of Ethan. "I love you too, darlin'. You're my sweet girl, you always have been, and you always will be. Don't you ever forget that."

For the rest of the ride I laughed and cried with my dad. We hadn't been alone for a long time, and I appreciated the way he was so caring when he needed to be. Even though I'd watched him and my brother having it out, this soft side of him proved that he was the best dad in the world. Besides, my brother sometimes needed a good kick in the ass.

I hadn't seen my sister since she'd gone to rehab. I remember her looking so fragile, with eyes glossed over. The girl that was walking toward us had put on at least ten pounds. Her hair was styled, and she was smiling. Though she still looked tired, I could tell she was thrilled to see us both standing there. We hugged her at the same time, and that's where my emotions went awry. We never bonded like this, yet both of us needed each other more than we'd care to admit. "I'm sorry for what happened to you," she whispered in my ear.

"Same here," I said back.

My dad let us stand there embracing for quite some time. I could tell from his grimace that he appreciated the way we were behaving. He had tears in his eyes, which was a rarity.

He put his hand on my shoulder. "Let's get you both home. Mom's been cookin' all day."

"I can't wait to eat something with taste," Addy said as we began walking toward the exit.

In that moment I wasn't thinking about myself, my failures, and what I hadn't yet overcome. I was grateful for my beautiful family and content knowing that above anything else, they were what I needed the most right now.

I'd been looking everywhere for a best friend, feeling like nobody would ever understand, yet my sister, who was only one year apart from me in age, was right beside me, needing the same kind of companionship. It was a true revelation.

My love life was going to have to wait, because it was time for me to accept what I couldn't change, and look forward to the person I was meant to be.

Chapter 31
Ethan

I couldn't wait to tell her the news. I was both excited and worried. She was going to be so angry with me. Still, I felt like I had good reason to stay away. My timing may have sucked, but I needed to figure some things out for myself. Mostly I needed to come to terms that there were things in life I'd never be able to change. I couldn't look at my friend and see someone fragile. I needed to be able to know for sure that without her strength she wouldn't have come so far.

Pulling up at the ranch made me a bit leery. There was a chance that Chris had told her father to make sure I never stepped foot near her again, though I don't think she'd still be leaving me messages if she felt that way. Still, my guilt over not being there stressed me. How was I ever going to make up for betraying her friendship? How was I going to look her in the eyes, knowing I'd loved her for so long, and tell her that my decisions had been the reason for everything that happened to her? I should have made better choices, and not relied on damn scientific results about relationship odds. How incredibly selfish I'd been to assume she'd wait around for me to wise up?

After I'd made it through the entrance gates, and found my way down the long dirt lane, I pulled up in front of the large log home belonging to her parents. Facing her dad was going to be a challenge in itself.

I looked in the rearview mirror at my reflection, trying to psych myself some courage. "You've got this, dude. Be honest with them."

When I climbed the porch steps and knocked, her mother answered the door. She smiled immediately, giving me a bit of reassurance. "Good afternoon, Mrs. Mitchell. I was hopin' to see Christian if that's alright."

She frowned. "It would be if she were here. Colt took her to pick up Addy. She was released today."

I smiled, even though I felt disappointed. "That's great news. I'm sure it'll be nice to have them all home."

"Why don't you come inside? I haven't seen you in a while, and could use the company." I stepped inside as she continued to speak. "I've got some fresh tea made. Would you like some?"

"Certainly. That would be great."

I followed her into the kitchen and sat down at the small table. She'd been busy cooking up a storm. There were pots of food on each burner, and the aroma was heavenly. "Here you go. I added some lemon, just like you always asked for."

I guess there was a time when I was a fixture at the ranch. It was nice having her remember little things. It made me feel as if she didn't have a problem with my visit. "How's she doin', Christian, I mean. How is she?"

"She's improving every day. Sometimes it's still pretty tough on her. She's in therapy, and seems to be doing well with that. She misses you, Ethan, she doesn't talk about it much, but I can tell."

Right away I felt that guilt-punch again. "Mrs. Mitchell, I-."

"Savanna. Mrs. Mitchell is my mother-in-law," she corrected.

I smiled and continued on. "I never should have stayed away. I know that. It's just that I couldn't be the person she wanted me to be. It was a dumb decision, brought on by years of regret. The truth is I've been a coward, hidin' behind what could have happened, instead of lettin' it play out. My goals got pushed to the side, leavin' me to make bad choices, and to push the one person most important away."

She turned and leaned on the table, looking me right in the eyes. "Ethan, Colt and I have known you've been in love with our daughter for a very long time. If taking a break was what was needed for you to see that, then I'm glad you did it. It's never too late to tell someone how you feel. Sure, you might not get the expected result, but you'll feel better that they know. You can't regret what you've never tried."

Her kind words were reassuring, right at a moment where I was questioning my intentions. "Yeah, it's taken me a while to get my act together I suppose."

She got back to working at the stove as she continued to converse with me. "You should stay for dinner. We've got plenty of food."

"It seems like tonight's a celebration for family. I don't want to impose, ma'am."

"Ethan, you are family."

"I don't know if Chris would see it that way, especially now."

"Nonsense. You're staying. I insist."

I wasn't going to argue with the woman about a meal I knew would blow me away. Her cooking skills were amazing. She could make liver and onions taste like filet mignon.

We sat there for a time catching up on day to day life. After a while it felt like I hadn't spent any time away from the family.

It wasn't until we heard the vehicle pull up out up front that I started to fret. This wasn't like seeing her mom's welcoming smile. It wasn't like two star-crossed lovers finally finding each other after time apart. I'd walked away from her, abandoning her after I'd promised never to do such a thing. There was a good chance she was going to tell me to go to hell.

I stood up as the front door opened, watching as Chris' mother rushed over to welcome her family home. I stood there staring at the strength of one family, who'd been dealt several crappy hands all at once. Their union, and ability to strive together was what I longed to have someday with their daughter. Seeing her again was like looking out that old bus window on the first, autumn day of school and seeing her climbing aboard. Even towards the rear I could see those green eyes glistening. There had never been a time where I felt so drawn to someone before, and even in my adolescent state, I knew I had to know everything about her.

It would have been nice to see her running into my arms, taking comfort in the fact that I was there for her. She was too caught in up her family to notice me at first, and I didn't want to take away from their important reunion. After a few moments her father looked up and spotted me in the room. He cleared his throat before greeting me. "Ethan. Where you been hidin' at, boy?"

I shrugged, and put on a fake smile until my gaze met Chris'. "Hey."

"Hey yourself," she replied. "What're you doin' here?"

"I was in the neighborhood," I teased.

She took a few steps in my direction, never coming close enough for me to pull her into my arms, not that I would have been able to do that with her dad watching us. Something about that man terrified me, despite the fact that we were finally at eye level with each other.

"Are you stayin' for dinner?" He asked.

"If it's alright with Chris. I mean, your wife invited me already, but I wouldn't want to make anyone upset by bein' here."

He walked over and put his arm around me, dragging me into the kitchen with him. "Nonsense. This is a day of communion. We'd be glad to have you, ain't that right, Christian?"

I turned and noticed that she'd followed us into the room. Her arms were crossed in the front of her chest as she smiled. It wasn't her happy smile, but more her putting on a nice face to appease her parent's kind of gesture. I hated that.

For a few minutes the family talked to Christian, pretty much leaving me there to sip on my fresh glass of sweet tea. I didn't mind, since I'd missed being around. Every couple of seconds I'd catch Chris looking at me. I couldn't tell if she was angry or curious. I'd always been so good at reading her, but something had changed, and it bothered me not to be able to put my finger on it.

Since they wouldn't notice me missing, I walked out on the porch to get some crisp fresh air. The fall leaves blanketed the ground in a hue of reds, browns, and oranges. It smelled like autumn as I stood there admiring the landscape. A horse neighed in the distance, just as the sound of the porch door creaking open behind me caught my attention. I didn't have to turn to know it was her. Somehow I could feel her presence so close to me. With my hands on the railing I watched her come to stand beside me. She didn't speak, but remained silent, as if she was waiting for me. "I missed you, Chris."

"You've got a terrible way of showin' it. Did you think it was okay to ignore my calls; to ignore me?" When she turned to look at me her eyes were filled with tears. "I needed you, Ethan, and you weren't around. Do you have any idea what it was like tryin' so hard to heal without you?" She shoved me. "Do you?"

My heart was being ripped to shreds and it was my own damn fault. I deserved this. "I'm sorry."

"You're sorry? Are you kiddin' me? After all this time you come and say you're sorry. You didn't just break my heart. You shattered it. When I thought I couldn't get worse, you drug me down to a level I never knew existed. You were all I had, my last hope at someone I could trust. How dare you come here and think that apologizin' would fix things. I can't even look at you. You took my hope away, Ethan. I loved you, and you cast me aside as if I meant nothin' at all."

"Chris, please." I tried to reach out and touch her, but she batted me away for the second time.

"Don't touch me. Don't you ever touch me again."

"You heard my sister." Noah's voice caught me off guard. I took a step back seeing him standing at the far end of the porch with his fiancée, Shalan.

I threw my hands up. "I'm not goin' to touch her, man."

"Did he hurt you, sis?" He asked.

"Not physically."

Noah stepped closer. "I think you should go, Ethan. It's obvious my sister's in no mood for visitors."

Since I respected this family, I knew I couldn't make a scene. I had to walk away, even if I was leaving my heart on that porch. Christian didn't want me near her, and I was not able to handle it.

Chapter 32
Christian

I'd gotten the shock of my life and handled it terribly. The look on his face was something I'd never forget. It was strange to see him so vulnerable. Had I not been so angry with him, things could have turned out differently.

My parents said nothing when I headed back in the house, and I was pretty certain my brother knew I was a force to be reckoned with.

During dinner I refused to speak, letting my sister get all the attention. She needed it more than I did. While I silently chewed my food, hoping to disguise my trembling lips, I listened to her telling her struggles to my family. Ignoring my situation wasn't going to get me anywhere. I'd have to face my demons, no matter how painful they were for me. It was part of moving forward, part of learning how to love myself.

After I helped clear the table and load the dishwasher, I retreated with everyone else to the living room. It felt nice to be together, but my thoughts weren't on another happy moment to add to my list. They were focused on Ethan, and how I'd pushed him away for a second time.

I hated myself.

The anticipation of seeing him again had gotten the best of me. As much as I wanted to spend the evening reminiscing with everyone, I knew I wasn't good company. That's why I excused myself for a late night walk.

There was only one place I'd head, and it wasn't far away.

The barn had always been a refuge for me, even when it wasn't filled with horses. It was also where I'd lost my virginity. Since I'd pushed Ethan away, it was the one place I could feel close to him.

In all honesty I just wanted to be alone so I could cry in peace. My hopes were that I'd become exhausted and fall asleep on a bed of hay like I used to when I was distraught and hiding from the world.

It would have been nice if I were born immune to getting my feelings hurt, of being vulnerable. What was screwed up was that I'd forced Ethan out of my life, after jealousy had showed its ugly face. The severity of losing my friend hadn't only stunted my recovery, but caused the pain to be so intense that I felt like I'd never heal.

I was finally beginning to feel better.

I was making progress with my doctor.

Then he showed up.

Now I was a wreck.

The lantern I'd always used was still in the same place I'd left it the last time. It took me a second to get it lit and secured back on the hook. The loft was a cozy place. On many occasions I'd climb up and read a book from cover to cover. I'd bring stray kittens in and feed them, and sometimes I'd hide when my cousins came to visit. Of all the places on the ranch this was my own personal private spot.

Just as I'd found a spot to sit down, I began to cry. My pent up anxiety from seeing Ethan had set me back. I knew I had to let it all out, so that in the morning I could figure out a way to get back on track.

It wasn't too long after that I heard footsteps beneath me. I stopped sniffling and peered over the ledge. There wasn't anyone there that I could see, so I backed away and attempted to calm down, just in case someone was listening.

I heard the footsteps again, this time confidant that there was someone else in the barn with me. That's the moment when I looked down and saw who it was. He'd known where to look, and I honestly wasn't surprised that he'd assumed that's where I'd be. For a few seconds we just stared at one another. This was my opportunity to apologize for being insensitive. It was the time to admit that I'd overreacted; except, I couldn't move. I had all of the words right there on my tongue, but they wouldn't come out. Ethan walked over to the steps, but didn't climb, not yet. "Did you think you could get rid me of me so easily?"

I refused to stop looking at him, at his dark wavy hair, and those deeply sexy eyes. I'd missed every detail of his face, and the way it felt when his hands were laced with mine. In that moment I knew I wouldn't let him go away, even if a friendship was all he'd ever offer. "Honestly, no. Somehow I knew you'd be back."

"I never left. I got halfway down that lane and pulled over. You see, I've had a lot of time to think. I know you think I abandoned you, but I didn't. I couldn't."

"You've been MIA for weeks. You've ignored my calls. If that's not abandonin' me, then I don't know what is."

"It's more complicated than that, Chris."

I hated that we were beginning to argue already. Here I'd thought I'd lost him again and I was right back to accusing him of things. If I wanted to make amends and have him in my life, one of us was going to have to give. "You're right." I was prepared to make that first move. "We both made mistakes. Maybe my life was a little too hard to keep up with. I know it was for me, so I can't imagine how it felt to watch me goin' through it."

"It wasn't that. I can assure you. I'd never turn my back on you because of somethin' terrible."

He lurched forward, putting his hand on the ladder leading up to where I stood. With each step he spoke one sentence. "I told you before that I had a secret." Step. "It's time I come clean." Step. In all honesty I figured he'd gotten someone pregnant. I knew he'd had other partners, but expected him to always use precaution.

Ethan was on that last step, staring directly into my eyes. My chest rising made it apparent that my breathing had increased. As much as I tried to contain my emotions, having him so close to me, in such a special place, left me vulnerable. "So what's the secret? You've got me where you want me. I can't run away. Spill."

He climbed up into the loft with me, backing me up against the far wooden-planked wall, never taking his gaze off of mine. The moment was intense, but all I could think about was feeling his embrace again. I longed for it, as if it were the lost piece of my recovery puzzle. "I think I've loved you since that first day you stepped on the school bus."

I shook my head. "What? What do you mean?"

"I'm in love with you, Christian. I have been in love with you every single day for as long as I can remember. God knows I've had a shit way of showin' it, but it's the truth. I love you, and I get that I don't deserve it, but I'd like a shot at makin' this more than just a friendship."

I was frozen, completely unable to speak, more or less move an inch. Ethan brought his hand up to my face. I never pulled away from his touch. His warm palms sent a heat wave through my core.

Hot tears fell from my cheeks as I continued staring hopelessly into his eyes. "All this time. I don't understand."

"I thought that if I waited we'd have a better chance at a real future. I wanted to be certain that I'd never lose you." He paused and looked away for a second, furrowing his brows and seeming conflicted. "What happened to you broke me, Chris. It tore me up. No matter how hard I tried I knew I'd never be able to take it away. Because of my stupidity you'll be tormented forever. I don't know how to live with that, babe. It breaks me."

"You love me." I kept going back to that in my mind. I supposed I'd waited so long to hear it with meaning that it was messing with my ability to comprehend everything else.

He touched my face again, taking one step closer in my direction. With only inches separating us I could feel the air as he exhaled. In that moment nothing else existed.

There was no more pain.

There was no time missed.

There was no attack.

It was as if I'd left my body and entered a new one; given a second chance at happiness. I want to feel this rush of invigorating euphoria. I needed to know what it felt like to let myself fall, without being afraid of what I could lose, because I'd already lost too much.

This was my path to recovery.

This was my eternal escape.

This was my salvation; my reason for wanting to overcome my demons.

Our lips brushed ever so gently and I closed my eyes, allowing myself to get lost without fear.

His touch was familiar, and welcomed. My body trembled for all the right reasons, and as his fingers laced in both of mine I knew he'd never leave me again. I could feel his intent as if it were my own. We were in sync, riding a new wave, but this time together as one. This was the moment where I found my happy place. It was the moment where I knew I'd be able to let go of my past and slowly move forward with my future.

This was everything to me.

Our kiss was short lived. I had to hear it again; a million more times before it would begin to be too much. "Tell me again."

He pulled one hand up, rolling his thumb over my lips. "I love you, way more than a friend. I love you like I want to be with you for the rest of my life. I always have and I always will."

Chapter 33
Ethan

Her kiss sent pleasure throughout my bones. No longer did I have to hold back. She was mine, like she should have been all along. Realizing how fragile she still was, I went easy, backing away from our kiss after only a few moments. I brushed the hair back behind her ears, never taking my eyes off of hers. "I don't want to get carried away."

"It's okay. I'd tell you if I needed to stop."

"I've thought about you so much. It's killin' me to want you this bad."

I could tell she needed a second to comprehend what I was implying. I'd never force her into a decision that could be damaging to her recovery, so I had to be patient and let her decide where this reunion was going to go.

"I want you too, Ethan. It's just...I'm a little apprehensive. I know that I'm physically able to be with you, but mentally I'm scared it's too soon."

"I get it. Just know that these hands," I held them up to show her. "Were meant to touch you.

My arms were meant to hold you, and I know for a fact that my heart was meant to love you."

Trying not to look disappointed in what wouldn't come next, I leaned in and kissed her again. As it began to progress into something deeper; something more intense, we both stopped. "Maybe I should go." I began backing away while holding one of her hands. I couldn't get carried away.

She pulled me back. "When you talk like that it makes me crazy. Don't go. Stay here with me, like we used to. I want to wake up in your arms, so I know this ain't just a dream."

Kissing her forehead was comforting. "It's not a dream. You have my heart, Chris. You always have. I'm surprised you didn't notice, especially after everything that happened. Couldn't you tell how jealous I was? Couldn't you see that it killed me to see you with someone else?"

When I said it I worried that speaking about her time with Seth was going to set us back, but she smiled, reassuring me that I hadn't screwed up our moment. "You were actin' weird, that's for sure, but I believed you were always tellin' me the truth. I think I wanted you to love me so badly that I couldn't accept you actually might."

"I should have told you the truth a long time ago."

"You're here now. My doctor says that I need to stop dwellin' on what I can't change. If everything led us to this very moment then I'm not goin' to complain anymore. This is all I've ever wanted."

"Me too."

She pushed me to the side and made her way over to the ladder. "Wait here. I'll be back in ten minutes."

"Where're you goin'?"

A half-smile formed in the corner of her lips. "You'll see in a few minutes. Don't you dare leave."

"I won't!" I promised.

I watched her walk out of the barn, all the while with a huge smile on my face. I'd made a ton of mistakes. My immaturity could have cost me everything, but somehow I'd found my way back to my girl.

I knew I'd have to tell her about Amber, but for now I wanted our time together to be special. This place was sacred to us. I'd never ruin it with painful conversations about the past.

It took her a little more than ten minutes, not that I was counting. While she was gone I sat down on a bale of Timothy hay and took in the ambience of the loft. I recalled an array of lit candles, and the two of us tangled up together in one sleeping bag. Our first time wasn't like other teenagers experiences. We took our time, exploring every inch of one another, with patience and compassion. I didn't believe it back then, but our love was already so powerful. She owned me, utterly and completely. My constant battle to accept that had cost me dearly, finally proving without a doubt that everything I was experiencing was the proof I required.

I peered down watching her approach the ladder with both of her hands full. She lifted up a large duffle-bag, and stuck another one over her back as she began to climb. With a giant smile covering her face she starting unzipping each bag, revealing her intentions for the rest of our evening.

"Please tell me your parents don't know I'm here."

"My parents helped me pack all this stuff. Stop worryin', Ethan. We're adults. They'd rather know than not. Although, my dad did leave you a note in the lower, left pocket of that bag." She pointed to the bigger bag. "He may have mentioned the removal of your lower appendages, but he's probably kiddin'." She giggled.

I squirmed as I unfolded the letter and began to read it out loud.

"Ethan,
It's a difficult time for a father to accept that his daughter is a grown woman. I've watched her struggle throughout life, but she's always had one constant.
It's you.
Thank you for lovin' my daughter. I'd appreciate it if you respected her, and promise that you'll always be her best friend.
If you don't, just know I'll find ya.
Colt Mitchell,
Your someday-father-in-law"

Christian was already laughing. I shrugged and folded up the note, sticking it in my back pocket. "I reckon I better do as he says."

"Probably."

"So what's in the bags?"

"Flameless candles, some snacks, a container of tea, two pillows, and two sleepin' bags," she explained.

"Are you certain that your dad ain't goin' to come out here with his rifle?" I just needed verification on that before I agreed to spend the night with the guy's daughter.

"My father and brother know we're out here together. Don't get your panties in a bunch."

"I won't be closin' my eyes all night, that's for sure."

"That's just silly. They want me to be happy, Ethan, even if it means bein' a little more lenient when it comes to you." She slapped me lightly, laughing again. I'd forgotten how good it felt to make her smile. "Besides, I'm pretty sure they know I'm takin' things slow."

"Come here," I ordered.

She nudged forward so I could pull her into my arms. "I'll do whatever it takes, Chris."

She took me by the hand and pulled us down on one of the sleeping bags. I knew I had to be gentle with her, even though the urge to take her was very apparent. Our kisses were slow-paced. I savored them, like it was the first time. Her body shook beneath mine, reminding me of her fragile state. When I pulled away to give her a moment to gather herself, she seemed disappointed. "What's wrong."

"Nothin'," I answered. "I thought you might need a second."

She haplessly stared at me for a second. "I know you'd never hurt me. Bein' with you is natural. It's always been easy."

I pecked her before responding. "I will love on you all night long. I'll hold you, and kiss you in every place imaginable, but I won't do that. I can't. Not yet. We're goin' to go slow, because we've got plenty of time."

"Ethan, if I don't give you what you want, are you goin' to go out and get it somewhere else?"

"Hell no! That's somethin' you'll never have to worry about. You're the only woman I want."

She smiled shyly. "Okay."

"Good. Now let's get back to that kissin'."

As much as I wished this night could be more, I appreciated bein' able to stay with her. I needed this just as much as she did.

A little while later I lay still with Christian wrapped in my arms. We'd climbed into an oversized sleeping bag and zippered up to keep warm on this particularly chilly night. Even though the barn kept out the wind, it had no insulation to provide us with any type of comfort.

She slept so peacefully next to me. Her warm body nestled up against mine allowed me to be content. We didn't need intercourse to take us to another level. We'd been sleeping together for years. There wasn't an inch of her that I didn't know. I would wait to have her again, because I knew it would be well worth it.

While she rested peacefully, I thought about what was to come, where we would live, and how our lives would intertwine. Chris knew my plans to keep my roots grounded on a farm. She'd accepted that I never wanted to live in a busy city. I wouldn't have to worry about taking her away from her dreams, because we'd shared the same one for as long as I could remember.

While the crickets sang, and the moonlight sky moved about the horizon, I finally closed my eyes. Even if her father or brother came to kill me I'd die a satisfied man. God had given her to me, and I knew I'd never take that for granted again.

I couldn't wait to wake up to her beautiful smile, every single day until I took my last breath. That's how life was supposed to be; simple and kind. We'd want for nothing as long as we had each other.

Chapter 34
Christian

The sound of the rooster woke me up from a deep sleep. I realized right away that I was zippered in a blanket with Ethan. He opened his eyes noticing I was struggling to free myself. "You okay?"

"I'm about to pee my pants," I admitted.

He chuckled and helped free me. An immediate chill overwhelmed me, causing me to cover my chest with my arms.

"Holy hell it's freezin'," he complained

"Let's go inside. I'm sure my dad's already up," I suggested.

"I don't know, Chris. Maybe I should head home for a bit."

"Get up and come inside with me. I promise you'll survive."

When I started to march away he caught my arm, pulling me back against his chest. "Hold up. I think we should properly say good mornin' before we go anywhere." His lips found mine, and I closed my eyes, savoring the gesture.

"This feels right," I admitted.

"Yeah, it sure does."

I led Ethan inside of my parent's house, spotting my dad as soon as we walked through the door. "Good mornin'," he announced.

"Sir," Ethan replied.

"It's chilly out there. I thought you might end up inside last night."

"I didn't notice," I admitted proudly.

Ethan was very quiet, acting as if he was about to piss off my dad. I was getting a kick out of it, so I grabbed his hand and began to pull him up the stairs. "Where are we goin'?" He whispered.

"To brush our teeth. Mom keeps extra toothbrushes for when family comes, in case they forget. There's a container under the sink in the hall bathroom. Help yourself. I'm just goin' to change my clothes and brush my hair."

"Alright then." He entered the bathroom, leaving me to walk to my room. My sister opened her door looking like she was still asleep. "Hey, Chris. You just gettin' in?"

"Yeah," I said proudly. "We slept in the barn."

"I heard. Listen, I'm real sorry about what happened to you back at school. I feel like I should've been there for you and it hurts that I couldn't. I messed up so bad. Dad and mom look at me like they don't know what to do next. Noah's not speakin' to me because the wedding got postponed again. I feel like I can't win. Anyway, I just want you to know that I'd trade places with you if I could. I envy your life, sis. You're beautiful, intelligent, and you have Ethan, who's crazy about you. I hope one day I can have that."

I hugged my sister. "All that matters is that you're home. I need you now. I need you to be well. We all do."

"I don't want to be that person anymore, Chris. I swear I don't."

"I'm not goin' anywhere, Addy. If I've learned anything, it's that the best place for us is here with our family. We can get through everything with their help. I promise."

I didn't like seeing my sister cry. I'd never known what it was like to be addicted to drugs. I wouldn't understand the trials of withdrawals and the difficulties of bein' around people after havin' done so much wrong.

Despite the fact that we were different, we both needed the same kind of support. I'd be there for my sister, and she'd do the same for me. Together we could get through this.

Ethan met me in the hallway, but refused to come into my room when I changed. It was cute how worried he was about my father. Last night, before I'd come back out to the barn I'd given it to my dad straight.

He'd learned about Ethan sticking around, and how we'd made up. I think once he'd heard that he took a second to contain his concerns. With my mother's assistance I was able to convince him that I was old enough to make my own decisions, and out of everything I'd ever done in my life,

Ethan was always something I'd been serious about.

I think in some ways my current struggles helped him to be more lenient. In all honesty I never thought I'd see the day when he allowed any man to spend the night, even if we weren't under his roof.

Ethan's actions only reminded me how much he knew my family. He acted as if he was walking around on eggshells, and it was extremely amusing.

Once I'd changed my clothes and freshened up, I found my family, including my boyfriend, in the kitchen. My mom had prepared a large breakfast, and for the first time in a long time, she seemed happy.

My father kept pinching her butt when she walked by, winking when one of us would catch him. I placed my hand on Ethan's leg once I'd sat down. He gave me this worried look, as if I was putting him in a lion's den. I wanted to laugh, but respected his desire to stay in my dad's good graces.

The five of us sat at our little kitchen table enjoying a meal together. I can't even describe what it felt like to look around and see everyone in a good mood.

"This is nice," I admitted.

"It is," my mom agreed.

"We need to do this more often," my father suggested. "Now let's bow our heads and thank God for all he's given us."

"Can I do it, dad?" We all looked up to see Addy waiting for an answer.

My father got the biggest grimace on his face. It brought tears to my eyes as I watched him reacting to her request. "Go on, darlin'."

While listening to my sister's prayer, I silently thanked God for everything he'd given me. Mostly I thanked him for my second chance with Ethan, because somehow I knew his love would help me to heal.

Later that morning Ethan and I walked hand in hand out to the old willow tree, where most of us kids always liked to retreat to. The bright sky was shining through gaps in the trees, lighting the path to the clearing. Birds sang all around us, and it was the perfect definition of peaceful.

"It's nice bein' here with you, babe," Ethan said as we continued on. "It makes me want to get done with school and come home. With what I've learned, I think I can increase our agriculture growth by fifty percent. Do you know what somethin' like that could mean for my parent's farm?"

"As a matter of fact, I do."

He chuckled and pulled me closer. "Yeah, I guess you do."

"I've been thinkin' about school as well. I've made my mind up about goin' back. It's probably a good idea if I put my last year on hold for a while. It's just that even if I transferred, I'd have to leave home again. Right now this is the only place where

I feel safe. My sister's here and she needs me. I suppose there are a lot of reasons."

"So if I were to take a plot of land from my parents and build a nice size house, would you consider movin' a couple miles down the road, with me? It will be a while, so I don't need an answer this minute." His question was more than a dream come true for me. It meant forever.

"Yes." There was no hesitation in my answer. "I would love to."

We stopped walking and had another moment where we stared at one another. He took both of my hands and leaned forward to press his lips over mine. "I love you, Chris."

"It makes me smile when you say that."

"There's somethin' I think you should know. I meant to tell you about it last night, but we got a little lost in translation."

"What is it?" I stepped back. "Is it bad?"

"You weren't the only person that got attacked, babe."

I began to worry, not about me, but whoever had been a victim. "How do you know that?"

"It's a long damn story, but let's just say I met someone who happened to be in a bad way. She told me about bein' attacked, gettin' pregnant, and losin' her child."

I thought I'd feel like I wasn't alone. I assumed that if someone else ever stepped forward I'd be able to connect with them. All I felt for this person was sympathy.

I sank down to the ground listening as he told me who it was, and what had happened to her, before I even came into the picture. As he finished, he took my hand and kissed it. "I didn't tell you this to upset you. I'm tellin' you because I feel like maybe you could help each other. Amber's not like the other girls, Chris. She's got a soul, and she needs a friend. She tried to take her own life because of this asshole. Together maybe you'll have enough to take him down."

Amber, the one girl I'd felt the most connected to.

I wondered why she'd hadn't told me the truth, not that it mattered now. There was nothing anyone could do to change the past.

"If she wanted to press charges she could have a long time ago. You're right. I would like to talk to her, because I think we could help each other, but I'm not interested in doin' anything else. I want to put this all in the past, especially since I have a reason to work toward a future. Can you understand that?"

He nodded. "Yeah. I get it."

"I have faith that he'll get what's comin' to him. In the meantime I'm not goin' to let his actions hold me back. Everyday I'm makin' progress, and now I've got goals I want to achieve."

"Do you want to tell me about them?" He asked.

"How about I show you?" I pulled him along until we reached the old willow tree. Once we fell down underneath it, we immediately embraced in a deep kiss. Slowly, to make sure I was ready for what I was about to do, I let my hand slip down in his pants. It wasn't surprising what I felt inside, but it was how my body naturally reacted to being in this situation with the man I'd always loved.

They say that time heals all wounds. I'd like to think that saying is true. I definitely wasn't healed, not all the way. I had a long journey before I could claim that victory. For now I was prepared to gradually make progress with intimacy again, one kiss at a time.

Chapter 35
Christian

When the next Thursday rolled around I couldn't wait to tell my doctor how Ethan was back in my life. While he was at school, getting his work done before Thanksgiving break, I strolled into her office feeling like I could conquer the world.

I think she knew before I even sat down that something was different with me. I watched her give me a once over. "I can already tell you've made progress since our last meet."

I crossed my legs and prepared to shock her. "Well, Ethan came back in my life this week, and he's in love with me. All this time he said he's loved me. I still can hardly believe it myself, but he's been over to the house every day after school, and he spent the whole past weekend with me."

She jotted something down like usual. "I see. How does it make you feel to have him back in your life?"

"I feel whole again. It's like I know I'm goin' to be okay, because I have my best friend by my side."

"What about intimacy?"

Immediately I felt uncomfortable. "What about it?"

"You've had a sexual relationship with Ethan for years, so naturally one would expect that to start back up. Have you attempted to be intimate with Ethan since he's been back?"

I looked down, as if she'd detected my conflicts right away. "We mess around and kiss all the time. He's gentle with me. I know he'll wait as long as it takes me."

"How do you feel when you're with him?"

"Obviously happy."

"No. How do you feel when things start to become intense? Do you withdraw or does he?"

I twiddled my fingers. "I suppose it's me. Sometimes he tells me to slow down. Ethan's good like that."

"Are you frightened by the idea of being with a man again?"

"Should I be?"

She looked up from her desk and dropped her pen down. I watched as her hands folded together. "I can't answer that for you, Christian. Every patient manages trauma differently. I've had some patients that were victims who took years to overcome their complexities. Others prevail quite easily, going back to the life they had before they suffered their experience."

"Is it possible that my love for Ethan is so strong that I'm able to move on so soon?"

"What do you think?" Sometimes I hated how shrinks turned things around. Why couldn't they say what they meant, instead of making us solve some crazy mind game? "I think that when I'm alone with Ethan I want to take things to the next level, because it's always been special. It's a happy place for me. When I'm with Ethan, I don't think about that night. Does that sound weird?"

"I think you won't know until you try. It sounds like Ethan's willing to be patient if you need him to. Why don't you discuss it more with him. I know sometimes spontaneity is enjoyable. I'd make your first encounter a planned one. Set a date and work your way to it. If it doesn't work out then we'll know what we have to focus on."

For the next hour I told the doctor my concerns. My fear was that I'd get halfway done with the deed and freak out. Perhaps I'd watched too many movies where girls acted that way. When I was alone I did think about that night, but I also thought about all of the other women who had it so much worse than me. Seth wasn't a stranger. Even though I hated the mere mention of his name, I was making progress with being able to move past it.

When I left her office I felt better. It wasn't like Ethan would walk away if I wanted him to go slow. I was fully aware that the final piece of being able to move forward would depend on this act. As much as I feared it, a part of me looked ahead to the new and improved relationship that I finally had with my best friend. Knowing he loved me had only given me the strength I required to pull it off. I was going to overcome this obstacle, because out of the evilness that besieged me, I knew I could see the light.

Since I had plans to meet Ethan back at the ranch, I didn't waste time heading home. My eagerness to be with him wasn't just to overcome obstacles. Every ounce of me wanted to be close to him, because even though I had issues with intimacy, I still felt the safest in his arms.

It wasn't surprising to find my cousins arriving. My stomach knotted up at the mere thought of approaching them with my doctor's suggestions. The last thing I needed was to hear them ridicule me to pieces.

With a steady focus I walked toward them, fearing whatever was to come out of their smart mouths. Jax spotted me first, just as he helped a female step out from the back seat. "Chris, you're just in time to meet my girl. This is Reese." I looked at the brunette, petite girl, with light colored eyes that may or may not have been gray, and smiled, even though I wondered what she was doing with my crazy cousin.

Then, before I could greet her, he cut in between us and wrapped his arms around me. I couldn't for the life of me reciprocate. This was something that had never occurred before. I mean, my mom probably had pictures of when we were kids, but this wasn't like that. "Are you ill?" I teased.

"I heard what happened, Chris," he whispered in my ear. "I know you've got a brother, but if you need me to kick some ass I'd be glad to."

I pulled away, wondering how I was supposed to react. "Thanks, but I'm just tryin' to move forward."

"I can tell. You look great."

His girlfriend interrupted the compliment. "When you said she was pretty you didn't do her justice. Girl, you are gorgeous!"

I was taken aback by her statement. My cheeks immediately became flustered. "Thanks, but you're too nice. Jax would never say that about me."

She looked back at him, and then toward me again. "No, really. He talks about you and your sister Addison all the time. You're stunning. I'm surprised you don't model. With your figure you could go places."

All of the sudden I felt modest. My arms hugged my sweater across my chest, and I searched for what to say next.

Jax put his arm around me at the same time his brother Jake approached us. He too leaned down and hugged me. "How're you doin'?"

I shrugged. "Did my mom put you up to this?"

"What?" Jake looked confused. "No. We talked about what happened to you on the way here. All fun aside, you're our cousin. Neither of us wants to see you hurt."

Reese walked over to the car and began pulling out her bags. I made sure I spoke so she couldn't hear me. "I thought you guys hated me."

They both laughed, as if my comment was preposterous.

"Seriously, you've made fun of me for as long as I could remember. Don't be nice to me just because of what I've been through. I'm stronger than you think."

Jake nudged his twin brother. "Look cuz, just because we pick on you doesn't mean what we say is true. If we weren't related we'd totally hit it," he teased.

Feeling disgusted, I smacked him on the arm. "You're sick."

He swatted me away. "I was only sayin' you were doable. Calm down. You know it ain't like that. All jokes aside, you're smokin' hot. Our friends have been givin' us shit about hookin' them up for years."

I could feel the burning developing in my eyes. This wasn't just some kind of confirmation for me. This was life changing. My whole life I'd felt out of place. It was as if I couldn't let myself see what apparently everyone else did. This wasn't like hearing my boyfriend, or even my parents telling me I was pretty. It was like asking the most critical skeptics. Not that I'd ever base my life on anything they said, the twin's honest response had left me speechless. I was literally stunned that this was taking place.

When I saw Reese moving toward us I decided to accept their compliments before I could feel embarrassed. "Thanks guys."

Jax quickly reached over and started messing up my hair. "No problem, nerd."

Jake laughed. "Yeah, don't go tellin' anyone we said you were pretty. We wouldn't want the family thinkin' we went soft."

I rolled my eyes, but nodded anyway. I didn't care if I was the only person who ever knew what they'd said to me. It was unforgettable.

I watched them gather the rest of their belongings and walk inside of my parent's house. At that same time Ethan's vehicle pulled down the lane. In that moment I felt more beautiful than I could ever remember feeling. It was then that I knew I'd be able to give myself to my boyfriend, both inside and out I knew I wasn't a waste of space.

Chapter 36
Ethan

Something was different about her. Even though I couldn't put my finger on it, I knew it had something to do with her cousins. She'd always been sort of uncomfortable when they came around. Now, all of a sudden, she was full of smiles as they walked away.

After obtaining the bouquet of fall colored flowers I'd picked up on the way, I climbed out of the car to greet my lady. I still couldn't get over how nice it felt to address her as mine. Her gaze filled me with warmth, as if to remind me that we were both finally where we knew we needed to be.

I wrapped my arms around her, and although it was nothing new, everything felt changed; so surreal. "I missed you," she said as she whispered against my face.

"Me too. How was your appointment?" I asked as I separated us enough to look into those green eyes.

"It was good."

I paid close attention to her cousins disappearing into the house. "How about them? Did they give you any shit?" I'd been around the family enough to know how things went. Her cousins were bullies at times. They didn't mean any harm, but she always took it so personal. Had I been in her shoes I'm sure it wouldn't be hard to understand her methods of reasoning.

"Actually," she looked down at the ground and I watched her face turn to a shy grimace. "They said I'm beautiful."

I could tell she was touched by their term of endearment. My hand lifted and coursed over her cheek. "You are."

Chris shrugged and looked away, as if she couldn't handle the compliment. "It's hard to believe sometimes. I've never looked in the mirror and saw myself that way. It's intense."

"I've always seen the beauty, both inside and out. Don't you understand that? You're the most beautiful, true, innocent, lovin', honest person I know. Darlin', you're nothin' but a treasure."

She began to giggle and shove me away. "Stop it. That's just weird comin' from you."

I tossed up my hands. "What? It's the truth."

"You're just tryin' to get in my pants." I watched as she continued shaking her head at my comment.

I crossed my arms over my chest. "I'm not goin' to lie. It wouldn't kill me to make love to you over and over until to the sun came up over the horizon, but that ain't why I said it. I feel all of those things for you; I see them when I look at you."

She stopped moving and just stared at me. It was impossible to stand so close and not reach out to touch her. Our hands laced together and with little effort I pulled her close to me. Her warm breath let me know she was near enough to kiss. I didn't dawdle when it came to something so necessary. In that moment it was just us.

Our embrace was short-lived when we heard whistling, knowing it was coming from either of her cousins. She squeezed both of my hands as she spoke. "I want you to make love to me tonight, Ethan."

"You know we can't," I replied quickly. "You're not ready."

"I am. The doctor says I'll know it and I do."

I refused to believe that she was. "I don't expect anything."

She pulled me closer so anyone lurking wouldn't be able to hear. "You were my first for everything that matters. You showed me what it was like to feel completely loved when we are together. You're my safe place, Ethan. Bein' with you doesn't make me feel nervous. It makes me feel alive again."

I reached forward and kissed the top of her head, holding my lips there for a long amount of time. "I will never hurt you."

"I know," she whispered. Then, as if she wasn't taking no for an answer, she continued. "Tonight. We're goin' to make love until the sun meets with the horizon. We'll take our time, and when it's all over I'll have that last piece of myself back. I don't just want this, Ethan. I need it. I need you. I need you to love me more than you ever have before. I need you to remind me that our love is stronger than anything that comes in our way." All of a sudden I felt her trembling and noticed she was crying. It wasn't a cry like she was in pain. It was more along the lines of being so determined that emotions were pouring out of her. I stroked her face and wiped away the residue.

"Okay, babe. You don't have to beg. I'll make love to you. I'll give you my all with little effort, because lovin' you is easy, it's natural. My only concern will be you, and if you tell me to stop I -."

"I won't." Chris shook her head. "I might need to pause, but I won't ask you to stop. Every inch of my body wants to be with you again. I know I won't want you to stop."

"But if you do...I will. I'll wait as long as it takes. Since I'm keepin' you around forever, there's no rush."

"I'd rather not waste anymore time," she said with an ornery snicker.

"Then I guess it's settled. Tonight I'll make love to you, and not because you asked me to, but more along of the lines of bein' that close to you somehow completes me."

"Keep talkin' like that and we won't make it to dinner." With the vibes she was sending I was half-tempted to escort her somewhere private and get started. The last thing I wanted to do was hold in my excitement around her family. "I'm just teasin'," I assured her. It was important to keep it together.

"No you're not! Don't forget how well I know you, Ethan."

We kissed one more time after I pulled her close with a little jerk. She squealed and gave me a shocked look as she pulled away. "Yeah, maybe you do. All the more reason to take you to our special spot and get started."

She pushed away full of smiles. While biting down on her lip she continued to step backwards. "When you're sittin' at the table near my father just imagine what you're goin' to do with me later. I might even give him a head's up that we won't be stickin' around for dessert." Chris took off running. Her laughter echoed off of the surrounding trees.

I stood there watching her go into the house, the whole time trying to rid myself of the image of being horny around her family. If they weren't on high alert before we came out as a couple, they certainly were now. I imagined death by salad fork and almost cringed. Instead of eating, I was going to be clenching my silverware, hoping I didn't have to use it for self-defense.

A couple hours later I sat there amongst her whole family with the idea of being intimate still lingering in my mind. I did my best to avoid eye contact, with not only Chris, but her father and brother. I only answered when addressed, and realized that they probably knew I was being ridiculously weird. It didn't matter. As long as I could sit there at the table, and not think about how good it was going to feel to make love to my girl again, I'd be fine.

Unfortunately my girlfriend had other ideas. Her warm hand reached under the table as she carried on in a conversation with her brother. I forced my legs together to prevent a sudden growth beneath my meal.

While she continued taunting me, Chris would purposely include me in the conversation, expecting me to answer straight-faced. She was doing all of this on purpose and I couldn't do anything to rectify the situation. It was quite obvious that I wouldn't be able to get up and walk out of the room. The closer her fingers got to my crotch the more apparent it became. I started thinking long-term; how many extra minutes it would take me to calm down enough to be able to stand up.

For a moment I peered over and saw the fire in her eyes. Her cheerful mood lifted some of my anxiety, although it wasn't enough to shake my fear of being forever known as the guy who got up from the Mitchell family table with a woody. Finally I came to the conclusion that I'd have to take matters into my own hands. As gently and not obvious as it could be, I removed her hand from my pants and gave her a look. She shot one back, but didn't attempt to torture me again.

When everyone retreated to the living room for dessert I picked a chair that I could sit in by myself. It was vital that I have a good relationship with her family, since I knew I'd someday be a member.

Just when we all started talking about football, Chris came in with some kind of cake. It was covered in icing, and she was purposely taking her finger to draw up some and lick it off, all the while watching me react. I slowly gulped down the lump forming in my throat as I turned to ignore her innuendos. Of course, it wasn't fast enough to defer wandering eyes. "Hey Ethan, you alright over there?" Noah asked. "You look like you're about to bust a nut."

As shocking as his remark came out, I watched as the room filled with laughing bodies.

"Whatever!" I spat out and crossed my legs. Directly in view was my girlfriend, steady eying me up. She was never going to hear the end of it if I made it out of the house alive. "Pick on someone else, Noah. You ain't gettin' me in trouble."

"I'll let it go, if you tell me when you started bangin' my sister. You see, you never asked us for permission. We don't take that kind of action lightly."

Chris stood up and started marching toward me. "Shut up, Noah. You should have asked him that question a long time ago."

I was petrified to look in the direction of her father, especially when she came to sit on my lap. A part of me wanted to run out before they located the hunting rifles.

"He's just messin' with ya, Ethan," her father explained. "You have our blessin', you know that."

I nodded. "Thanks, sir. I appreciate that."

"Boy, quit your worryin'. I think we all knew you two would end up together," Noah teased.

Chris wrapped her arms around my neck. Her smile was comforting until she leaned up and whispered in my ear. "Let's get out of here."

I pulled away and looked at the vast amount of eyes staring at me. With little nerve left I refused to respond. Chris seemed annoyed as she waited for an answer. Out of nowhere she jumped up and went for the stairs. I watched as she climbed each one, never looking back at me.

"Now you've gone and did it. She's pissed."

"She is not," I exclaimed, even though I didn't know.

Not even a minute later she came downstairs with an overnight bag strapped to her shoulder. She walked over and kissed her dad on the cheek, whispering something in his ear, the whole time he was staring at me. Then he nodded.

She called out to everyone that we were leaving and took my hand. Before I knew it we were out on the front porch. "What are you doin'?"

"What's it look like?" She asked.

"Chris, we can't just leave."

"We can. I asked my parents if we could sneak away and they said it was fine. Stop bein' a worry wart. Don't you want to be with me, Ethan?"

I sighed, feeling like I wasn't in control at all. "Of course I do."

"Then let's go."

Ten minutes later we were at the main house. The house was quiet as we entered and charted up the long staircase in the direction of the left wing. Chris took my hand and pulled me along the way until we reached the last bedroom in the hall. Since they were expecting a ton of family to come in, all of the rooms had been made up. This particular one was my girlfriend's favorite.

She tossed her bag down on the king-sized bed and turned to face me. "I'm goin' to take a bubble bath." She began to back away. "Do you want to join me?"

"Does your Gram know you're here?"

"Yep. We have the whole wing to ourselves tonight."

Knowing we'd be alone me feel better, so I followed her toward the master bathroom. She kissed me slowly when I caught up to her, leading us both onto the cold, ceramic tiled floor. "We don't have to go all the way, Chris. I'm puttin' it out there, so you know."

"Take off my clothes," she whispered against my lips.

I think this was the moment I knew she wasn't going to back down. I felt her determination as our lips pressed together, and from years of being with this woman, I was sure she wasn't going to tell me to stop.

Chapter 37
Christian

I could feel him entering the room behind me. His presence allowed me to stay motivated with my plans. First I lit a few candles, placing them around the tub. Then I set the temperature of the water and poured in a little bit of soap to create the bubbles.

That was the easy part. The next steps would require me to be confident. In my honest opinion this task would be harder than intercourse.

Even though he'd seen me naked a hundred times, I trembled at the thought of revealing myself to him. Within a few steps he was up against my body, his hands clenching the fabric to my shirt. My chest rose and fell rapidly as I anticipated it being lifted over my head. Ethan peered into my eyes, saying nothing when he raised it up over my breasts. Even with a bra on, my nipples were tingling. I couldn't contain my heavy breathing.

When the shirt came off of my head completely I parted my lips, accepting another kiss from Ethan. The taste of his tongue lingered on my own when he pulled away.

It took me a second to open my eyes, even when I felt his hands reaching around my back. With little effort my bra strap was unfastened. Ethan kept his focus on me as he pulled it away to fall at our feet. I kept my hands at my sides, watching him step back and take me in. The way he made me feel was indescribable. It was so obvious that he was consumed by undressing me. The lump in his pants was only half the proof. His heavy eyes told me that he was high on the idea of continuing.

Very slowly Ethan crouched down and took hold of my pants. With a light tug they came down over my hips, sinking until they sat at my ankles. I stepped out of them while watching him looking up at me.

I expected him to remove my underwear quickly so that he could undress and join me in the tub, but Ethan wasn't in a hurry. His eyes traveled down my body until he stared straight forward at my lace panties. I felt so warm, even with the cold tile beneath my feet.

The pressure of his initial touch between my legs almost made them buckle. It wasn't only about the anticipation. My desire to make love to him, without regret, or worries, was causing me to shake profusely. I wasn't afraid, but more excited. I knew it was important to be able to let go and get lost in the moment. His touch only sparked a fire that I knew would burn all night long.

I watched Ethan's face slip forward until he was only an inch away from my covered pussy. He teased the elastic that clung to my hips, only to let go again. His hot breath blew over the fabric, heating between my legs. His eyes, focused on mine, blinked slowly as he leaned forward to drag his bottom lip over me there. It was just a trace, nothing with enough force to cause a reaction. Still, I found myself craving for it to happen again.

Next Ethan pulled down my panties, revealing my sensitive sex. He leaned forward and kissed my pussy, only to stand up as my underwear fell to the floor. I watched my boyfriend ripping off his shirt, followed by his pants and boxers. For a few seconds I wondered if we were going to make it to the tub before he tried to touch me again. Just standing there, seeing him so hard because of me made me feel desirable.

Ethan grabbed my hand before slipping it down in the warm soapy water. I stepped in after him, appreciating the temperature and the fact that bubbles would prevent him from seeing any imperfections on my naked skin.

I knew it was silly. Besides my parents, this man had seen all of me. He'd seen me laugh, cry, and lose myself. Hiding from him only meant I wasn't ready to accept what I couldn't change. Knowing how important it was for me to change, I stood up from the bubbles and sat back down on the edge of the large soaking tub. My skin glistened as the remaining suds began to pop, exposing more of me for Ethan's viewing pleasure.

He adjusted in the tub, slipping his wet hands up my legs. When he reached my knees he stopped, and I got an inkling that maybe he was worried about how far to go. "Don't stop," I whispered.

Ethan inched his way up to my thighs, all the while watching my reaction. It was apparent that he was prepared for me to stop him, in which I wasn't going to. When he paused I used my toes to push him away, not because I was done, but for the purpose of grabbing his undivided attention.

He sank down in the other end of the tub waiting for me to do something. Feeling completely out of my realm, I slipped my wet hands over my breasts, sliding easily over my hard nipples. I could feel an intense burning between my legs as I fondled myself this way. It had been a while since I was able to touch myself without cringing. Ethan's eyes watched me, while I continued massaging my body. I ran one hand down between my legs, coursing over my clit once before going back to my breast. I had to bite down on my bottom lip to keep from crying out loudly. This intense teasing was only making me hotter, so much that my body felt like it was burning up. "Touch me," I managed to say.

He grabbed a washcloth that was folded on the ledge and lathered it with some scented soap. Starting on my left leg, he scrubbed my skin until he made his way to my inner thigh. I could feel that rag so close to my sweet spot, taunting me in ways that only Ethan could. When he pulled it back I felt disappointed. Then he rinsed it off, splashing the water all around my most private of areas. He peered at it, inching closer as if to touch it with his mouth. I gasped when I could once again feel his hot breath blowing over it. "I want you so bad, babe." He kissed me there, slowly without tongue, letting his soft lips linger there.

It was almost too much to bear. My increased breathing was more obvious as I attempted to tell him to proceed. "Ethan," his name played off my lips. "Taste me."

His tongue felt like a million kisses all at once as it flicked over my clit. He slurped my pussy into his mouth, sucking it just enough and then letting go. My body arched at the moment I felt his warm tongue drawing circles over my bud. I tangled my fingers into locks of his hair, clenching them as he took me to places I never thought I'd go again. I could feel him pleasing me everywhere, in every crevice of my existence. I was losing myself in him, exactly what I knew would happen if I'd just let go.

Ethan didn't let me come down from my euphoric high. He pulled me down into the heated tub, positioning my legs to wrap around his back. His stiff erection was apparent beneath me, and unlike the night before, I was prepared to take it to the next level. Nothing was going to stop him from sliding inside of me, and I was about to make sure of it.

While Ethan took his time, savoring each kiss, I obtained his hard cock with my right hand, scooting my pussy over it to the perfect spot. He halted me at the last second. "Are you sure?"

I couldn't explain why it happened, but I felt the hot tears filling my eyes even before I could answer. "Yes. I love you, Ethan. I'm sure."

He kissed me again, this time mingling his tongue with mine. I felt his fingers rubbing over my clit, like he was warming me up for penetration. My body reacted to his touch, and he knew it as well. Right before he slid inside, Ethan moved me to the side and climbed out of the tub. He located a towel and held it out for me. "I need you in bed, Chris. I want to fall asleep inside of you, just like our first time."

My mind took me back to that night when everything was perfect. It was then that I secretly gave him my heart to keep.

I followed him into the bedroom, letting the towel fall before I made it to the mattress. Ethan sat down with his focus on me standing in front of him baring all. "God, you're so beautiful."

In this moment I felt it.

"Please make love to me," I begged.

"Gladly," he whispered as he pulled me onto the bed.

Ethan began at my feet, kissing my toes, then my ankles, and up to my calves. He massaged my knees and tickled behind them before moving up to my thighs. The anticipation of feeling him playing with my pussy sent me into a frenzy. I yearned for his touch again, and when it happened I couldn't contain my enjoyment. He licked and then sucked on my clit again and again; each time giving me absolute pleasure. By the time he came up for air I could hardly breathe myself.

Ethan massaged my breasts as he lifted to suckle on each of my nipples. His gentle bite at the end caused me to cry out. I clung to his hair, pulling as I lost control over myself again.

By the time he made his way to my mouth I was unable to even consider that we hadn't had intercourse yet. He'd satiated me to the brink of feeling as if I was flying. Then it happened. I could feel the pressure up against my sex. He was there; stiff, and ready.

This was the moment where he stopped moving and waited for my permission. I kissed him eagerly, tasting his sweat over his lips. The salty residue glistened over his cheeks as I searched for his eyes. Once I met his stare I knew what I wanted; what was about to happen.

I let one hand reach up and graze through his thick hair. "What are you waitin' for?"

"I don't want to hurt you."

I shook my head. "That's not possible."

Then it happened. With careful precision he entered me, filling my channel with his familiar love. Like our first time together, it felt tight in the beginning. I clung to his body, digging my nails into his back. Beads of sweat covered our bodies as we continued grinding together. He gripped my hair and pulled me into a deep kiss. At the same time I could feel my body losing control. He slowed his pace to allow me a few moments to catch my breath.

We flipped positions with me on top. Our hands laced together as I began rocking my body over his. The friction caused jolts of vibrating sensations from my lips to my toes. He held onto my hips, guiding me to a perfect stride. Then I felt it happening. He'd held out for as long as he could. I didn't want him to stop, because being with him felt so right, but I knew it was his turn. Then he tightened up and exploded.

Just like he'd given me, I waited a few minutes before attempting to move around. He pulled me down over his chest and wrapped his arms behind my back. I didn't care that we were sweaty. Being with him made everything worthwhile. It was all I'd ever wanted. He was gentle, caring, and above all patient.

We spent a little while lying there together talking about what was to come. We spoke of the bad times and he held me close when I had to cry a little. Speaking to Ethan about what happened wasn't like talking to my doctor. He saw into my soul, and was the only person able to reach in and comfort me back to life again. He gave me hope, and promises that I knew he'd keep.

I'd overcome my biggest hurdle, and all I could think about was being with him again, feeling him pleasuring me until I lost myself in momentary bliss.

He didn't push me away when I persuaded him for another round. In fact, with only a simple slip of the tongue I had him at my beck and call. I'd never felt so empowered, and perhaps it's what he wanted me to feel. At any rate, he knew what I needed, and I was appreciative.

I could feel his overwhelming emotions taking over as we continued to make love again and again throughout the night. By the time the sun started to rise we were exhausted, both in mind and body.

Ethan had kept his promise, never taking a single moment for himself. The night had been about me, and I suppose it was important for my first time. The weird thing was that I never thought about Seth while we were intimate, and even in the hours afterwards. Being with Ethan occupied my mind, allowing me to savor each and every moment we were together.

With the sun shining through the blinds I stayed wrapped in Ethan's arms. He kissed me good morning and moved the hair out of my eyes. "Good mornin', darlin'."

I hugged him tightly. "I could get used to this."

"I already am," he replied.

"It's a good thing you got my dad's approval to date me."

"Why is that?" He asked as he played with my hand.

"It'll be easier when you have to ask for my hand in marriage."

Ethan sat straight up and rubbed his face. I giggled, thinking my joke had gotten to him. "I'll have you know that no matter what your family says you're goin' to be my wife. I'd like for us to wait until I graduate, but it's goin' to happen. You and I have a long road ahead of us. Besides, your dad sort of already gave me the go-ahead. I've got it in writing."

"Well then it sounds perfect."

He pulled my hand up to his lips. "It will be. I promise."

Epilogue
4 months later

Ethan

I hated waking her up, but after reading the text message I knew she'd want to know about this. It wasn't every day that the person who attacked someone finally gets caught.

"Chris, wake up." She stirred and rolled over to my side, never opening her eyes. I walked over to that side, sitting down on the mattress beside her. After removing the hair away from her face, I leaned forward and kissed her. "Darlin', wake up. I've got somethin' to tell you."

"Five more minutes, Ethan. I was up late studyin'." Since she'd enrolled in online classes Chris had spent quite a few evenings buried in books.

"It's important. You can go back to sleep as soon as I'm done."

She sat up and cracked open both eyes. "This better be good. I was dreamin' of us bein' at the beach already."

"It's only a few weeks away, babe." I waited for her to smile before continuing. "So I woke up and had a text message from a number I didn't recognize."

"Is it from an old girlfriend?" She asked as she stretched out her arms. Since moving back into my parent's house, Chris had been staying with me. She hadn't technically moved in, but it was only a matter of time before we made it official. I think I was more concerned about what her parents would say about it, but so far they'd been pretty cool.

"No! It's not from an old girlfriend. It's actually from that girl Amber. Do you remember her?"

Her eyes shot open. "Of course I do. What about her? Why is she sendin' you messages?"

"Seth got arrested over the weekend. Accordin' to Amber's text he got trashed and attacked Mila at the frat house when he found out she was seeing someone new. Apparently he thought his friend was asleep in the room they were in. Halfway through the guy got up and started beatin' the shit out of him until the police came. I don't know the details other than what I've told you, but I'm pretty sure he's not gettin' out of this one. Amber said she wanted me to let you know the detective might be contactin' you about your statement." I waited for it all to sink in. While Chris remained silent I crouched down in front of her and took her hands. "I'm tellin' you this because I know you're strong now. If you want to pursue this we'll do it together. If you don't then we'll go about our lives as if this conversation never happened."

I could tell she was thinking about it. "Is Mila okay? She was a bitch to me, but nobody deserves what happened."

"I guess. Amber didn't go into details. She just basically said Seth was arrested and why."

"I'll testify." Her answer was short and to the point.

"Are you sure?"

She nodded. "If the detective gets in touch with me I'll do whatever it takes to ensure this never happens again."

I pulled my girlfriend into a big hug, noticing right away that she wasn't freaking out. She'd been going to therapy for months, and our relationship was also going strong. Chris was happy, and we both promised to never look back at what we could have done differently. "I'm so proud of you."

She pulled away and looked right into my eyes. "I couldn't have done this without you, Ethan. The other girls aren't as lucky as me. They'll need to find something to help them heal. It's somethin' they'll never forget, but will be able to let go if they learn how."

"You're so beautiful when you're strong and determined."

The smile that followed let me know she felt as beautiful as I saw her. Out of something horrible my girlfriend had learned to love herself. I didn't want to feel thankful for what happened to her, because it was awful, but I was glad that through it all we were able to come together and I was finally the person she needed me to be.

No matter where life took us we'd be together. From the very moment she stepped inside of that bus I knew she was my future. I'd spend the rest of my life making sure she knew it too.

The End

Look for Noah's Wedding in All I Want (A Christmas Anthology) December 13th 2014, and Jake's Book Coming January 2015.